Welcome, Wanderer

The one whose beard was like flowing water spoke, and his voice was deeper than is common among Elves, rich and melodious with wisdom. "It is a long way you have come. Few among men have ever dared seek out this city. Great striving should be rewarded, surely."

Ingulf forced himself to stand and be polite, while his heart drove him to strike aside these frail figures with a sweep of his arm, and run to find Airellen. . . .

"A great warrior you have been in the seas of the East," said he of the silver beard. "That you may be a greater one—look!" He held out a sword. It glittered like frost in the moonlight. "With this sword, great deeds lie before you. With it, perhaps, you may win to your heart's desire."

Ace Books by Paul Edwin Zimmer

A GATHERING OF HEROES
THE LOST PRINCE
KING CHONDOS' RIDE
INGULF THE MAD

INGULF THE MAD

PAUL EDWIN ZIMMER

ACE BOOKS, NEW YORK

This book is an Ace original
edition, and has never been
previously published.

INGULF THE MAD

An Ace Book / published by arrangement with
the author

PRINTING HISTORY
Ace edition / July 1989

ISBN: 0-441-37094-2

Ace Books are published by The Berkley Publishing Group,
200 Madison Avenue, New York, New York 10016.
The name "Ace" and the "A" logo
are trademarks belonging to
Charter Communications, Inc.

PRINTED IN THE UNITED STATES OF AMERICA

10 9 8 7 6 5 4 3 2 1

For Lisa,
who pulled Ingulf
back from the Sea . . .

CONTENTS

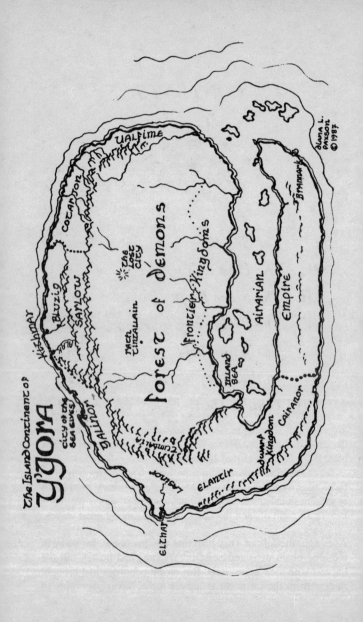

The Island Continent of
Ygora

City of the Sea Elves

UALFIME

Forest of demons

The Lost City

Frontier Kingdoms

AIMARIAN

Empire

INLAND SEA

dwarf Kingdom

Cainanor

BRANNARK

ELANTIR

Cumbria

BALLNOR

CUINLLAIN

SARLOW

BLUZID

COTAMPTOR

KICHWAY

LATHOR

ELCHAY

Mach Tinzallain

diana L. PAYSON
© 1987

The Sea-Elves

THE CITY OF the Sea-Elves stands alone—all but unknown in lands of men—by Y'Gora's northern strand. There come the ships from beyond the world.

And there, one evening, came Ingulf of the Isles after long wandering, as the Twin Suns sank in rainbow splendor. They had risen and set many times on his quest: long had he sifted legend and myth, seeking a clue that would lead him here.

He heard the roar of surf hissing on the shore as he turned his horse's head toward the sea. White towers rose in sight, and the unvisited city lay before him. Sea-wind stirred his copper hair: the salt smell stirred his mind.

Waves of blood poured strongly through his veins: tiny chill thrillings swept over him. All the days and dreary months of searching faded from memory, and instead it was a woman's face he thought of, and the shape of a seal among great waves.

Ages ago, the folk of Tray Ithir that was his home, far away in the long chain of islands east of Y'Gora, had beaten out the harvest with their great flails. But recent centuries had brought raiders from the far north at harvest time, savage servants of the Demon-Lords of the icy waste, and so the great flails had found new work to do. So deadly were they at this task that the men of Tray Ithir became far-famed warriors. Generations of the Airarian Emperors, who rule many of the wide-scattered islands east of Y'Gora, as well as the great Airarian peninsula that makes Y'Gora look on a map like a great cat's skull, with the Inner Sea its open mouth, had sought the men of Tray Ithir to bring their war-flails into their armies.

Ingulf, son of Fingold, had followed this path. His father had been sword-master to his clan, and his war-flail and skilled sword-arm won him some small fame in the Emperor's service.

When one raiding-season ended, he found himself in the dull and barren isles of the Scurlmard chain, far to the north of his home, beyond the isles of the Curranach.

The folk of the Scurlmards will not hunt seals, for they say that the Sea-People travel in this form.

But Ingulf laughed at such tales.

Boredom came upon him in the Scurlmards. He went hunting alone in his small boat. Hills of water rose and fell about him: the Twin Suns were fiery eyes above the sea. Barren, stony islands appeared and vanished behind restless, blue-green waves.

He was returning to harbor with the few fish he had caught, when a long brown shape skimmed up the side of a rippling wave.

A seal, he thought, and plied his oars. He was skilled at hunting in the water: he crept up on it and laid down the oars and gripped his harpoon.

He stiffened, and raised the long straight shaft. The seal balanced on the crest of a wave. Ingulf rose and threw, and the harpoon flew. It struck further back than he had planned, and the seal wailed in a woman's voice.

His harpoon line tightened in his hand, and his boat was drawn swiftly through the water. A dip in the waves showed him the rocks of a stony little island ahead.

The rope hummed. Black, jagged stone pierced the creamy water on either side, but the seal swam safely through, dragging the boat behind, toward a tiny gravel beach. A cave gaped in the cliff above.

A wave lifted the seal and laid her gently on the little beach. Ingulf jerked out his long dirk, ready to leap from the boat; for a seal upon land is easy to kill.

But the brown shape reared up, and the seal-skin seemed to fall away. It was a woman there, crying and tugging with slender white hands at the harpoon in her hip.

As he stared, Ingulf almost lost his life to the sea. Powerful currents seized the boat and whirled it toward the rocks. He seized his paddle and drove the pitching boat to shore.

She let go the spear-shaft then, and tried to escape, but fell, with blood pouring over her white legs.

He leaped from the boat and ran to her side. The ends of the long brown hair that was her only garment were bright with blood. Huge eyes stared at him in wild terror.

He tried to speak soothingly as he wrestled with the harpoon, working the barb loose. Her pain would haunt his nightmares forever.

Had it been her long brown hair he had seen in the water, and thought was a seal? It hung below her waist.

His mind went round and round, numb with guilt. He got the harpoon loose, and she sobbed and screamed with exhaustion while he tried to stop the blood.

That was the beginning of it all, and terrible it was. He bound up her wound as best he might, stuttering helpless words of guilt and sorrow, and made her drink from the wineskin that was slung on his back. She controlled her weeping at last, and gazed at him with eyes that were larger and softer than the eyes of any woman of mortal blood.

But a strange thing it was, that he could never afterward remember what color those eyes were. Sometimes he seemed to remember that they had been gray as the sea at twilight, and then again they would come into his mind a transparent blue, like the night sky between the stars, or again as brown as her hair, or sometimes golden. . . .

But whatever color they were, he would see those eyes looking at him for the rest of his days.

He built a fire, and brought from the boat those few fish he had caught, along with his fur-lined cloak to cover her. The Twin Suns settled into the sea. She ate the fish he cooked, and slept wrapped in his cloak, while he sat and piled driftwood on the fire until he fell asleep with his back against the stone.

A time of happiness came with the sunlight into the cave, for then she spoke to him, and her voice in speech seemed more beautiful than any song.

Her name was Airellen, the daughter of Falmoran, and she had never before spoken to a mortal. Something she told him of that strange city by the waves where men do not go, and more of the green mystery of the sea, though all she said was to him a maze of strange names and riddles. But her eyes glowed on him, and he was happy.

He found himself trying to tell her of Tray Ithir and his people, but now they seemed drab and colorless, and his tongue stumbled into silence. Then he tried to tell her of the battles he had seen in the service of the Emperor, but it came to him that he was boasting, and he was silent once more.

Yet he lived as in a fever of happiness, hunting for shellfish in the shallow water, tending the fire each night while she slept.

It came to him more than once that he should take her to Lonnamara in his boat, to the healer there; but when he spoke of this to her, he found himself lost in her wide eyes, while she told some tale of marvels that he could never afterward recall.

The thought faded from his mind. The days passed, and her wound healed, while he served her in a joy that seemed half-dream.

He loved her. He knew that he loved her, and he tried in vain to make himself speak of it. But when her eyes turned upon him, he could not.

Far more swiftly than mortal flesh, her wound healed. A terror came upon him then. Soon she would be able to return to her own people. He tried to picture life without her, and a hostile, empty future rose before him.

In a panic, then, he rushed to tell her of his love—and failed, his will drowning in the oceans of her eyes.

Out of her sight, he could think again, and his resolve

returned. He fell to shaping words into a speech that would make his feelings clear to her, and he rehearsed it again and again to himself as he gathered driftwood on the beach.

But when he tried to say these carefully-chosen words to her, again he found himself silent before those huge and beautiful eyes, while she spoke to him of persons and places that were but a tangle of names he did not know.

He found himself dazed outside the cave, and realized he still had not spoken. He rushed back inside, the vision of the empty world he had foreseen a terror within him, and clenching shut his eyes he forced his lips to move—not in the careful words he had labored on, but wild, stammering words.

Her small breasts moved in a sigh.

"But you are a mortal man," she said. "The old songs of my people say that when a mere handful of decades have passed, your youth and strength and beauty will fall from you, and you will wither like a leaf, and die. I have no need of sorrow. Let us part as friends, and let me remember you as you are now."

She rose from where she was sitting, and tried to walk by him to the mouth of the cave. But he, stammering words he could never remember after, seized her arm; thinking only that he could never, ever live without her.

Her wide eyes filled with the same terror they had held when he had leaped with his knife from the boat. Suddenly her beauty flared around him; his passion burst and drained away in an instant of unendurable ecstasy, and he fell stunned to the floor.

He lay helpless as she limped past him, out of the cave and down to the sea. He tried to raise himself, to follow her, fighting his weakness, but could not even crawl.

Then the sweetness of her singing was like an icy wave in his blood, as she walked singing into the sea, and he heard the words of her song—

> But mortals turn to dust and bone
> And leave you crying all alone . . .

Mastering his weakness, he dragged himself to the mouth of the cave. But all he saw was a seal skimming over the crest of the waves.

* * *

Far had he journeyed since he had lurched at last from the cave, where he had lain mindless for two days. A madness had driven him to his boat, a madness to find that secret city and harbor of the Sea-Elves, where men do not go.

In Elthar, where the Guardians of the World watch over Y'Gora, and where dwell yet survivors of those first Elves who came to the world in the Age of Terror to join the battle against the Dark Powers, he got little help. It were best, he was told, that Mortal Men stay away from the Sea-People, for so little do they know of men that they do not realize how dangerous magic can be to them. For the Elves live by magic, and strong spells are nothing to them.

Tales were told him of men who wandered for years witless, lost in lovely dreams that Elves had woven for them, to ease, as they thought, the burden of mortal life.

But such tales did not turn the son of Fingold from his purpose. The Sages of Elthar shook their heads.

"He, too, has been touched by an Elf," they said.

He had told none his own story. But ancient maps and curious scraps of legend gave him hope, and he left Elthar. He tried to charter a boat to search the northern coasts, but none would consent to sail into those waters. Slave galleys of Sarlow hunted there, and sailors told of seeing white ships with glowing sails, and one of a far glimpse of white towers. But mortal ships avoided those waters, unless driven there by the lawless wind.

So he rode north and east from Elthar, asking questions of the friendly forest Elves. Silence he met most often, and a look of pity from star-keen eyes. But sometimes he got warnings, and some of these had helped him to guess regions worth searching.

He wandered long in the great forests of the northern coast of Galinor, near the edges of the Forest of Demons, and the western borders of the dreaded land of Sarlow. Once he escaped from a Demon by sheer luck, and once had to fight his way out of an ambush of goblin rat-folk. Once he blundered into a raiding party out of Sarlow, driving home their bound and weeping slaves. The great iron blade of his flail had sung a new song for them, and left bodies sprawled among the tangled roots of trees, and the slaves weeping with joy.

South of him men dwelt in scattered farming villages, but along the coast he found only a single tiny fishing village, whose people grew silent when he spoke to them of Elves, and ran away when he asked if any had seen the white ships upon the ocean.

Hunters told him of paths in the forest where Elves had turned them aside. He found one of these and followed it.

A voice hailed him from a tree. Looking up, he saw peering between the leaves the wide eyes of an Elf.

"Turn back," the soft voice said. "This is no path for a Mortal Man to be taking."

"I have business with Falmoran of the Sea-Elves and his kin," Ingulf answered, his heartbeat unnaturally loud. The wise eyes looked at him in grave silence.

"Ride on, then," the Elf said, after a time. "And may all powers protect you among my kinsmen of the sea."

His quest ended, he sat on his horse and listened to the sad song the sea pours upon the shore. The towers reared up, as white as bone. Tales said they shone at night. Sailors feared to see their light.

The Twin Suns vanished in the opal sea. Slowly the peacock colors of the afterglow dimmed.

In his mind, her eyes were on him.

He spurred the horse down the long green slope, toward the towers and the sea. He saw no shapes on sand or stone between the towers; no sign that folk lived there, save that once he thought he saw a hint of motion near the sea, where the docks would be. But the street toward which he rode was empty.

Yet eyes were on him, ageless and bright.

Fiarril of the Sea-Elves stroked the strings of his harp.

"One comes," he said, "who has about him the sadness of Mortal Men."

His fingers moved with that sadness, and wrung it sobbing from the strings of his harp. But his companion, Curulin, looked keenly at the man riding toward them through the dusk.

"There is more sadness than that upon him. . . ." And

Curulin's harp took up that sadness, fingers hunting across the strings for some precious thing that had been lost.

The mourning sound of the strings reached Ingulf's ears, and he slumped in the saddle. Despair choked him; his worst fears rose in his mind. He pulled the horse to a stop, seeing again terror in her eyes, seeing her feet limping past, leaving him, leaving him forever. She might yet be far away in the sea, or perhaps the dangers of the sea had taken her. . . .

"There was a joy in him too," said Fiarril. His fingers danced across the strings, in a shimmer of delight and of love. "Listen! It is to a tryst that he comes!"

Ingulf pounded his heels into his horse's sides, urging him on. Like an echo of his elation the music was around him, pulsing with the joy in his veins. Airellen! He would see her soon, tonight. . . .

Against Fiarril's music the fingers of his companion played an undercurrent of lust.

Ingulf rode between tall towers, and in his mind her eyes glowed. Unseen Elves watched him gallop through the twilight, their music all around him. White stone rang beneath the horse's hooves. Wild music filled him; and drunk with it, he spurred the horse recklessly.

The boom of the waves filled the streets like the snores of a giant.

He pulled his horse to a stop. All about him tall figures stared at him with huge eyes that were inhumanly bright. There were women among them, slender, fine-boned—

Was *she* here? Airellen! Where was Airellen? He leaped from the saddle and ran into the crowd, searching for her. Where was she? These were her kind, frail-boned, with wide eyes in fragile faces, and hair like cloaks of shadow on their backs—but she was not among them. Emptiness and longing battled the joyous music. Where was she?

Beautiful as these might be, none was she, none was Airellen, none could quench the longing in him. The center of his life had been taken from him; the heart of the universe was gone! Where was she? Where was she?

He ran, searching frantically through the crowd. Beautiful

inhuman face after face turned wide eyes on him, and was not hers. Panic filled him. Where was she? Where was she?

Fiarril's fingers followed his mood, shifting to a mad quest across the strings.

Cold stars pricked through the sapphire of the sky. Was it the color of her eyes? He could not remember, could not remember—

Where was she? Where was she?

The people of the city made way for the madman who charged through them, looking from face to face. Wide, innocent eyes stared at him, wondering. The towers glowed silver light on white stone streets. Moons hung in the sky like pearls.

Where was she? Where was she? Fiarril's fingers hunted on the strings. Panic flooded Ingulf, and sickened him.

Then, far away down the white avenue, he saw her.

She wore a gown of velvet blue, and walked with another woman of the Sea-Elves. Joy leaped in him, and Fiarril's music echoed it.

He began to run toward her, then controlled himself. Wrestling with his breath, he made himself walk to meet her, while music swirled around him in surges of glory.

She looked up. Her eyes came to him. For just a second, terror flickered in their depths.

Then she looked past him, through him, as though he were not there at all.

Harpstrings crashed in a tangled discord. He stood rooted, staring at her through a blur of tears.

She walked past him, without a glance. His heart was lurching crazily in his chest. Panic hunted him up and down the strings of Fiarril's harp.

She walked on with the other, and he, scarcely knowing what he did, followed, like a moth flying to a flame.

Perhaps, he thought madly, she had truly not seen him. Perhaps she had not known him in the twilight. Perhaps—

What other hope had he?

He followed, and then he was walking beside her. Surely she must see him!

He reached out, timidly, and touched her hand. She went on walking.

"Airellen!" His voice was a thin sea-bird's wail, the cry of some lost thing. She walked on, as if she had not heard.

Fiarril's harp sobbed out a sorrow that could not be borne, and stopped.

Booming surf echoed between the towers. Ingulf stared into the darkness. The crashing waves called to him, promising peace, promising forgetfulness, in deep salty pools. His thoughts shattered in spray on the stone of her silence.

He walked toward the ocean, toward forgetfulness. The sea had brought Airellen to him, and only the sea could help him now. The deep tides would take him; the eels would feast; the churning sand would polish his bones.

Fiarril stirred, blinked the tears from his eyes, and set his hands to the strings of his harp.

Water hissed on sand. Fiarril's fingers rippled over the strings.

Music that was filled with the beauty and glory of life shimmered in Ingulf's ears. His feet dragged on toward the sea; and the music did not slow them or turn them.

Without Airellen the beauty of life was only emptiness and mockery. Sand blew across white stone by his feet. Pallid towers pointed at the stars. Sea-surge purred before him: harpstrings tinkled behind.

Fiarril plucked wonder from the strings of his harp; wonder, adventure, glory. The wide world unseen; perils not yet faced; women not yet taken. The music ran along Ingulf's nerves and sent chills to his shoulders, but he did not turn aside.

What adventure could be as great as death? All mortal lands were poisoned now; no wonder was greater than the depths of Airellen's eyes; no peril more terrible than the attempt to approach her once more.

Ingulf passed out of the long street between the towers, to see the black water frothing on the beach in starlight, and beyond, the long moving folds of ocean falling toward the shore. Almost the chiming of harpstrings was lost in the pulse of the waves. In a moment, he would be free of its torment, and soon, of all torment.

Lastly, and in desperation, Fiarril struck *fear* upon the chords of his harp, evoking the worm that hides within the spine, and flinches instinctively in its bony armor when death comes too near.

Ingulf's feet stopped on the sand, and his body rebelled against his will. Sand shifted under his feet as he struggled to move them.

And Fiarril called others of his kindred to join their harps to his, and herd the unhappy mortal back from the beach, away from the call of the sea.

Shocked by his sudden cowardice, Ingulf stared at the surging waves. He had faced the foeman's steel in a thousand fights. All his life he had traveled in tiny boats over the broad ocean. How, then, could he be afraid of death? Afraid of the sea?

He strove to drive his body on, but his limbs trembled, and would not move.

About him Fiarril and his kin wrapped a tune of illusion and enchantment, and phantoms thronged toward him over the sands of the beach. And Fiarril played shyness and embarrassment on Ingulf's nerves, as he looked up to see people coming toward him over the sand. The music put the thought into his head that, if he went into the water, these people would drag him out before he could drown, and question him, and Airellen might not wish to be talked of.

And a tall young man stood forth, and his voice was strong and proud as he called to Ingulf:

"Well met, Mortal Man! I hear you are a swordsman. You shall match strokes with *me!*"

And the rage which had smoldered in Ingulf since Airellen had turned from him wrenched at his muscles, and he and the young man fought up and down the beach with swords that seemed at times to have dulled blades, and at times seemed to be sharp.

The youth fought like a skilled warrior and practiced, while Ingulf himself had not drawn blade in many months of wandering. Yet the skill in his arm had not deserted him, and only once did the other blade slip past his guard, and that was a harmless glancing touch on his left shoulder, with a blunted blade. But Ingulf touched the other again and again, while warlike music stirred the air around him, and almost, for a time, hid from him his sorrow.

Then, as they fenced, he saw Airellen, watching him from beyond the crowd. His heart leaped, and he sprang boldly in, to show her the sword-skill for which he was justly famed. . . .

She turned away, and walked back into the city.

Black rage overcame him, and he struck off the youth's head with a sword that was suddenly sharp in his hand, then threw the blade aside and paced on the sand.

Fiarril's fingers whirled over the strings as he tried to use pride to drive away despair. But Ingulf's sick hopelessness was too deep.

Ingulf strode up and down the beach, and the pain that was inside him turned the whole world bitter and evil.

Then a woman who wore Airellen's shape came to him, and took him to her bed. He knew she was not Airellen, but he went with her.

And the Sea-Elves clustered about Fiarril, questioning, for the madness and sorrow of this mortal filled them with wonder. But Fiarril shook his head sadly, while his fingers wove spells on the strings of his harp.

"It is the rushing by of his days that makes him so," said one Elf, gravely. "He knows that he cannot wait, as we can, to let time soothe his hurts. For he knows that each day that rushes by brings death that much closer."

"Mortals are always throwing away their lives for some silly reason," said another, shaking his head. "They set no value on their lives, for they know their lives are forfeit from birth, and there is no reason to fear death."

Fiarril left them still talking, and went to find Airellen. But when he had found her, he feared there was no help there; for she seemed to care nothing for Ingulf's despair.

"He is a beast!" she said. "He *hunted* me! He stabbed his spear in me, as though I were an animal, and hurt me! Now he dares to hunt me again, this death-bound man! I am *still* an animal to him!" And she turned away, and fled.

Fiarril stared after her, fingering his harp. There was

something strange in her voice; he felt her words did not reveal her mind. Surely she could at least speak to the man!

Fiarril's mind was deep, and kindly, but he knew little of Mortal Men. He had heard that they could be more easily moved or bound by spells than could the Elves. But it had taken strong spells to draw the man back from the sea. . . .

Time would make all clear, but time the mortal did not have. He thought of things he had seen in Ingulf's mind. Surely in time Airellen might be brought to take pity on the man—but would the mortal live that long?

Not if he kept walking into the ocean with no sea-magic about him! And if the man had to watch his life slipping away, and no words for him from Airellen, then surely the despair would be upon him again. . . .

Fiarril tried to imagine what it would be like, to know that the fleeting days and hours were stripping his life away, and his strength and health with it. He shuddered.

Perhaps he should cast the mortal into a sleep, until at last the girl would be willing to talk to him—but sleep-spells were chancy things, sometimes, and besides, Airellen would be easier to persuade if the man were up and wandering about.

But his awareness of time could be taken from him. If it seemed to him that only the one night was passing, then he would not suffer as the days and months went by.

Ingulf came down to the streets again. Elves stared at him. There was a lump of ice in the bottom of his heart, but the madness that had held him had passed, and he could hear the moan of the surf without longing to lie down and vanish in the deep salt pools.

She did not love him. That was the terrible thing he had to face—and could not face! But hope was in him once again; hope that he could make her see that he was not a worthless man. But he'd not made a good beginning.

Elf-folk watched him warily, with glittering eyes. No doubt they thought him a madman. Indeed, he'd acted the madman: down their streets he'd galloped his horse at full speed. . . .

A harp was playing. A tall Sea-Elf stood before him, with a long beard swaying like seaweed in the salty wind. Ingulf had never before seen a bearded Elf, and looked at him closely, wondering if this were a man, or a being of some strange race unknown to him. The hair of the beard was as fine and soft as a child's hair, or a maiden's, and golden like old honey; the face beneath the beard was like a frail-boned young girl's face, and the eyes were huge and ageless. Long fragile fingers opened and closed on the harpstrings.

For a long time the wide eyes looked at him in silence, and when at last the Elf spoke—or did he sing?—his voice was gentle and soft as the dawn call of some forest bird.

"It is from far away that Ingulf the great swordsman has come among us," the Elf's voice came. But did he speak or did he sing? Ingulf could not tell. "Ingulf the Wanderer out of far eastern isles, famed in the service of mortal kings." Fingers on harpstrings flickered, and tiny chiming notes rippled and rang above the booming echoes of the waves. "Come to us across the weary miles, to rest from the trials of his journeyings. . . ."

Music wrapped around Ingulf, as the voice shifted between speech and song. The music grew swift and wild, and he found himself dancing, Elf-folk merry about him, whirling gaily through the white stone streets, while something clawed at his heart.

He did not see the Twin Suns when they rose. His long night had begun. When the dancing ended, they brought him wine and bread. Elf-women gathered about him, and many a sweet thing said, and he ate as he had danced, scarce knowing what he did: for the center of his life was gone from him, and the world was hollow.

He wandered the white stone streets, lost in a mist of spells, and sunlight was moonlight to him.

Waves throbbed on the shore. Sea-Elves danced and sang old songs. But Airellen kept her eyes turned from the lanky figure that haunted her.

He moved among the Elves, not taller than they, but heavier, bigger-boned. Their bones were like fragile lacework. As the long night wore on, his grew too large for the flesh that was on them, for he never hungered, and the Elves did not always remember to feed him.

Airellen danced through the city in her blue velvet gown.

Once, he circled cunningly ahead of her, so that she must either meet him face to face, or turn and run openly from him. He rehearsed in his mind words to say.

They were in the angle of a broad white square, with benches all around, and a fountain surrounded by grass in the center. She hesitated, trapped in the angle of the square, with no way to turn. She half-turned to flee, paused, turned as though to face him, kept on turning, turning, whirling, her blue dress belling about her hidden legs in sunlight that he saw as moonlight, and her grace and beauty trapped him where he stood. Tenderness and love filled his frozen mind, and he stood in courteous silence as she walked past him and away, out into the sunlight he could not see, leaving him hopeless in the dark. . . .

Fiarril's fingers clenched on the strings of his harp. He called to one of his kin to harp the mortal away from the destroying torment that flooded his mind, while he himself sought out Airellen.

"It is a glamour you have on him!" he raged. She shrank back from him. "No wonder my strongest spells cannot keep his mind from you!"

"I did not mean to!" she cried. "What could I have done? He wounded me! He put his hands on me! And it was nothing that I did! Only this—"

Her beauty flared, and passion and tenderness softened Fiarril—for a moment.

"But have you not tried to take it off? And why do you not speak to the poor man, who is dying for a word—even a look—from you?"

Terror widened her eyes. "I *cannot!*" she sobbed, and ran from him, down the pale street.

Ingulf ceased to wonder at the harping that was always in his ears. It was like the air he breathed, unnoticed. The harping and the slow drum of surf never stopped. Bewildered in a maze of magic, he wandered through the night of his coming, while beyond the city men counted away the days of a month.

He saw only moonlight and starlight and glowing stone.

Neither candle nor torch lit the towers, but their walls were filled with light.

And Airellen moved through the city like a ghost that haunts a dream.

Again and yet again he tried to close the gap between them, to make her see him, speak to him, somehow. But the spur of his mad desire always melted in a reluctance to bring her pain.

Once he followed her through starlit streets like a werewolf stalking, his mind inflamed with the need to hear her voice, to speak to her—but a part of him shuddered with the thought of frightening her. Clear in his mind he heard her scream, saw her blood welling about his harpoon shaft. . . .

Tenderness tore his heart, and he hesitated. She turned aside, closed a door, was gone. In the moonlight outside her door he ran to and fro in torment, until the harps lured him away once more.

The beat of the waves on the shore measured no time. The night went on forever.

A white ship came swaying across the sea, its sails like glowing clouds. The Sea-Elves went dancing down to the wharves, and Ingulf with them, lending his broad shoulders to unloading bales of mysterious, sweet-smelling cargo.

Airellen, too, was in the crowd by the dock, but she kept her eyes turned from Ingulf, and a curious shyness kept him from pursuing her.

Stately mariners stared at him with eyes bright with knowledge of other-world seas, startled to see a mortal in the streets of their city; but they were newly come from the Elvish lands that know not change or sorrow, and all in this world was new to them. They stared at the Twin Suns he could not see; they marveled at the familiar host of moons.

There was feasting and song in the city of the Sea-Elves, but Fiarril got little joy of it, for he was busy with his harp, keeping Ingulf back from the sea after this new meeting with Airellen.

And if Ingulf wondered that the ship from beyond the world could arrive and depart after long feasting, all in a single night, and that night not yet over, Fiarril's harping took the thought quickly away.

Thus Fiarril fought the mortal's despair with dreams; harp-

ing illusions about Ingulf so that he walked and talked with a
phantom of Airellen. Yet Fiarril saw that Airellen's spell was
still the stronger, and that though Ingulf's heart rose a little
from its despair, he still knew, somehow, that it was only a
dream and a shadow.

Then Fiarril began to fear that he would never be able to
wake the mortal, but must keep him wrapped in dreams until he
died. He sought out Airellen, hoping that he could convince
her to take charge of his illusion, and speak to Ingulf through
its mouth. But when he had spoken, she did not answer, only
fled from him with wounded eyes.

Dimly, then, Fiarril guessed what her secret must be.

Deeper and deeper he drew Ingulf into a net of enchantment,
wondering if he would ever be able to release him.

Then, out of the deep forest, wild Wood-Elves came to claim
the cargo: and with them Dorialith, who has more to do with
Mortal Men than any other among the Sea-Elves, save,
perhaps, for Ethellin the Wise.

When Dorialith saw the mortal and his invisible companion
walking between the towers, he quickly followed the strands of
the spell to Fiarril, and great anger was upon him.

"What is this that you have done?" he demanded sharply.
"And how long have you been—playing with him? The man is
as thin as an eel, and weariness clogs his flesh! He will die if
you do not stop this!"

Fiarril's fingers plucked golden chords of hope and relief
from the strings of his harp and wove them into his spell as he
sighed. Now the mortal could be helped!

"It is not as you think, Dorialith! The man would be dead by
now if I had let the killing despair that is on him have its way!"
Hurriedly—for Dorialith's anger was very great—he explained
the story he had picked from Ingulf's mind, and what he
guessed about Airellen.

"It is great harm you have done him," Dorialith said sadly,
shaking his head so that his long beard, colorless as water,
rippled in the light breeze. "The man has lost a month out of
a life that was short enough already."

All around them harpstrings and bagpipes raced with pounding drums, while Wood-Elves and Sea-Elves danced in greet-

ing, whirling wildly over the white stone. Dorialith had Fiarril charm the mortal closer, and studied Ingulf dancing with his phantom lover. "This month might have healed him—no knowing—but you have taken it from him, and given him instead a single night in which Airellen has still had a month in which to hurt him."

"Do you think that she means to hurt him so?"

"I do not," said Dorialith. "But the pain is there, and there is no time to heal his hurt before she wounds him anew."

"I should be taking the spell off of him, then," said Fiarril, stretching out his fingers to strike a chord of waking on the harp.

"No! You will drive him mad indeed—or kill him—if you jerk him from under such a heap of piled-up enchantments as you have made for him. And you'd best feed him now. And if ever you have dealings with men in the future, remember that you must let them eat at least once a day! Preferably more often than that! And sleep, too, they need. They are not like us, Fiarril." He rose, and stood watching Ingulf. "After he has eaten, put him to sleep for a while. His body needs rest, whatever your spell tells his mind. I will speak to Airellen before he wakes. As though I had no other work to do!"

Ingulf had long since given up trying to tell dream from reality. He knew he must be dreaming now, because Airellen was with him—only it was not *really* Airellen. She did not draw away when he tried to touch her. Although somehow he never quite seemed to touch her. . . .

She was far more pleasant than Airellen had ever been. But it was the real Airellen he loved—even angry at him, even wrapped in that terrible, soul-killing silence. . . .

His nails drove into his palms at the thought.

Why could he not hate her? Why did he have to go on loving her, hopelessly? If he could only make himself be angry with her, make himself blame her for the pain he was suffering . . .

But he was helpless in his love. Did she know what she was doing to him? Perhaps she was laughing at him, perhaps she enjoyed watching him suffer. He tried to make himself believe that, to overthrow this horrible nightmare of love. . . .

It did no good. He loved her. Even if it were true, he must still love her! Tears filled his eyes. Why could she not be kind to him?

And her image brought him to a place where there was food, and urged him to eat. He needed no urging. He seemed always to be hungry now. It was strange, for hadn't he been stuffing himself all the night through, at one feast after another?

His head whirled as he tried to remember everything that had happened that night. The white ship, and all of the feasting, and following Airellen again and again through the streets, Airellen who would not speak to him, would not look at him. . . .

If only he could make himself hate her.

She was with him now, but that was only a dream. Only a dream. Though the food tasted real enough. . . .

Then it seemed she led him into one of the glowing towers—but he knew it was only a dream. Perhaps the surest sign of that was the warm dreamless darkness that crept down his face the moment he joined her on the bed.

Harpstrings chimed in his ears.

Dorialith helped the Wood-Elves as they sorted out their part of the cargo—rare herbs from beyond the world, that could not grow in mortal lands; magical treasures and weapons of power sent to them to use in their long war against the powers from the Dark World.

When Dorialith sought out Fiarril, after the Wood-Elves had gone, he bore one of these in his hand: a sword that had been forged in the Land of the Ever-Living.

"This may help to balance, a little, the harm that we have done him," he said, as Fiarril stared at the sword. "And, if I mistake not what I see in him, this is a man who can do great good with such a blade, if he can be freed from the trouble that is on him now. He is sleeping?"

"He sleeps," said Fiarril, and led Dorialith to the tower chamber where Ingulf lay alone. Dorialith studied the sleeper carefully for a time; then, taking Fiarril's harp, stroked from the strings soft notes of rest, of peace, of unbinding. Slowly, carefully, he unknotted the layered strands of illusion and spell that Fiarril had laid.

The Twin Suns soared across the sky and settled in the west, and still Dorialith played. At last he played a spell of healing slumber, and gave the harp back to Fiarril.

They left Ingulf in the dreamless sleep of exhaustion, and went to seek Airellen. The rainbow light of sunset shimmered in the west. The Elf-folk thronged the streets; immortal, untiring, gay.

Airellen was walking by the sea, and the damp wind spread her hair into a pennon. She did not seem pleased to see Fiarril coming, and began to turn away, but when she saw Dorialith she stopped, and her eyes fell, for he is mighty among the Sea-Elves.

His wise gray eyes, shining like silver in the twilight, looked long at her, while his pale, silken beard floated in the wind, a white banner opposing the dark one of her hair.

"Daughter," he said at last, gently, "you have done greater harm than you know." The last rainbow glimmer of sunset faded from the edge of the sky, and the icy stars stared down. "In the heart of this man I have seen the seed of a great hero. Yet now he has not even the will to be angry with you for what you have done to him."

She had been looking at the ground, but her head snapped up at that. "Am I to blame that he followed me here? He hunted me, not I him!"

"Even the simplest glamour, that an Elf-Woman will throw about herself without thinking," said Dorialith, "is a deadly snare for a Mortal Man."

"And if it is a glamour that is upon him," she snapped, "cannot *you* take it off, Dorialith Mac Mananawn?"

But he only shook his head, sadly. "Some spells struggle against a man's nature. Easy it is to take those off. And some neither oppose his nature nor harmonize with it; those, too, are a simple matter. If he had felt no attraction to you other than that caused by the spell, then I could take it off him easily enough. But this spell rides too well with his own mind. Only *you* can take it off."

She closed her eyes, and her face twisted. Her hands closed around each other and writhed as though in pain. But her voice was level.

"What must I do, then?"

"You must be sure no liking for him clouds your mind—not even pity. You must take your dislike of him, or your indifference, whichever you truly feel, and you must cast it into the mirror of his mind, and forge a spell of emptiness, of petty rage and ugliness, of self-centered, careless mockery, and callous disregard, so that he will wish to be rid of you as much as you wish to be rid of him. Truth always conquers illusion: you must make him feel towards you as you feel towards him—"

"No!" Her voice broke, and a kind of terror came into her face. "No, I cannot—"

"You do care for him, then," said Dorialith, quietly. "I feared as much."

She looked at her hands, that were shaking, and knotting about each other.

"I did not mean to make him love me!" she cried. "He frightened me. He hurt me, but he was sorry afterwards, and very kind, and him so different from anyone I had ever met. But he frightened me—he laid his hands on me, his warm hands—" Her voice faltered in confusion; her hands took turns twisting her fingers. "I—I had to make him let go of me! I could feel—he is a beast! I felt his need for me, throbbing through him, through us both, and I—and I—"

"I know the spell you used," said Dorialith, gently. "No pleasure for you in that parting, only shame and fear: yet the moment's ecstasy you gave to him is more to him now than the rest of his life." He sighed sadly, and shook his head. "With no magic between you, he would still have come to love you. . . ."

"But he *doesn't* love me!" she cried wildly. "It's not *me* he loves, not truly *me* at all! It's only the glamour, only the pleasure I can give! He doesn't love *me*, he only loves—" She sobbed, and quieted, but still her hands writhed in protest.

"Can you create anything which does not spring from your own nature?" asked Dorialith wryly. "If so, treasure this gift,

as one unique among living creatures. But no, Daughter. Were
it only the illusion that he loved, Fiarril would have drawn him
from you long since, with his own illusion, with the illusion of
you that he wrought.

"But if you were to strip yourself of all illusion, and Fiarril
and I together were to harp up the most radiant and compelling
vision of you that might be dreamed . . . the mortal would
turn from it in an instant to find the real you. *It is you that he
loves.*"

"He is a beast!"

"Perhaps. But a beast that loves you, and will die without
your help."

She stood silent, shrunken, hunched in upon herself, staring
at her hands. "What the old songs say about Mortal Men—is it
true?" Her voice was a ghost of a whisper. "About age—
and—and—"

"It is true, Daughter," said Dorialith sadly. "In a mere
hundred years, all that will remain of his flesh and blood will
be his children—if ever he has any. And that, Daughter, is the
only thing you will ever be able to give him."

She shuddered convulsively, and looked up at him. "I do not
understand—I thought—I thought, perhaps, if I did not speak
to him—"

"You were afraid to speak to him," said Dorialith.

"And how should I dare to speak to him?" she cried wildly.
"Oh, you talk and talk of *his* suffering, but do you think I do
not suffer? There is nothing I can do! You say he will die
without my help, but he will die anyway! Nothing I can do will
save him from that!"

"Yet if he lived out his span of years," said Dorialith, "or
even if he died in battle, there might be great good he could be
doing. But you have taken away his will to live. If you gave
him hope—"

"And what hope have I to give him? You have told me I
cannot remove the spell, not if—what is it you would have me
do? Tell me how I *can* help him!"

"Talk to him, if nothing else. Let him know, at least, that
you can see him, that the poor creature can hope. . . ."

"Hope again! I have no hope to give him. I could not bear

to watch him age and—change and—die. No creature could bear that!" She buried her face in her hands. "What mournful lives Mortal Women must live!"

"He will not age right away," said Dorialith. "He is young yet. A good twenty years or more must pass before he begins to fail, and even in as short a time as that, a great many things may happen."

"Oh, indeed!" she said. "For one thing, if we keep talking till then, I may be able to make sense out of your hints and riddles! *Is* there a way to help him? What is it you want me to *do*?"

"There is one thing you can do, which will help," said Dorialith. "Since you do love him, a little. Take him as your lover. Use the spell I gave you. It will not stop him from loving you—it may not even take away all the glamour. But if his desire is fulfilled, time can do that. If he comes to love you as you love him, and no more—then, as you tire of him, he will tire of you."

"And if I do *not* tire of him? If I find that I love him more, instead of less?"

"Then you can live happily until he dies."

"No! Have pity on me! You cannot ask that!" She broke into wild sobbing. "I cannot bear to watch him die! Have pity on me, Dorialith!"

"And how much pity have you shown him?" Dorialith's eyes flared in anger. "When he wounded you, he took the harpoon out, and cared for you until the wound healed. Can you not do as much for the wound you have given him?"

She shrank back before his anger. Her long fingers kneaded one another against the blue velvet of her gown.

"I—I will talk to him," she said, tonelessly.

Alone in the tower room, Ingulf opened leaden eyes and stared at the glowing walls. For a time his numbed brain could make no sense of what he saw. Where was he? And what strange dreams had he been having?

Then memory came to him, and forced his unwilling limbs to sluggish motion. *Airellen!* She was *here!*

He staggered to the door, and stood leaning against the wall with his head whirling. How much of what he remembered was real, and how much dreams? It could not *all* have been real, surely?

Airellen! She had turned from him, walked away without a sign that she had heard his voice calling—

Yet also in his mind was the memory of her in this room with him, of her skin against his. . . .

He staggered down winding stone steps, around and around, as his brain whirled around and around. Airellen! Had he hurt her again? Was she angry? What had *happened?*

He stumbled through a door into starlight. The host of tiny moons glowed between the stars. Crashing, hissing surf echoed from glowing towers.

Tall, bearded figures stood before him. Their eyes were gray and bright, and larger than the eyes of mortal men. Their long beards rippled and swayed in the wind like a woman's hair, and one beard was yellow like old honey, and the other was like water pouring in the starlight. But the faces behind the beards were children's faces.

"Welcome, Wanderer!" The one whose beard was like flowing water spoke, and his voice was deeper than is common among Elves, rich and melodious with wisdom. "It is a long way you have come from your stone-beached islands, Ingulf son of Fingold, and a tangled path that you have followed."

Ingulf blinked, his mind too muddled for such talk. The one with the honey-colored beard—had he not seen him last night?

"A hard road," the silver-bearded Elf went on. "Few among men have ever dared seek out this city. Great striving should be rewarded, surely."

He must force himself to stand and be polite, while his heart drove him to strike aside these frail figures with a sweep of his arm, and run to find Airellen. . . .

"A great warrior you have been in the seas of the East," said he of the silver beard. "That you may be a greater one—look!" He held out a sword. It glittered like frost in the moonlight. But when the Elf moved into shadow, it still gleamed. "With this sword, great deeds lies before you. With it, perhaps, you may win to your heart's desire."

"*Airellen?*" he croaked, and wondered at himself.

"She is waiting for you," said the honey-bearded Elf, his voice like golden harpstrings. "But take the sword that Dorialith gives you."

He took the blade in his hand, and the warrior in him rejoiced at the weight and feel of it. The gold-bearded Elf pointed.

"She is waiting for you," he said, and Ingulf saw her, sitting on a bench in the moonlight: her eyes were cast down and her hands clasped in her lap. He ran past the Elves toward her, the gleaming sword forgotten in his hand.

Her face lifted as he came up, then dropped again. Fear shot through him. Would she look at him? Would she speak to him?

"Airellen?" he stammered, his voice weak with terror. Her wide eyes lifted.

"Ingulf," she said. "Come, sit by me."

He sat, his tongue trapped in his mouth. He must find words—but there were no words. Her eyes, her eyes were looking at him—

"Where—how did you get that sword?" he heard her saying. "Did Dorialith give it to you? Are you a hero now, Ingulf?" He had forgotten the sword he held clenched in his hand. He stared at the blade stupidly, and then laid it in the dust at her feet.

She had said his name! He had never known his name could be so beautiful.

"I—" He swallowed, forced words past his clumsy tongue. "If I am—if I am a hero, it is for you. It is all for you, whatever I am. I must make you happy. There is nothing else in the world. If you wish it, I will hurl the sword into the sea, or I will take it and go alone against the Demon-Lords of Sarlow."

She was looking at her lap again. All he could see was long, dark hair.

"It was for you I came!" His voice was frantic. "I wish for nothing else!"

Her head bobbed: her hands leaped from her lap; vanished behind the hair that covered her face.

"I know my worthlessness. I am no hero; no bard to sing your beauty, or to find words to tell you of my love. But I do love you!"

"No!" she sobbed. "You do *not* love me! It is only a spell I put on you. You cannot love *me!* After all I have done, after I have treated you so? Oh, Ingulf, what shall I do?"

"If it is a spell," he said, "never take it off. Oh, Beloved, do not turn from me. Hope of my life, Blessed Lady, do not make me suffer any more. Don't hurt me again. Stay with me, please, stay with me."

Her eyes met his. He had thought to find out what color they were at last, but then he was lost in their depths, and past caring. He heard her voice, crooning soft words. Strange visions swirled in his mind. For a moment he seemed to be Airellen herself, fleeing before a mad Ingulf who stalked between the white towers like a hunting scarecrow. He felt the harpoon bite into her side. . . .

His body faded. He could hear her voice crooning softly.

The warmth of his hands, the power of his voice, the strength and the tenderness of him . . .
But he will fade, he will fail, he will die. . . .

He was sitting on the bench beside her again, and her eyes were gazing into his. She loved him. He knew that now. He reached out and caught her hand, feeling her fingers cold and fragile in his grasp.

There was a curious vision in his mind, of himself, shriveling like a withered flower, and falling away to dust. What did it mean?

Her slender hand. Her fragile body. Her tiny shoulders. Yet he would die, and she would not. . . .

"I will bear your child, if that must be," she said.

He stared at her, then caught her hand and pressed it to his face, and kissed the frail fingers and the tiny palm, scarcely able to breathe.

My child, he thought. *Her child.*

"Your hands, your warm hands!" she said. "Oh, Ingulf, what are we to do? Where can we go? Should I go with you, among Mortal Men? It would not be good for you to stay here. Perhaps we could live with the Forest-Elves, or find a home in one of the cities in the West, in Elthar perhaps, where Elves and Men live. . . ."

His arms were around her. Her lips opened shyly to his. She

felt so fragile, so tiny, in his arms! He felt her, tasted her, smelled her, his beloved! He stroked her hair.

"What does it matter where we live," he whispered, "so long as we are together? Only stay with me, as long as I am living, never leave me again. . . ."

She stiffened in his arms.

"No!" she gasped, pushing away from him, and her face was a mask of terror. "No, not that! My love, you must not ask that of me! I cannot bear it, you must let me go before then! I love you too much to—you must let me go first!"

Her horror was echoing in his mind, but he thought it was his own fear of losing her.

"I can never let you go!" he cried. "Never! Not until death has me!"

"No!" she screamed, and wrenched herself away from him, and leaping from the bench was running from him, down the long white street that led to the sea.

He leaped up, leaving the bright sword of heroes gleaming in the dust, and ran after her.

His feet pounded hard stone. He heard shouts behind, but he cared not. He ran and ran, but ever the lonely slender figure before him drew away from him, growing smaller and still smaller, running, down to the edge of the sea.

She cast off her velvet gown. He saw the waves rise to greet her white body. His feet scuffed through sand as he ran toward the black night sea, calling her name.

A long dark shape like a seal darted away through the waves.

Starlight and moonlight above him, and the sea running up the beach to meet him with glass-dark waves. Water reared up and caught him in a cold embrace. He mounted the wave and swam.

Dimly he heard splashes in the water behind him. Out and away from the shore he drove, trying to shout her name, spitting out the salt water that leaped eagerly into his throat. He saw seals near him in the water, their bright eyes gleaming.

His limbs were heavy and weak, as though he had not eaten for a long time. He swam on, seeking for her, but his bones grew heavier and heavier, dragging him down. He felt himself sinking, and was glad.

A dark shape came up against him, and strong teeth fastened in his robe. He was being towed through the water. He did not want to live in a world where she did not love him! He started to struggle, but he was too weak for that. Water dashed into his throat and choked him. . . .

Then he was lying on sand, and coughing up water. Cold air seared his lungs. He rolled over, and saw the silver-bearded Elf between himself and the stars.

"Airellen!" he gasped, when he could speak again. "Where is she?"

"She will be swimming as a seal among the islands of the North," said Dorialith, "hunting among the salmon herds; trying to forget her sorrows in the salt tides of the wild ocean. It is a road that my people take when trouble is on them."

Ingulf stared. "Then I will stay here until she comes back," he said. But the Sea-Elf shook his head sadly.

"She will not come back while you are here," he said. "And she can stay in the sea longer than you will be alive. But aside from that, I cannot allow you to stay. It is a dangerous place for a Mortal Man. You have fared better than the last mortal who came among us, two thousand years and more ago.

"We welcomed him happily, meaning no evil, and I played music for him, that he might dance, and forget the sorrows of mortal life. He danced until he died."

Ingulf pushed himself unsteadily to his feet. Endlessly the breakers rolled upon the shore, smashed into spray, and fell purring back from the land. In the east he saw a pale glow, where tiny moons hung golden in the light of suns yet sunken.

For the first time in a month Ingulf was looking at the golden moons of dawn, but he did not know how long a night was behind him.

"But what shall I do?" he cried. "Must I seek her among the seals in the skerries of the North? I have no powers for such a quest! But my life is worth nothing to me, if she is gone out of it! What can I do?"

"Hope!" said Dorialith. "You cannot seek her. But in time her panic will leave her, and perhaps she will come to seek you."

Ingulf gaped at him, and the elf smiled, lifting something from the sand that gleamed with white light: the starlight flame of the sword from the Land of the Ever-Living. He pressed the hilt into Ingulf's lax hand.

"Take it," Dorialith said, "and go. Be bold and strong. Let your deeds become the seeds of song, and in time she will hear of them. I will see to that!" The Twin Suns rose, and in their light the froth that tipped the waves glowed like fresh milk.

And so it was that Ingulf of the Isles left the City of the Sea-Elves, gaunt and haggard, with nothing to show for his journey except the magical sword that he named *Frostfire*. Bright in his hands it shone, as he left—alone—the sands where the Sea-Elves' city stands.

II

The Loon's Cry

AIRELLEN RODE A wave to a rock that jutted stark and wet from the froth-creamy sea, and, casting off the seal-shape that was upon her, rested naked on sun-warmed stone.

Wind and storm had tired her: she was weary of the lonely waste of waves, and beginning to hate the taste of fish.

She saw another head bobbing in the water, and tensed, wondering who it was that found her; torn between the desire to flee, and the desire to hear a voice—any voice.

A white seal came riding on a wave-crest and slid smoothly onto dark rock. Wide elf eyes looked out from the white-furred face.

Then the seal-skin fell away, and a woman was there, her smooth skin lily-white against the black rock, her hair as snowy as Airellen's was lustrous dark brown.

In a jewel at her throat burned a spark of wandering fire.

"Cousin!" the newcomer cried. "I did not look to meet you wandering these waters! Is it not said that your father's ship has sailed from the Land of the Ever-Living, and will enter this world soon? I had thought to see you at the city!"

The smile on Airellen's face shrank and vanished. Red blood flooded her skin. Her eyes sought the pitted rock. Her fists clenched; then, quickly, she pressed her palms together, and her long fingers twined and knotted.

"Why, Cousin—what is this?" The white-haired girl's laugh was silvery and cruel. "What secret have I touched? Come! You can tell *me*! Is it your father you are hiding from? Or a lover . . .? "She laughed again, as Airellen flinched, blushing even deeper. "Indeed!" she crowed. "Have I hit on it, then? But who—?"

"Swanwhite! Leave me be!" Airellen cried. "Don't—don't—*dig* so! Leave me alone!"

"If you'll not tell me," Swanwhite laughed, "then you leave me no choice but to find out for myself! Let me see, now. . . . " She glanced quickly around the rock. "Ah!"

A swift, fluid motion, and she was leaning over a small hollow, where calm water reflected the sky. She bent, pink nipples brushing the rock, and breathed on the tiny pool.

"No!" Airellen cried, but Swanwhite only laughed.

Water misted, rippled, cleared, and then they both saw, there in the water, the big-boned scarecrow shape; the angular, long-nosed face under the red hair. . . .

"A *Mortal* Man!" Swanwhite breathed, startled.

Airellen gave a little shuddering gasp.

"Ingulf!" Her fists knotted: tears ran down her blushing cheeks.

A woman's scream sounded, somewhere in the endless woodlands.

Ingulf stopped, his eyes hunting through thick brambles, seeking between the pillars of countless trees. Somewhere above the leaves, he knew, the Twin Suns shone, but he could not see far in this green dimness.

Haunted, hopeless, homeless, Ingulf wandered aimlessly, helpless in these thick forests, so different from his native islands. Thorns had torn and shredded his tartan robe: his mind, too, was in tatters. It was a hateful world that he lived in now. Birds were nesting, hatching their eggs, feeding their mates, and surely it was all to mock him, to remind him that he was alone. . . .

Long months had passed since Ingulf, guided by helpful

Forest-Elves, had blundered into a poor fisher village and there learned that a month had gone out of his life during the night he had spent in the Sea-Elves' city.

Not once in that time had Airellen's face left his mind; not once had he slept without dreaming of her; not once had he halted in his mad quest for deeds to do, that Dorialith might make good his promise.

He saw her eyes in every sunset, her shape behind every tree. A patch of blackness on birch bark would suddenly seem to shape into her hair, and he would see her face framed in it, feel her eyes upon him. . . .

Blundering ever deeper inland, he wandered at last out of Galinor over the hills south, through the Elfwoods, and on into the Forest of Demons itself.

And always it seemed that some malign fate had come between him and the hope of his heart, and more and more bitter he became, until he felt that all the world had joined to mock him, and hold him from his love.

Lost in the forest, he blundered ever deeper. . . .

Another scream. Ingulf's heart twisted. Could Airellen be *here*, and in danger?

He began to run, blundering clumsily through brambles, his heart leaping with crazy hope and fear.

The scream died away, and Ingulf could hear only his own feet, crashing on leaves, and the frantic pounding of his heart and sobbing of his breath.

Where had the scream come from? He paused to breathe, trying to listen, while his eyes scanned the forest.

Surely the trees must hate him, surely there was some malign fate in the world that would not allow him to aid another in pain, mocking him with underbrush and echoes, and baffling twists between trees, and hills that cut off vision worse than sea-fog.

In the open ocean it would only be a matter of waiting for the waves to move. But where in these tangled trees could she be?

Even if it was not Airellen, somewhere a woman was suffering pain and fear. . . .

Was the scream only to mock him? Or was he being lured into a trap of some kind?

The screaming sounded again, and mingled with it, men's voices shouting and the clamor of steel.

Ingulf's fingers clenched on the haft of his great war-flail, the flat iron blade dangling loose, ready to swing in its deadly arc. His ears hunted the woods, tying to find direction among the clustered trees and occasional maddening echoes.

Gathering up his flail again, holding the blade tight to the shaft, he began moving slowly to the left. The sound seemed to come from there. Again the woman screamed, and now it seemed louder, and Ingulf began to run, adjusting *Frostfire's* scabbard in his belt with his left hand.

Suddenly he blundered into a trail, and went running along it, hearing, louder, the battering of steel ahead. He came to the brow of a knoll and looked down into a ravine.

The very land conspired against him! Why did fate hate him so?

He ran down the slope. Roots clawed at his feet. Ahead, the trail led uphill into tall pines with wind booming in their boughs.

Crashing through a screen of leaves came the glittering figure of a man in armor, reeling back onto the pine needles at the rim of the rise, to fall sprawling down the bank, smearing the needles with blood.

Another man reeled over the knoll, clutching at a dripping red leg, and slid, shrieking, down the hill. Other men appeared, under a shimmer of swords, the drumming of their shields all but drowned by the wind in the pines.

Ingulf sprang forward. Here were those he had come to aid!

Another mail-clad corpse pitched down the slope, and behind Ingulf glimpsed a tall blond figure, clad in smoky green plaid, sword crusted with blood. *One of the forest savages*, Ingulf thought.

Roots caught at Ingulf's feet. He saw men running down the hill as they fought, but he had to look down at the roots and loose earth that were trying to trip him, to keep him from the heroic deeds that were his only hope of love and sanity. . . .

Armored men were running and shouting; one screamed piteously, trying to crawl away, dragging behind him the spurting ruin of a leg.

Ingulf sprang between the wounded man and the tall, deadly, unarmored figure that bounded toward him.

The dark iron blade of the flail flew free, spinning out above the blond man's shield. The blood-crusted sword lashed into its path.

Most blades would have shattered under that terrible stroke; but this one held. The steel bent like a bow, and tore itself from the hand that held it. Ingulf stared. The blond man dodged back, disarmed but unhurt.

"Islander!" he shouted. "Is it mad you are, or a traitor, that you aid slave-hunters out of Sarlow?" Ingulf froze: the wheel of his flail faltered in its spin.

"Duck, you fool!" the blond man shouted, and Ingulf leaped to the side, his flail whirling around him as he turned, to drive down on the spear-shaft that pierced the air where he had stood. The spinning iron snapped the thick wood shaft as though it had been a twig.

He let the tip smash into the earth, showering pine needles and dirt. A convulsive swirl of his shoulders jerked it aloft again, its spin reversed. Mail-rings clashed deafeningly, and the man behind the spear staggered back, coughing blood from rib-pierced lungs.

The blond man was scrambling for his sword, and the armored men rushed, swords raised.

Ingulf hurled himself into their path, the flattened iron bar a deadly wheel. In the madness of battle, he could forget, and here at last was an evil on which he could vent the seething anger and hatred that boiled within him; to fight back against the unjust world and avenge his ruined life. . . .

The bare foot of dull edge at the very tip of the flattened iron went through a man's neck as easily as a sharp blade might have; its terrible weight whirred around again, spraying blood, and a helmet crumpled under the stroke.

Slavers backed away as the madman drove among them, his flail lashing, humming in the air, and his face twisted and his eyes wild.

There was a sudden loud crashing, a rending of wood, and thin branches and leaves showered on Ingulf's head and shoulders, as the handle of the flail tugged at his hand.

Ingulf's foes had backed under the low branches of a tree; the chain and the long iron bar were tangled in shattered boughs.

Ingulf let go the handle. Sneering, a slaver stabbed with his sword.

Ingulf's leg crumpled: his hand flew to *Frostfire's* hilt as the point passed over his head.

A cold, glassy wheel of flame blossomed as *Frostfire* whipped from its scabbard, ripping through mail-rings as easily as cloth: red threads rippled on the shimmering wheel of steel.

Then Ingulf sprang up, past the toppling, bleeding figure, and red drops flew from his sword.

Blades rang: blood reddened ring-mail. Harried, milling like sheep, mail-clad shapes fled, and suddenly Ingulf and the other man were eyeing each other across a slope strewn with shattered corpses.

"Well, Islander!" the blond man said. "You have a sword-arm indeed. I'm glad you came, and glad to welcome you! It is Carroll Mac Lir I am. Who is it I am thanking?"

"Ingulf, Son of Fingold," he said. "It was in Tray Ithir that I was born."

"It is a long way to Tray Ithir," said Carroll, shaking his head, "and you are far from your home. But it is glad I am to welcome you! But come!" He stepped to one of the bodies and stooped, to lift something that dripped with blood. "Here is the key. Let us free the poor wretches that these carrion-eaters were dragging back with them."

Ingulf followed him back into the trees, and through brush. Where had Airellen brought him now?

Wailing rose ahead, and then a clangor of chains. A strip of sunlight on an open trail cut through the forest's shadows. Here lay more mail-clad bodies, and others among them: forest men, naked but for kilts. Carroll called out, and the underbrush crashed and swayed: iron clanked, and a long line of haggard people pushed through the leaves, dragging the chain that bound them together.

Once before Ingulf had seen such misery, on his long quest for the City of the Sea-Elves. But that caravan had been smaller, its captives newly taken.

Some here were gaunt and hollow-eyed, their ribs ridges in scarred skin. They wailed and cursed as they fought to free the long chain from the trembling, grasping bushes.

Long before the chain was free, Ingulf had given up counting. The chain seemed endless. Misery-haunted eyes met his: scared eyes of recent captives, still full-fleshed; of women with bruised breasts and bloody thighs; of wounded angry men, with whip-strokes crossing fresh sword-cuts.

Worse than these were the dulled, haunted eyes of starved, scarecrow men and women, with long-healed scars.

"Aye," said Carroll, seeing his face. "Thus the *Sarloach* treat their prisoners even before they get them home. Starved folk struggle less, and the weight of their chain keeps them quiet. Yet these are lucky; they would be worse off in Sarlow."

The blood-stained key in Carroll's hand opened collars and wrist bands, and in a madness of joy and sorrow the freed people danced, wept, laughed, wailed, embraced each other and their deliverers until Ingulf was sure his ribs must break. Carroll had to break up a fight. Some of the stronger men stripped the bodies of their captors and armed themselves, and then chopped heads from dead slavers and hoisted them on spears. Voices bayed in wild acclaim.

"Savages!" Ingulf muttered. Carroll gave a snort of bitter laughter.

"Judge them after you have seen your own village burned, your own kin raped and butchered and eaten! Had you been on that chain, you would be howling as loud as any," said Carroll.

"Why do they allow it?" cried Ingulf. "Why have the Hasturs not destroyed them? Why do the tribes not unite to wipe out these evil, murdering, enemy monsters?"

"The Forest Clans unite?" Carroll said. "A few have, but the old feuds die hard. And the tribes nearest to Sarlow, that are most aware of the danger, are already wiped out. But even if a large number of clans could be united, or even all the clans of the forest, they would still not be strong enough to break Sarlow. Many times the Three Kingdoms have gathered their armies against them, but always the host has been turned back in the passes of the mountains."

"And what of the Hasturs?" Ingulf asked.

"There are limits even to the powers of the Hasturs. The Sorcerers of Sarlow are very strong."

Ingulf watched. All around them freed people danced, weeping and shouting hysterically. It was an evil world into which he had come.

What had Dorialith said? *Be bold and strong. Let your deeds become the seeds of song, and in time she will hear.* . . .

Perhaps there was a reason for all his suffering: perhaps he was being tormented thus in order to force him to take the actions which no one else dared.

Perhaps everything, from the time of his seeing Airellen in her seal-shape in the water, had all been planned for this! Perhaps it was not some unknown sin of his own for which he was being punished, but in order to destroy this other evil. . . .

"Then I shall go to Sarlow," Ingulf said. "It is time the slaves were freed."

"What?" Carroll stared at him. "What are you saying? Are you joking or mad—or—?"

"I mean what I say," said Ingulf. "I shall go into Sarlow, and free the slaves there, and—"

"Are you mad?" cried Carroll. "Have you not heard a word I said? Did you not hear me say that an army—?"

"One man may go where an army cannot," said Ingulf. "And *She* will never hear of me if I skulk in these trees and do nothing."

"She—? Who—?" Carroll shook his head. "I do not understand, and I do not know who you speak of, but it is plain that you know nothing of Sarlow! Are you thinking you can just walk in and then walk out again? If you get over the mountains at all, you will be a slave in their pits or meat for their table! You have never seen what is beyond these mountains!"

"Have you?" Ingulf asked.

"I have." Carroll's voice was grim. "I was chained on one of these chains once. I saw my father and sister cut up to feed the slavers that drove us. And I worked in the Slave Pits of Sarlow, with the whip on my back, until a knife fell from an overseer's belt, and I saw my chance. I killed the man with the keys, and freed others, and we killed the guards with our picks and hammers, and escaped. But not for long." Memory haunted his face.

"We made for the mountains. We heard howling behind us, and knew that the Hounds of Sarlow were on our scent. We had taken weapons from the guards, and when the first pack came, in daylight, we were ready for them, and we fought and we slew and we drove them off, though many of us were dragged down. Then we went on . . . on toward the mountains. . . ."

He paused. His breathing was harsh and ragged, his face twisted.

"The second pack came at night," he said. "A werewolf led them, and him no weapon of plain steel could harm. Swords went through his flesh, and the wounds closed and healed behind the sword. Man after man he dragged down, and we would all have died there, had the Hasturs not seen our need. . . ." He bit his lip, and closed his eyes.

"One of the Hasturs looked over the mountains, saw our fight, and came. He appeared out of the air, and burned the werewolf with a bolt of need-fire." He paused, and stared into the air before him. "But by then, there were only five of us left. There had been more than a hundred. . . ."

"Plain steel cannot hurt a werewolf," said Ingulf. "But that is why Dorialith gave me this blade." He pulled *Frostfire* halfway from its scabbard, then slammed it home again.

Around them the freed slaves were slowly quieting, though some still wept, and a few others still capered wildly and fiercely, stabbing at the dead slavers with shrill war-cries.

"Even with such a sword . . ." said Carroll, "it is madness to—" But a shriek from Ingulf cut him off.

"I am tired of talk! Why are you doing this to me?" His voice was as shrill and as wild as those of the frenzied savages around them. "Why do you try to destroy my only hope? Did *they* send you here to test me? Are they trying to keep me from her?"

Carroll stared at him, jaw dropping, while around them both, the freed salves reeled unheeding, dancing and weeping and shouting with fury. Ingulf's outburst had gone unheard, lost in the mingled jangle of passions.

"You *are* mad," Carroll said, stunned, wondering. "You are truly, simply—"

"Mad or sane, I go to Sarlow!" Ingulf shouted. At last, he thought, fate had guided him to the deed he sought. "You may fight me, guide me, or leave me be!"

"Will you not turn back *now*?"said Carroll. "Can you not see from here how hopeless it is? Do you think you can get past yon fort?"

Ingulf did not answer. He was studying the long ridges of the mountain-chain that ran all along the northern horizon. Carroll had guided him to the great mountains of Sarlow's southern borders, and now . . .

From the hilltop where they hid, he had a clear view of the broad road that wound around the hill and then up the mountain slopes, toward the narrow notch which divided two sharp peaks. He could see as well the high, frowning walls that closed that pass, and atop the walls, the tiny moving dots of pin-prick brilliance where sunlight flashed on the armor of distant men.

From behind them, from the little lake that lay in a hollow between hills, came a shrill, eerie sound like frantic laughter. Ingulf started.

"What was that?" he asked.

"A loon on the lake," Carroll answered. "Do they not have loons out in the islands? They are water birds, after all."

"Not on Tray Ithir, at least—or not often. I've heard the sound before, but never when there was anyone to ask what it was. So it's only a bird! It sounds so strange! And—evil!"

"It's only a bird," said Carroll. "A crazy bird. Like you."

Ingulf did not answer, but went back to studying the land ahead. There were trees about them, but ahead, between them and the road, were only chopped tree-stumps. All up the side of the mountain the trees had been cut.

To right and left, away from the road, spurs of forest swept up the steep slopes.

"If we go along the edge of the wood, there," said Ingulf,

pointing off to the right, "the trees will give us cover almost to the top."

"And what then?" asked Carroll. "Do you think you can climb the cliff there? Or do you plan to walk up to the wall and knock it down?"

"Ah, that cliff is no worse than the cliff of Scuriniscariv on Tray Ithir," said Ingulf, "and I used to climb that every morning when I was a boy! Almost every morning, anyway . . . and do I not see a stream there, falling down the rock?"

"Indeed," said Carroll. "There is good fishing in the lower reaches of that stream—or was, when I was young. Where it flows off to—"

A sudden loud, rumbling roar rose from the east, drowning his words. They looked, and saw one of the tallest of the distant mountain peaks veiled in a black, writhing vapor that seemed to eddy in the air.

Carroll leaped to his feet and stood staring, face stricken. Ingulf shaded his eyes with his palm, trying to see.

A shrill whining seemed mixed in the roar. The dark, whirling cloud seemed to be sliding down the mountain's face. For a moment he saw below it the soft green of distant pines; then that was blotted out by a swirling rough-textured gray—but then that, too, was hidden by the falling black curtain. . . .

Then the slopes of a nearer mountain blocked that view, and there was only a tall blotch of writhing, swirling darkness.

The top of the spinning, ink-black mist began to move down. Something showed behind, but it did not look the same. . . .

The mountain now had a broad, flat top, as though its tip had been sliced with a knife.

The cloud continued to settle. Now a rounded, greenish slope appeared. . . .

Ingulf gasped, and straightened. A vast space had been gouged out of the side of the mountain, and where a gentle, wooded slope had been, there was now a sheer, polished wall of pallid, yellowish granite.

"*Sgur Alain!*" Carroll cried, pain in his voice. "*Gone!* The

Golden Well, the aisle of stones, the Lone Oak tree . . . all
lost. Shattered in a single stroke, with all that remained of the
home of my kin!"

"What?" Ingulf could not speak. He stared at the sheer cliff.

"They have started on this side of the mountains now!"
Carroll snarled. "Thus their sorcerers use their power! *Now*
will you turn back?"

"You may," Ingulf said, glaring. "I will not."

"Loon!" Carroll shook his head, and stared at the broken
mountain. The echoes of the roaring had died away. There was
no sound of bird nor beast; all creatures crouched, fearful,
listening. . . .

Then, after several moments of tense silence, a jay called,
somewhere in the branches of a distant pine. A blackbird
answered, and then a squirrel chattered from one of the trees
above their heads. The loon cried from the lake. The forest
came to life again.

A chorus of shrill, baying cries sounded from deeper in the
woods. Carroll stirred, and loosened his sword in its scabbard.

"The Hounds of Sarlow!"he exclaimed. "If they have found
our scent, it is already too late to do anything but run."

"You will not stop me through fear!" Ingulf snapped.
Carroll looked at him sharply.

Ingulf's eyes went to the mountains, and the guarded pass.
It seemed to his mad mind that the path through them led to
Airellen. Surely, this would be a deed she could not ignore!

What matter if he died? That would end his suffering, as he
tried to do when he had walked into the sea, and the seals had
dragged him back. . . .

He started off, away from bitter memories, his flail on his
shoulder, along the wood's edge toward the north.

"Ingulf!" Carroll shouted after him, but he trudged on, the
long iron blade of his flail dangling behind his back. The other
was only trying to keep him from the glory that was his only
hope, the chance of deeds that could draw her back from the
sea. . . .

He did not look back until he heard great bodies crashing
through brush behind him, and heard Carroll's war-cry.

Turning, Ingulf saw gray wolves pouring from the forest, a

single horseman riding at their head. He whirled and ran back. Carroll was in danger, and Ingulf knew himself to be the cause.

Wolves turned as Carroll rushed up: one leaped. Carroll's keen blade split the slanted skull. A second wolf reared at his throat as he ripped his blade free. His shield held it away, while steel wheeled beneath it to slice the beast in half.

The lead wolf leaped at Ingulf. The flail flew, iron shattering bones. The Islander charged, the long iron bar whirring in a blur around him.

Carroll's bright blade whipped round. As wolves sprang to slay, their bounds met steel. Blood soaked the ground.

The iron bar of Ingulf's great flail sailed hissing on air, lashing around him as he fought his way to Carroll's side.

Hooves hammered as the horseman bore down upon them, bright sword flashing in a silver wheel. The wolves scattered away from the hooves. Ingulf sprang out of the sword's path, his flail flying high above the horse's back, sweeping the foe from his saddle with a sound of snapping bones.

Wolves wailed: the pack scattered and fled.

"Quick!" cried Carroll. "It will not take them long to bring others. We can lose them in the stream. Follow me!"

He raced up the slope, keeping in the shadow of the trees, with Ingulf close behind. Carroll dodged deeper into the woods, then suddenly leaped high into the air, to the top of a huge granite boulder.

"Here!" he called, stretching a hand down to Ingulf. "Jump! Jump as high and as far as you can. That will confuse them."

Ingulf jumped, caught Carroll's hand, and as soon as he was steady on the rock, Carroll sprang away to another boulder.

From there they jumped high up a slope, almost to the top of an embankment. Ingulf heard clearly the gurgle of water.

They ran to the top of the ridge, and saw in the ravine below a slow, shallow stream, crawling lightless under spreading willow branches at the foot of a steep drop.

Already Carroll was lowering himself over the edge.

"Drop into the stream!" he said. "It's not far. Downstream it flows into another that leads deep into the wood."

But Ingulf looked upstream, and saw water pouring down a sheer dark cliff.

A long howl sounded behind, then a chorus of wild yapping cries. Ingulf turned and ran along the ravine's lip, toward the falling water.

"Come along!" He heard Carroll, behind him, shout. "Where are you? What are you doing? 'Tis not a far drop!"

Ingulf slipped the thong of his flail over his head, and let it drag on the ground.

Before him, trees climbed the hill in steep ranks, but earth walls flanked the gully where the water fell. Tree-roots groped out into the air, reaching for the stream. He gripped one, then another, as he worked his way toward the cliff.

"You loon!" Carroll shouted from below. "What are you doing?"

He reached the rock and found a narrow place to stand. Turning, he saw Carroll below, thigh-deep in the stream, very small and far away.

Wolves howled in the woods beyond.

"Madman!" screamed Carroll. "What do you think you're doing? Loon! Madman! Come down!"

"They will not think to look for me this way," Ingulf called back. "I will be safer than you, indeed! But this will give me the path I need over the mountains."

"Fool!" Carroll's voice raised echoes. "Come back!" Wolf howls shuddered in the air.

"You go back!" Ingulf called. "Get safely home. But be quiet now, or they'll not need our scent to find us."

He turned and climbed, fingers roving over rough rock. Once he glanced over his shoulder, and saw Carroll still staring up at him. Holding firm with one hand, he waved the other to motion the blond man away. Then he climbed on.

The worn, rugged rock gave no trouble to one who had spent much of his boyhood stealing gull's eggs from the seacliffs of Tray Ithir. His flail dangled down the center of his back from the thong around his neck.

He pulled himself over the lip of the broad ledge, and looking back saw Carroll, a tiny figure far below, wading morosely down the stream.

From here he could see the boulders where they had jumped. Wolves were sniffing the ground around them, milling angrily.

Beyond, the road swarmed with mounted figures gleaming in ring-mail.

He watched until Carroll had vanished in the trees, then turned to work his slow way up the mountain.

He soon found himself wishing that gulls nested here. Or anything he could eat. He came to places where the rock slanted enough that he could walk, wading in the swift stream that tugged at his legs with icy-fingered currents, while his hands rested.

Higher he climbed, and higher, while the Twin Suns crossed the sky. Evening found him curled in his cloak on a high ledge, sleeping soundly, and dawn found him scrambling among weather-shattered jagged boulders near the mountain-crest. Now he could look down and see the fortress that straddled the pass.

Thick walls blocked the notch; dawn light glittered on the mail of patrolling guards. Horsemen rode out, with packs of wolves running behind.

Other packs came in, but the men who led them were naked and unarmed.

At night, these would be invulnerable wolves that his flail could not slay. He loosened *Frostfire* in its sheath, and climbed on.

He heaved himself up between two boulders and found himself looking out over a broad, blurred landscape.

Great masses of cloud or smoke covered much of the land, but there was something profoundly disturbing about what he could see. He frowned, and turned to look behind him, back over the endless sea of trees that stretched to every horizon. He heard distant howling.

He forced his way between the jagged boulders and started down the slope, toward the evil land below.

Airellen had trapped him into this evil world, where every hand would be against him, and the bond of common humanity would not matter: a land filled with creatures in human form who joined willingly in the work that would lead to eventual destruction of the world and its people, of the universe itself. . . .

He stared out over the landscape of the evil world, trying to understand what was so jarring. There were gaps in the smoke, and through them he saw woodlands, deserts, city.

The land was so flat! There were only the faintest hints of swelling here and there—as though rows of little hills had been sheared off by some gigantic axe-stroke.

The more he stared at the land below, the stranger it appeared. He saw wild woods and cities cheek by jowl. As the slow-moving mists parted, flat land, gray as filed stone, appeared.

A wind began to blow the smoke aside. He gasped.

There, like a tiled floor in a prison, land lay in patterned blocks of city, forest, farm, barren rock.

Shuddering at the sight, suddenly in a sweat, reeling, Ingulf of the Isles wondered what he was trying to do, as it dawned on him at last that this land of Sarlow was not merely larger than Tray Ithir, but larger than all of the islands in its chain.

What was it he had planned? This patterned landscape ran to the horizon! He could not see the sea. . . .

And what force could have so shaped this immense plain?

He remembered suddenly the whirling mist that had planed away a mountainside while he had watched.

Airellen had driven him to this madness. It was for her he had come! But surely she would see him after this!

He saw again *her* eyes, staring past him, or through him, pretending he was not there. Surely, after this—

If he lived. If he was not simply swallowed up in this vast land. Dorialith had promised to sing of his deeds to Airellen, but how would Dorialith hear of his deeds if he could not escape from Sarlow?

He allowed himself a sparing sip from his waterskin. Hunger was at him, too, but he had already eaten, the day before, the little oat bread and dried venison Carroll had pressed on him.

The singing of birds grew rarer as he picked his way slowly down the mountainside, keeping well away from the road that ran down from the fortified pass.

Long grass grew here, pallid yellow-green, and away from the road some sparse scatter of trees that gave him a little cover.

He glimpsed on the road the bright shimmer of mail, where armored men rode with their wolves.

Through the pale grass loping came tough, shadow-coated warders; red tongues hung dripping from the white-fanged jaws. Their panting, rapid breath and the rushing paws crashing through the grasses mingling with thudding hooves and the jingling squeak of the mail of the master riding in their midst was loud in Ingulf's ears as he crouched hidden in tall pale grass at a tree-trunk's foot.

They missed his scent, passing in a rustle and clatter and a chorus of hoarse, rasping breath: the glittering proud figure on the red-brown horse never turned his blond head. Ingulf watched them go, the wolves bounding behind the arrogant rider.

Rising, he slipped from tree to tree behind them, for further down the mountain the road curved to cut across his path, and this was the way that he must go to get around it.

The scrubby hillside forest thickened ahead. Far below, mail-rings sparkled as, to and fro between plain and fortress, armies marched.

He remembered how, as a small boy, he had amused himself by pretending he was going into some deadly danger. Now, as he descended toward true and deadly danger, he comforted himself by pretending to be that small boy, stalking imaginary dangers.

The Twin Suns moved steadily across the sky. He heard horse and wolves turning, heard rushing of heavy bodies through the grass, and sank down behind a tree while the great gray shapes bounded past him, the mailed rider gleaming in their midst.

They raced back along the road. He waited till they were well away, then moved down the hill. He could see through trees the ground below, divided by a line, on one side of which cattle grazed in a green field; on the other, the bared rock of the mountain's foot was anchored in a plain of mottled stone.

He saw now that that plain was not as smooth as he had thought it from the mountaintop, but was scarred with yawning pits and craters, some of them half-hidden under columns of dark smoke.

He heard faint, distant hammering, far across the plain, and under it sounded a wailing of voices.

He worked his way slowly down the hill. The Twin Suns were dipping toward the west, where thick haze hid the mountain border of Galenor, when he drew near the boundary of the green pasture. A cow saw him, and eyed him placidly, but there was no one else in sight.

The cow's eyes followed him as he worked his way cautiously toward a line of trees that ran along the edge dividing pasture from stone.

The wailing rose, under the hammering, and now he heard other voices, laughing and shouting, echo from the stone.

Now mingled with the wailing came sharp, distinct screams.

At the edge of the field, earth dipped away in a steep bank to a broad road, made for marching armies. On the far side, another embankment fell to naked stone.

Beyond the stone to the west was a field green with grain; to the north he could see towers and great halls of cheerless stone. Beyond the pasture he could see tall trees.

He looked up the slope and down the road. There was no one in sight. He scrambled down the drop and darted across the road quickly, daunted by its width and the mass of its stone. Far down the road, tiny figures swarmed by the city wall.

He slid down the bank and onto jagged stone. A wolf howled somewhere on the heights above, and he wondered if they had struck his trail.

He dashed across the flat, sheared stone.

Screaming and laughter grew louder ahead, and the clamoring of hammers.

The sounds all seemed to rise from one great gaping pit: all around it lay piles of some soft black stone.

Above the screams he heard wolves howling on the mountainside, and broke into a run, hurrying across the blank, bare rock, where any eye would quickly pick him out.

At last he reached the heaped black stones, and dodged between two piles, breathing hard. Hammering and maddening shrieks of pain battered at his ears.

He peered out, cautiously. The Twin Suns almost touched the jagged teeth of the western mountain ridge. A cold east wind rushed out of the gathering night. Shivering, he crept toward the light and the smoke that poured over the edge of the pit.

The smoke stung his eyes and made him cough as he looked over the edge. A red glow pulsed near the heart of the smoke, and in its dim light vague shapes moved.

Below him, at the pit's edge, strange black shapes were hammering, gouging out the black rock with picks.

Glaring shapes flaring points of red light strode among them. Whips rose and fell.

Blinking, Ingulf saw that the black shapes were starved, bony, naked men, caked with soot.

Armored men guarded them, firelight glimmering on mail-rings.

And near the fire something writhed and screamed.

It was smeared with black dust but underneath it was red, like a skinned animal. But it was alive: it writhed and screamed and pleaded in a human voice. . . .

Suddenly Ingulf was trying to vomit his empty stomach into the pit, as he realized what that screaming red thing was.

He sat shivering and weak at the edge, trying to force himself up. There was a ramp carved out of the edge of the pit. He should get up now, while the Twin Suns still peered over the hills, and run down the stair and kill the guards. But when at last he forced himself to stand, his knees shook.

Below, whips whistled and sliced backs coated with soot and blood, and picks pecked at the rock of the pit, and hammers drove chisels into it, and the beaten men moaned and cried, while the skinless man screamed by the fire.

Ingulf forced himself toward the ramp. Firelight gleamed on mail-rings as a metal shape strode toward the skinless thing and stood over it, laughing.

Ingulf reached the trail and started down, his great flail raised and ready to kill.

The armored man by the fire began to take off his mail.

Rainbow glints of sunset swirled across the sky above the smoke, as the Twin Suns sank. Mail-rings shimmered as they jingled to the floor beside the fire.

The great bladed flail was poised in Ingulf's hands, the

muscles of his chest tensed, ready to bring it swirling out.
Screaming and hammering echoed all around him from the
sides of the pit. His mind seethed with rage and pity, but his
knees had stopped trembling. He must be swift, and silent.

The slaves had picks and hammers and chains, but they were
starved and skeletal, as scarred in spirit as in skin. A few might
still have the courage to strike, but he could not depend on that.
He would have to kill most of the guards, at least, himself.

A slave working near the stairs looked up and saw him.

Ingulf tried to sign for silence, but the man reeled back
shrieking in a cracking bass voice.

The sky overhead grew dark: the light of the fire bright.

Ingulf realized that no one had heard the slave's scream, or
cared. All eyes, of slave and guard alike, had turned to the fire.

The stripped man threw his tunic down atop his mail and
turned, pale skin glowing in the firelight, and stooped above
the writhing, skinless thing. Leaping shadows seemed to twist
his body.

Ingulf stared, and a chill crept through his veins. Fire-
shadow twisted—but no! It was the man's flesh that twisted.

Stooped, humpbacked, the naked man lowered his hands to
the floor. The glow of white skin in firelight faded as hair crept
over it.

Flesh flowed and changed. Ingulf had heard tales of the
werewolves of Sarlow all his life, and he had seen his beloved
change from seal to woman and woman to seal. Still his pace
faltered and he stared at the shape-changer. Icy hair lifted on
his spine.

The shape-changer's crouching, apelike figure raised its
lengthening muzzle and screamed a howl into the sky. Skinless
red flesh shrieked as strong jaws closed.

A shout rose among the screams; mirror steel rippled red
from a sheath at a mailed man's side. Drumming feet ran at
Ingulf, darkness veiling mail. A sword wheeled in air.

The iron bar was a pendulum upon the bladed flail. Tense
muscles surged, lashing the iron bar out; steel belled and broke
as the thin sword snapped like glass. Ingulf leaped, gliding iron
looping in air. Bone shattered under steel.

Ingulf sprang to the dark pit's floor. Hammered iron hummed, air droning as death whirled around him.

But beside the fire, a dark head turned. Sharp ears pricked at death-shouts and battle-cries. Blood drooled as crushed bones dropped from the mighty jaws.

Chained slaves were trying to scramble out of the way. Shouting soldiers halted in their rush; a few among them had raided in the Outer Islands and recognized the rare but deadly weapon that they faced.

"Get your shields, you fools!" one shouted. "Form a shield-wall round him, it is the only—"

Ingulf sprang for the speaker, letting the flail's whirling weight pull him through the air in great, spinning leaps.

The whirling iron bar crunched mail, shattering bone in a wheel of whistling death.

Chained slaves, screaming, scrambled out of the way as a black-furred shaped shot through the crowd toward Ingulf's back.

Screams and the scrabble of claws brought him around. Red eyes met his. White teeth in gaping jaws were flying toward his throat.

The whirling iron bar lashed down, hurling the black-furred shape back, with red blood oozing from its shattered skull.

It rolled to a crouch. The bleeding stopped. Bone and fur crawled as the wound healed.

The guards had fallen back. Why rush in, risking death under that terrible flail, when an invulnerable ally could take your place?

The massive beast gathered its haunches under itself and, eyes still askew in its crushed head, snarled and sprang.

Ingulf let his flail go free, spinning of its own weight into the midst of his mailed foes, and dropped to one knee, hand flying to hilt, as the furred beast reared for his throat.

Frostfire flew from its sheath, a wheel of pallid flame.

The snarling roar changed to a shriek of pain as a line of light lanced the black fur.

Shouting stopped: slaves and guards alike gasped and were still in the sudden flaring moonlight of the sword. Blood poured over the frosty glow of the blade, dimming it.

Claws shrank back into fingers. The black-furred shape twisted with a monstrous rippling of bone; and it was a man's shape that fell kicking to the ground, the black hair writhing as it thinned.

Silence was broken with a wild shout as a slave threw himself onto a guard's back. The chain between his wrists fell over the guard's helmet and down to his throat.

Wild shrill shouting echoed from the walls in a chorus of hate.

Mail-clad men raised their swords as slaves with chains and picks and hammers swarmed upon them. Some snatched up the swords of fallen guards; one seized Ingulf's fallen flail and crushed a guard's helmet before the tricky whirling weapon twisted back upon its wielder, a glancing blow that snapped the unskilled arm like a twig.

And *Frostfire* slew, lashing in its own white light, as Ingulf leaped in. Slaves swarmed. Some shrieked and ran into the darkness. Yet still the guards' swords slashed at a wave of whip-scarred flesh, and in the midst of the madness *Frostfire* wheeled and hissed and slew.

Ingulf dodged a falling blade as *Frostfire* slashed through mail, and suddenly he saw no foe standing, only writhing mounds of struggling, heaped figures, beating and stabbing at things that screamed and bled.

"Free!" A man's voice howled. "We're free!" Other voices took up the shout, and still others drowned it with wordless weird cries.

A tangle-haired, skeletal man came capering like a shadow into *Frostfire*'s light. Ingulf saw teeth flash white in the sword-light as lips lifted to mouth words that were drowned in the crowd's sound. He stepped nearer, ears straining to hear. . . .

"—weapons," he heard, "—armed! The wolves are coming, the Hounds of Sarlow and their masters! Soon we'll hear them howling!" The voice faded, mumbling under the shouting. Then a bony hand seized Ingulf's arm, shouting in his ear, "—wolves and werewolves too! Can you not hear me, man? We must get this rabble calmed!"

"We must indeed!" Ingulf shouted back. "But how?"

The man let go his arm and scampered off. Ingulf stared at the mob about him, naked and bloody and covered with soot. Soon the men of Sarlow and their wolves would come.

But he felt like a man in a dream, cut off from the madness and joy all around him, as though behind a wall. What had this to do with Airellen? He looked about wildly, as though to find her eyes upon him, but saw only savagery. Soot-streaked figures in the dim red glow shrieked and raged as they robbed their captor's bodies, pulling free the bloody coats of mail.

A loud gong tolled. The pit's walls echoed, cutting through the shouting with the hollow metal boom of a rapidly battering hammer on a gong.

Cheering, jeering voices faded. Men looked up, afraid. Ingulf saw, across the dark pit, the man who beat upon the gong lower his hammer and turn to speak.

In the sudden stillness, they heard, far off in the night, the baying of the wolf-pack.

Vartheg rode with the wolf-pack, while his lieutenants loped beside his horse, armor and humanity laid aside.

His wolves bayed on a scent. A runaway slave, no doubt, for surely no enemy would dare the mailed soldiery of Sarlow.

Though tales whispered of Elves haunting the night, eluding even the wolves, Vartheg did not believe them. Elves might be hard to find, and hard to kill, but he had found and killed them.

A wild shriek ahead told him that his wolves had found their prey. Grinning, he spurred his horse cruelly, rushing toward the kill.

"Please!" The voice screamed. "I've come to find you! Let me tell your master—*No!*" Vartheg grinned as he rode up. He always enjoyed it when they begged.

"Call them off, please!" the voice shouted. A pit-slave, covered with coal-dust. Kaynvang and Vlujyagar had him down, but their jaws only held his bare limbs lightly.

"Please, Master!"

Vartheg laughed.

"You were looking for me?" he purred.

"Yes!" the slave screamed. "In the pit! A foreigner with a

sword of fire—*No! Don't!*—killed all the guards! Please make them let go!"

"What?" Vartheg exclaimed, then gave a soft whine at the two wolves, and they took their teeth out of the man's flesh. Vartheg urged his horse nearer. "Don't think lying will save your skin! Why are you telling me this? What do you hope to gain?"

"I'm not a foreign slave, Lord!" It was true, Vartheg realized; the accent told it. "I was a thief, Lord, and they sent me to the mines! I was underboss, and spy for the commander. They'd kill me—and I have nowhere to run to!" His voice was a wail. The pack milled all around. Vartheg rose in his stirrups. His voice was grim.

"If you are telling the truth, I'll see you are . . . rewarded." He sneered. "And if you're lying, I can reward that too! Which pit was this?"

"Pit forty-seven, Lord. Captain Svardvar's—"

Vartheg turned to the werewolf at his side.

"Vildvang!" he ordered. "Run to Klufbirk. Report to Sekthrig or to Vildern Blackbeard." He turned back to the slave. "How many slaves, do you think, will join this foreigner?"

"There were at least a hundred foreigners, Lord. Though some were killed—"

"Tell Sekthrig to send down two companies," said Vartheg, "and to watch the pass closely. Hurry!" The werewolf barked and sprang away. "I *think* I believe you, thief," he said, "so I may as well reward you now."

"Lord, I—I—"

"Vludric!" He called to his other werewolf. *"Bite him!"*

"No!" The slave screamed as a bolt of black fur leaped across the moonlight, knocking the other wolves aside as it caught the man and bore him to the ground. Vartheg laughed.

"So!" he called out, laughing. "Now you have been rewarded, thief! In a few nights you will be invulnerable, and there will be a place for you in the Army of Sarlow! Unless, of course, you have lied to me, in which case Vludric will find you and finish you off!"

A sobbing moan was his only reply. Laughing, Vartheg

called his hounds to heel, and wheeled his horse toward the pit, clawing its flanks with barbed spurs.

"Listen, men!" The man who had beaten the gong shouted across the pit. *"Listen!"* The shrill baying of the wolves blew ghostly down the nighted mountainside. "They will be here soon! Even if they have not heard you fools cackling, a patrol will be by in an hour!

"They will soon be hunting us, but we are free and armed! The keys to our fetters are in Untarr's belt. Find his corpse! We have swords and shields and mail; we have hammers; we have picks!"

"Now let us thank this warrior who freed us from the fear of the werewolf by arming ourselves to aid him!" Wild cheering echoed, and men began tumbling corpses about, searching for the keys.

Ingulf found his flail lying beside a groaning man who clutched a broken arm. Picking it up, he made his way toward the gong. *Why is this happening?* he wondered. The noise and confusion made his head feel sick and ghostly.

"Spread the weapons among you!" The man by the gong was shouting. "Let the man with a mail-shirt take a pick; let the man with a shield take a hammer, and then give the sword to another! A mailed man with a pick in both hands is as good as an axe-man! Give me a sword and I ask for no more. But a line of shields with hammers—Hah! We can form three lines, and we will crush any that come against us!" He broke off, and strode to meet Ingulf. Wet red blood dripped from the links beneath his still-chained, soot-stained hands.

"So what now, Islander?" he asked, low-voiced. "I talk bravely, but I would never have dared move a finger to help if you had not killed the werewolf. And I fear—all of us are filled with terror! Will that bright blade bring Hasturs to aid us? Or must we fight our way over the mountains, and through the forest beyond, with only one blade among us that can slay a werewolf—or whatever else the Sorcerers may choose to send after us?"

Ingulf stared at him.

"Who are you?" the Islander asked. "These folk all seem to take your orders."

"I am Rakmir Mac Mennis, of Orragut. And I have had to give orders before: I was the captain of the *Bennora* before it went down in the battle off the Scurlmards seven years ago, when Prince Alacar led the Imperial Fleet against Norian raiders, and the Sarlow fleet surprised us in the Troj Strualpoq between Sgronoq and Glocorrik."

"Alacar is Emperor now," said Ingulf, staring at this man who had endured seven years of this captivity. The eyes in the soot-blackened face vanished: the head shook back and forth.

"Old Emperor Hiduin, dead! Ah, that is harsh news! Alacar will be no well-loved ruler. What will I be going home to? A changed world!" His head shook again. "A changed world. Worse for me than most of these others. But let us hurry, swordsman. They will be after us soon enough. You have but the one sword, and there will be many werewolves."

Sudden rage swept over Ingulf.

"Is it a rabbit you are, that can think of nothing but running away?" he hissed between clenched teeth, glaring. "Now you wish to flee, when there are still others left to free?" His voice rose to a scream, and those around turned to stare. "Is no hatred on you for those with whips? Is there no pity on you for those still beaten?" He whirled, and sprang across the bottom of the pit.

Leaping up beside the gong, he struck it with the butt of his flail.

The gong's mellow tone boomed. As it died, they heard in the night the high, eerie keening of the wolf-pack.

"Do you hate the men who wield the whip?" Ingulf shrieked above the wolf-song. "Now that you are free, will you flee, leaving other hands bound? Do you wish to save your own lives, without striking a blow to free another?

"What makes your lives more precious than those of others still toiling under the lash? When we have freed the last slave we can reach, when we have killed as many of the foe as we can, then it will be time to find a road back!" The crowd murmured and shifted nervously. The howling of wolves grew louder.

"I did not come here a prisoner! I came of my own will over the mountains, to free slaves—to free men and women—to free *you!* There are still more of you to free. I go to find them, to set still others free! Those who wish may follow. The rest of you may flee! Arm yourselves, then flee or follow as you will!

"How do I get to the nearest pit?" he said, turning to Rakmir. The other stared at him.

"I should kill you," said Rakmir softly. "I should kill you and take that sword and lead these men out of here."

"Indeed?" Suddenly the iron blade of the flail dropped away from Ingulf's hand to dangle loosely from the shaft. Rakmir shook his head.

"Oh, I know well enough I can't do it. I saw you fight, Islander! But you are leading all these men to their deaths! I know I can't stop you, but my curse is on you for every man that falls."

Sekthrig the Flayer, Commander of the Pass, was boasting of his cruelty before his officers and his guests.

". . . and every time she caught her breath between screams, she kept babbling, over and over"—he pitched his voice in high falsetto, mimicking—'*Why are you doing this? Why are you doing this?*' He burst into loud guffaws, and most of the men in the room joined in. Vildern Blackbeard, pretending to laugh and determinedly hiding the weakness that kept him from enjoying the favorite sport of his fellows, noted that the two renegades, Calmar and Kelldule, did not laugh. But with their power, none would dare challenge their weakness.

And did you ever answer her? he found himself wondering, his false laughter dying while others laughed on. But that was foolish. Had not tSarl, the First Man, been created that his suffering might amuse the Dark Gods?

It was he, Vildern, who was different. There was some failing in him, some sinful weakness, which kept him from enjoying the struggles and screams of the weak as they—

Someone touched his arm. Startled, he looked up into the face of the boy Sigreth, who was with the guard that night.

"Sir," the boy whispered, "a werewolf has come with a

message—either for you or for the commander—" He shot a
sharp glance at Sekthrig, who had launched again into his tale
with relish. Vildern understood well enough. He slid from his
chair noiselessly and slipped from the room.

Outside, Ulvard waited with Rothgalin, the Beast-Speaker
for the Wolf Corps of the 22nd.

Beyond, a great black beast glowered red-eyed from the
shadows.

"Captain," the Beast-Speaker began, "there has been a
revolt in Svardar's Pit. And—a foreigner, Lord, or a *Liktalp*,
with a fire-sword—"

"What? A fire-sword?"

The werewolf growled from the corner, and burst into the
snarls that served as speech from the dog-jaws. Vildern
listened; he could not follow entirely, but he could recognize a
word sometimes. The Beast-Speaker turned back.

"Vildvang says he did not see the sword himself, or anything
else. A slave overseer—a criminal, not a captive—got away,
and said all Svardar's men were dead. Vartheg says you should
send at least two companies."

"At least," said Vildern. He sighed heavily, then grinned.
"For this, I must tell the commander. Vildvang," he said,
gesturing to the werewolf, "come here with me. You too,
Rothgalin!" He waved the other two back, and as the werewolf
came, he threw the door open and let the gigantic, red-eyed
creature precede him into the room.

He hid his glee as he heard Sekthrig's voice fail in the
middle of a word.

Ingulf and Rakmir glared at one another. Suddenly Rakmir
stiffened.

"They are coming!" he said. Ingulf turned.

He heard no wolves now. The howling had stopped. The
men in the pits were passing weapons and armor and shields in
a nervous silence, with low murmurs when they did speak.

And now, listening, he heard even that murmuring die.

Mail-rings glimmered at the pit's edge. A man stood there
looking down, his armor catching the faint gleam of the
firelight.

Eyes shone: dozens of slanted green eyes, and one red, glaring pair.

Ingulf sprang away from the gong and rushed toward the trail that led down into the pit.

"*Vludric!*" A voice shouted from the pit's rim. "Take him!"

The iron bar hung free, ready to move; but he saw the red eyes move and dash toward the top of the path. He shifted the flail to his left hand.

A darkness rushed out of the dark; a single pair of red eyes rushed at him. His right hand closed on *Frostfire's* hilt.

The red eyes neared. Green eyes clustered behind.

Sudden black fur and white fangs showed clear as the werewolf sprang.

Sprang into a wheel of cold white light as Ingulf whipped the blade free from the scabbard in a lightning cut.

There was a roar from the men in the pit: a howl of rage from the wolves.

Red blood pulsed from the black-furred throat. Without a cry the leaping body flew past Ingulf and pitched over the trail's edge to the floor of the pit.

Frostfire's flame vanished into its sheath; wolves leaping down the trail met instead the whirring iron bar.

"*Up now!*" Rakmir shouted. "Follow him!" The sea captain himself seized a torch from the fire and sprang to take the lead. Some held back, but other men surged forward, heavy miners' hammers raised.

Wolves yelped and whined as the iron bar whirred among them, shattering bones. From the pit's edge came a shout, and suddenly the wolves turned and were running swiftly away up the trail. Ingulf ran after them, while behind him surged a roaring mass of angry men.

He heard hoofbeats pound away, saw receding mail-rings glimmer in the light of tiny moons, and around them the fleeing shadows of the wolf-pack.

From the heights of the pass above them came the roar of a horn, and then mingled with it on the wind was borne the mournful choral howling of wolves.

Looking up, he saw the tiny light of a distant, opening gate. The men behind him all fell silent, huddled like sheep.

Now the distant voices of the wolves filled the air. Down the mountainside the echoes carried. Across cold, bare stone the ghostly echoes trembled in the icy air of night, and the newly freed slaves shivered.

Even brave men might have wavered, bursting into panic flight, running on—on—on until hunters dragged them down, had Ingulf not laughed loud and gaily before he shouted:

"Come! You are free men! Free more!"

Free! Pride reared over terror of the wailing of the wolves. Fire flared in men's eyes, and hands gripped hammer-hafts.

Loud on the wind still shivered the cry of the wolf-pack. Out in the night, hunters were gathering. What of it? Free men were marching—marching to free the rest!

Something of Ingulf's spirit had seized them. One man had freed a hundred, or more! That done, what was impossible? Even Rakmir was caught up in the mood as they marched.

Vildern's well-trained horse followed the wolf-pack down the dark hill. Mailed riders galloped all around him, mail-rings jingling. Ahead of them a sea of bobbing lupine backs surged through night-shadow: the werewolf-led pack of the Hounds of Sarlow.

Up the dark slope behind them, columns of footmen were marching more cautiously on the road. Vildern wished he were with them. He preferred to march with his men. But Sekthrig wanted him here, so he rode unwillingly through the night, behind the thrashing black backs of the carpet of wolves, surrounded by the hoarse panting of their breath.

Out of the night below came a sudden short bark, and the surging mass halted, milling. A chorus of whines and growls told of meeting, and the pack opened to admit a surging current of wolves sniffing and licking, with a horse and his rider in the middle.

The rider pulled his horse before Sekthrig and Vildern with a sharp salute.

"Vartheg here, Commander. The slaves from Coal-pit number ninety-seven have rebelled and killed all their guards. There are about a hundred men marching on the stone, with perhaps twenty swords among them. The rest are armed with picks and hammers. But they won't get far. I have wolves trailing them—"

"Why did you let them out of the pit?" Sekthrig snarled. "You had a werewolf and a pack. You could have blocked the trail out of the pit, and held them until we came!"

"I tried to do that, but . . ." Vartheg's voice had grown shrill; now he took a deep breath and paused. When he spoke again, he sounded tired. "There is a foreigner leading them, Sir, and he has a fire-sword. A fire-sword and another weapon I've never seen before. He killed Vludric—took his head off with one stroke—and then maimed and killed nearly a dozen of my wolves, single-handed. And he had a hundred men at his back. If I hadn't ordered my wolves back, I'd have lost them all! What was I supposed to do?"

"Is it an Elf?" asked Sigrat, Sekthrig's other lieutenant.

"I—don't know, sir," said Vartheg, shaking his head. "I've not seen enough of the *Liktalp* to know. But—I didn't think—he looks ordinary enough—but his hair is the color of the Nameless One. His clothes are all raggedy—he wears one of those plaid robes. . . ."

"An Islander?" said Sekthrig. *"Here?"*

"And he has—I don't know what to call it, Sir! It's like a long pole with a—a sword-blade chained to the end of it—flops around, but—"

"A bladed war-flail, from Tray Ithir!" Vildern exclaimed. "By the sound of things, sir, I'd say we have a Swordsman of the Isles on our hands." Sekthrig's breath hissed sharply.

"But—he must be some kind of a magician. The fire-sword just seemed to—appear in his hand—"

"Yes," Vildern said, with a satisfied nod, "that sounds—"

A sudden sharp bark from the werewolf Vildvang cut him off, and Sekthrig gestured imperiously for silence.

Men quieted; listening ears pricked up atop a sea of silent wolves.

Across the flat lands below, a long and complex wolf-song quavered and wailed—a message.

"Pit eighty-six, that would be," said Vartheg, his voice questioning. "But—that doesn't make sense, Sir! They're marching *away* from the mountains! I'd have thought they'd be moving up into the mountains, looking for a way out."

"It means they are not trying to escape!" Sekthrig snapped, impatiently. "It means they have seen our weakness at last, and are building up a slave revolt, here in the lands beyond the Lumrof! I have warned the Council, and others have too, that we have not a sufficient strength of troops here to hold the slaves down if they had help from outside! The Council says terror is the answer! *Hah*! Quickly now, I need two messengers! One must go back to Klufbirk, and beg the Sorcerers there for aid—the other must ride all the way to Bluzig, to warn the Council!"

Vildern was already turning, calling up a messenger on a swift horse for the ride to the fort. For the rider to Bluzig, he selected an officer—rank would help—and chose for him an escort of wolves, with a werewolf to lead them.

"Alert all the pits!" Sekthrig was saying, and wolves howled out warnings across the stone. "It is likely there are more of these swordsmen."

There was a frenzied milling and stamping, and then horses and wolves were running again, pouring down the dark hillside in a rumble of hooves and a storm of padded paws, and ragged hoarse breath from the wolves.

Vildern heard the horse-hooves ringing on the stone under them as they swept from the grassy bottom of the hill onto the planed rock at its foot.

Two hundred bare feet murmured over stone. Ahead, red-lit smoke glowed above the pit. Wolves howled on the nighted plain behind them.

Ingulf called a halt, and whispered to Rakmir to take charge and station men around the pit's edge to guard against the army they could hear behind them on the hill. Picking out twenty men—most with shields and hammers, some with swords, a few in mail with picks—he told them to be ready to follow, and then crept to the pit's edge and looked down.

A glowing pile of orange coals was the only light. Through the smoke he saw the sprawled shapes of sleepers and a single, drowsing guard. He began to turn, to speak to his men.

A savage growl sounded behind him, and a black-furred, red-eyed bulk hurtled roaring out of the dark.

A man went down, skull crushed in the mighty jaws, while Ingulf rolled to his feet. Others scattered out of its way as the raging shape rushed. A hammer-blow sent it reeling with a crushed skull, but it was up in a moment, shattered bone healing.

Ingulf dropped his flail at the pit's edge and ran to meet the beast, springing into its path.

Red eyes flared in *Frostfire's* light as he freed its blaze, slashing the black fur.

Questioning shouts rang from the pit as the bloodied beast screamed and fell, its shape shifting as it hit the ground.

Wolves howled out in the night, and horse-hooves hammered on the stony plain.

"Follow!" Ingulf shouted, *Frostfire* flaming in his hand like a comet to point the way.

Sheathing the sword, he snatched up his flail from the pit's rim and sprang down the trail, hearing behind him a rush of naked feet.

Whip-scarred slaves cowered as armored men, new-roused, snatched up swords and ran from sleep to death. Ingulf's whirling flail lashed out, cracking bones. Hammers crushed helms.

But the rage and hate of former slaves was the deadliest weapon. In a moment, they stood above the dead, while scared, half-awake slaves stared in fear.

Ingulf ran to the fire and threw on coal till it blazed.

"Listen, men!" he shouted. "You are free!"

They cringed in shadow, staring, not daring to believe.

"Rise up now!" he shouted. "Arise and arm yourselves! Do you not hear the nearing howls of the wolves that serve your foes? Would you die like sheep? You can see that your masters are dead! Rise up now!"

They crouched, numbly staring. Some wept.

"What is it that is wrong with you at all?" His voice grew shrill, high-pitched with passion. "Will you not act like men? Is it people you are at all? Will you crawl back to the masters that beat you and eat you, and feed you to werewolves? You unnatural animals! Is it dogs you are, or sheep? Why is this happening? What makes you act this way?" His voice shrilled falsetto; his hands clenched. The slaves cowered in confused terror. "Is there enchantment on you?" He pulled *Frostfire* from its sheath.

At first sight of that shining blade a keen wail burst from a hundred throats, drowning the wolves' howl in exultant savagery.

"Is it true!" a voice shouted. "We *are* free!" And other voices took up the cry. *"We are free!"* Some men wept. Others rushed the bodies of the dead, seizing swords out of the stiffening fingers and waving them wildly.

Through their sobbing and screams Ingulf heard a voice shout his name, and looking up saw an indistinct shape at the edge of the pit.

"They are coming!" It was Rakmir's voice. And listening, Ingulf heard, through the clamor around him, the nearing howling of wolves, and under that, the frantic drumbeat of hooves on stone.

Quickly, he sought out the men who followed him into the pit. A few he found embracing lost friends.

Sending his men up Rakmir's aid, he ran to find the gong that hung, as in the other pit, near the far wall, and beat upon it until the wild rejoicing voices were still, and every eye was fixed on him. In the stillness the wolf-howling was clear.

"Some of you have already taken swords from the dead," he shouted. "Take them with you and get up to the top of the trail. There will be a use for them there! The rest of you—you have hammers, you have picks. There are shields and mail-shirts. Take them! Avenge yourselves on your masters." He sprang down and ran to the trail, up out of the pit.

In the darkness above, Rakmir was ranging men in a line, the men with shields and hammers in the front, and the mailed men with picks spaced evenly between them.

Out on the darkness of the stony plain, waves of wolves surged like the front of a storm toward them. The men stood in a great dark mass, shoulders pressed together because they were afraid.

Ingulf could smell their fear: the sickbed-sweat scent of

terror that spreads from man to man. He smelled it, felt it trying to wash over him, to drown his mind, even as it quickened his heart and speeded his shallow breathing. What was he doing here? What was happening?

He could see, on the dark stone plain beyond, red eyes and green eyes in the froth of that first furred wave, which rolled toward them on the surf of the hoofbeats of the sword-crested wave behind it. What was he doing here? What was happening? What was he doing? Why was he here?

He looked up into the star-jeweled vastness of the night, and saw there Airellen's eyes.

Fear evaporated; he pushed his way through the huddled ranks, and *Frostfire's* sudden pale flame kindled their hearts.

"Now, free men!" His voice was miraculously calm as he shook the flaming blade in his fist. "Earn your freedom! Strike!"

He whirled to face the surf of hooves, the wave of wolves that rolled down upon them, like an ocean storm bearing down on some frail fishing-village.

He heard wind rush into lungs as every man behind him drew breath; but out of the sword-crested wave of horsemen a voice yelled.

"There! The fire-sword! Kill him: take it, and we cannot lose!"

But as the sword's light reflected from a mass of red eyes in the front of the wave of wolves, they veered sharply. A body of werewolves, running together in one black-furred mass, swerved to the right, splitting the wave, to crash against the shield-wall yards away.

The shield-wall sagged back. One man screamed, but others roared as they smote with picks and hammers, battering the black shapes back.

Ingulf turned, to run to their aid, and dozens of gray-furred, snarling shadows swarmed around him. Their toenails clicked on the stone as they lunged at him, their hot breath rasping through slavering fangs.

He jerked his wrist back, and teeth clicked where it had been. He whirled, *Frostfire's* keen edge flying on the wind, up under the opening jaw and the wet, white teeth. He felt slit skin and flesh open to his edge: the dead wolf fell, red blood running.

But more reared up around him, their harsh dog-stink in his nose. The flail in his left hand lashed out, but there had been no room for a proper swing between his body and the shield-wall, and he might as well have hit them with a stick. Even as *Frostfire* slashed back down, blunt-clawed, lunging paws drove him reeling against the shields. Teeth tore his tattered tartan robe.

Rakmir's voice roared. Men with shields surged forward, hammers lashing. Ingulf, slashing frantically with *Frostfire*, sensed lessening pressure as wolves fell back.

Teeth closed on his ankle, then loosened as he hacked off the head. Before he could bring his blade back up he saw fangs fly at his face: a wolf already launched in a leap above the piled dead—

He blinked, as a hammer smashed it, crushed, out of the air. *"Go on!"* Rakmir shouted. "Kill the werewolves! We'll keep these off your back."

He heard horses' drumming hooves check and falter, plunging, as the bloodied wave of wolves ebbed, back into the charging line.

Rakmir ran at Ingulf's back as he sprang, bright blade high, at the sagging wall where the black shapes clawed.

Hammers crushed skulls, picks ripped great wounds, and the beasts went down, but then the black fur rippled and crawled, and the werewolves rose, healed, and sprang back to attack. *Frostfire* flew in a steel-edged wheel: a wolf screamed in a man's voice as the bright blade bit. The bleeding beast reeled back, rearing in shock on its hind legs as it changed and died.

Milling werewolves fell back from the chill silver flame of the deadly blade out of Tir na n'Og. A few rushed, fear drowned in blood-lust. They died.

"Kill him!" a voice screamed from among the horsemen. "There's only one man!" Another werewolf rushed Ingulf, with a roar.

Well-forged bright Elvish steel-and-silver killed, and the others fled. Swift hoofbeats came pounding. A sword scythed from the sky. Rakmir's shield met it. The horse thundered by.

"*Sekthrig!*" a voice shrieked. A pickaxe whirled around, ripping the mailed man from his saddle, stretched him dead on the ground.

The mounted wave of horsemen loomed up, crested with steel. Picks and hammers met them.

Tiny white moons turned golden in the eastern sky. Changing werewolves wailed as they fled from the dawn.

Ingulf sheathed *Frostfire* and used his great flail.

"Retreat!" a deep voice shouted above the crash and the thunder of the battle. The horsemen fell back, then wheeled and cantered away in the twilight.

There was a wild cheer, and a few men broke ranks to chase the foe, but Rakmir's sea-captain's voice rose.

"Stand firm, you fools!"

Then the Twin Suns rose, sparkling on the armor of footmen that marched across the plain.

III

The Stone Plain

AT HIGH TIDE, when many little moons cluster around Domri and Lirdan, the sea-waves surge between the bone-white towers and up the streets of the City of the Sea-Elves. Deep tones throb in white stone as waves pluck the towers like harpstrings.

The white seal came riding the wave-crests into the white sea-froth that surged between the towers.

At the water's edge the seal-skin fell away, and Swanwhite, clad only in the jewel at her throat, waded up from foam that was no whiter than her body or her hair.

Dorialith was the first to see her striding up in beauty, dripping from the sea in the dawn, with the jewel of power flaming at her throat. He bowed low.

"Princess Ilsafewn!" The excitement of hope was in his voice. "Then—your father is here?" She shook her head, fine white hair whipping in the sea-wind, mute sharp pain in her far-seeing, sea-gray eyes.

"Neither Father nor Grandfather—or, at least, they did not come with me!" She smiled. "Indeed, it would be my dearest hope if they were here, but if not"—she straightened, proudly, and flame stirred in the jewel above her white breasts—"if not, the Seven still shall meet!"

"Who, then, rules at Tirorilorn?"

"Ocloqaran of the Mystic Shield rules in my name until I return," she said. Dorialith was staring past her now, down at the sea.

"But—your ship? Your escort?"

She laughed, "Why should I expose my warriors to attack? No ship could have taken the route I took without fighting. But the watchers have no time for hunting seal! And if they had"—suddenly rainbow flame blazed from the jewel at her throat, wrapping her white body with a veil of fire—"the Power of Tirorilorn is with me!"

"So I see," said Dorialith, shading his blinking eyes. He bowed again. "Thrice welcome, then, Lady of Tirorilorn! The Council of Seven has not been graced by such beauty since Etain was sent to speak for the Lords of the Living Land. But I fear it will be at least another day before all the Seven have gathered. Ciallglind is here, and Ethellin, but the Son of Awan is still far away upon the sea, and—"

"What of Falmoran?" she asked quickly. "Has the ship come from the Living Land?"

"It has, indeed, but . . . I must tell you that his daughter, your cousin Airellen, was not here to greet him, and that—"

"I know," she said. "I spoke with Airellen on my way here. Tell me of this mortal man of hers, this Ingulf. . . ."

The dawn light grew; Ingulf and Rakmir took stock of their losses, and counted the glittering mail-shirts moving slowly toward them across the stone plain.

Though a dozen of the freed slaves had been injured—including the man who had broken his own arm trying to wield Ingulf's flail—only four had been killed in all that day's fighting. And though the werewolves had ripped and torn the shields where they had crashed against the wall, they did not seem to have bitten any of the men behind them.

And in exchange, all the guards at both pits had been killed: more than a dozen wolves and werewolves, and three of the horsemen who had charged them. Including, Rakmir said, the commander of the fort in the pass.

And the man whose pick had killed him, Torvar Mac Valgar, had been a man Rakmir had thought long dead: the first mate of his ship. The two talked excitedly about old comrades and home, or about the torments of the years that had separated them, indiscriminately, glorying in the joy of each other's voice, even as they followed Ingulf, and planned the next move.

"Well, the *nearest* pit," Rakmir answered, "is on the far side of those glittering murderers out there!" He waved a hand at the advancing army. "But there is another, not too far off, that way." He pointed north on a line that crossed in front of the marching men. "But they'd be on top of us before we were halfway there. Our best chance will be the next pit *that* way, directly away from the enemy. Then we may be able to keep ahead of them—"

"No," said Ingulf. "We'll go north." They stared at him. He gestured toward the shimmering ranks. "If they were in any hurry to close with us, they'd be here by now. If we go directly away from them, they'll think we're running away, and they'll catch us. And by the time they catch us, most of the men *will* be running! But if we march out under their noses—"

"He's right," said Torvar. "We've got them scared. They can march much faster than that."

"Give the orders, then," said Ingulf. His heart soared. He was back where he had fought the werewolves now, and he counted them, looking at one naked blond corpse after another. Dorialith had said that Airellen would hear of his deeds! This was a deed that—

He froze. A woman's body sprawled, headless; and nearby a woman's head lay on its tangled yellow locks, the upside-down face snarling, while the dead eyes glared at him.

For a fleeting second of utter horror, it seemed Airellen's face. He screamed.

"What has brought this curse on me?" he cried, heedless of the stares that turned on him. "I strike a seal, and she is a woman! Now I strike a wolf, and she is a woman too! What is this curse on me? What is it that could make me break Hastur's Law, and turn woman-slayer?"

"You could not have known!" That was Rakmir's voice, and

it was his powerful hand that gripped Ingulf's shoulder and shook it. "Hastur will forgive you! Besides, Hastur's Law was to keep men from slaying the helpless—children and prisoners, as well as women. And she was *not* helpless when you killed her! *She* did not live under Hastur's Law."

"It is a curse that is on me!" Ingulf shrieked, heedless. "It is destroyed I am! Why am I being punished? Is it because I hurt Airellen, or was a curse already on me that caused me to throw the spear? Was it a curse that brought Airellen to me?" His voice grew shriller, wilder. *"Why do they hate me so?"*

Men huddled together, staring. Torvar turned to Rakmir.

"Why did you not tell me he was crazy?"

"I—I did not know that—" Rakmir shook his head. "I've not heard—raving like this before. I—don't know what—"

"How can there be such a curse on me?" Ingulf howled. "It makes no sense! *She* would not have cursed me! She cannot be so evil, or so cruel! And yet she turned from me, she destroyed me, she hurt me as no living being ever has before! Oh, my love, come back to me! Do not leave me in this evil world!

"Whenever I think of her, the evil world turns against me." His voice had dropped to a muttering whine. "They are trying to make me forget her! Ah, stop! Please stop! Why does the world conspire against me? I am not an evil man! I've done nothing to deserve this! Oh, please, stop destroying me! Oh, Lady, free me from this curse!"

Vildern had taken command when Sekthrig the Flayer died, and had ordered the retreat, although he knew the competing lieutenants would charge him with weakness, pretending that they would have fought to the last wolf and the last man, when the scramble for Sekthrig's position began.

But of course, if he *had* fought to the last wolf and the last man, then they would attack him for wasting lives. So what he did only mattered to the men whose lives were at risk. And Vildern always put his men first.

Bluish stone blushed in the dawn; mailed men marched slowly, cautiously, approaching the foe. Vildern knew well that two-to-one odds were not always decisive against desperate men.

And these freed slaves, facing death by torture, knowing there was no hope of mercy, had nothing to lose.

And so the terror which was to be our strength weakens us, Vildern thought. *Many of them must be very scared, and if they had any hope of mercy, would be happy to lay down their weapons and go back to the pits. . . .*

But they won't, because they know what happens to rebels. They've seen it happen to too many of their friends. . . .

We can't even promise them mercy and betray them, he thought, *because they know better than to believe us—and the offer would let them know we were afraid of them. . . .*

Loud voices broke into his thoughts. He reined his horse toward them. The loudest was a woman's voice.

In the chill dawn, naked werewolves, shivering, were being helped into the garments carried for them in the saddlebags. But one werewolf, an angry woman, was cursing as she snatched at clothing held out of reach by a grinning, armored man.

"Names like that won't do you any good!" The man sneered, lazily. "If you want these, you have to earn them! Now just shut your mouth and open your legs, or else—"

Vildern's drawn sword was in his hand: he brought the flat down, hard, on the mailed shoulder. The man staggered under the blow, and reeled around with a yelp.

"Hey! Who—what do you—?"

He recognized Vildern's face and shut his mouth, paling.

"You are here to fight!" Vildern snarled. "Give her that tunic and save your stupid games for *after* the battle!"

"But—it's just a woman!" The man protested, whining. "Why shouldn't I . . . ?" His voice died: his eyes crossed, staring at the point of Vildern's sword.

"Do as you are told." Vildern's voice was very soft.

"Yes—yes, sir." The man's voice was meek, yet Vildern knew he was plotting revenge inside, that he would be waiting for a chance. If he lived through the battle.

And if the wolf-woman didn't tear his throat out at nightfall. . . .

He became aware of gratitude in the girl's eyes as she caught the tunic the man threw, and he felt his ears burn with rage as

she pulled it over her head. Trolls take the bitch! He hadn't
done it for her! Did she think it mattered to him how many of
them raped her? She should be glad she was a werewolf and a
soldier, with nothing to worry about worse than rape and
occasional minor, harmless tortures. If she were an ordinary
woman, she'd be happy enough when a man stopped at rape!

But originally women had been created to be food, the
priests said, and had invented rape as a method of distracting
men. . . .

He frowned and turned away as the girl pulled on her
breeches and boots. There might be gratitude in her eyes, but
many of the troops standing nearby were turning away to hide
their resentment. When a man had a woman at his mercy that
way, how could he be expected not to take advantage of it?
Why should an officer interfere?

He spurred his horse angrily, aware of a perverse pleasure in
having interfered. It was part of that streak of weakness in him,
that kept him from enjoying torture like a Real Man. It had
probably come down from his slave forebears, along with his
black hair. . . .

"What are we to do?" Torvar asked, looking nervously across
the stone at the advancing enemy ranks. "Four hundred men
marching on us, and our leader a gibbering idiot! A fine time
he picked to be howling like a courting loon! He'll have half
our men running in a minute, if we don't do something quick!"

"Get them marching!" said Rakmir. "Follow his last sane
order. Maybe by the time we've got them under way, he'll
have calmed down."

"An evil day it was for me that I threw the spear!" Ingulf
lamented. "An evil day that I ever saw her! An evil day and a
shameful—and yet what was my life without her? Ah, Lady,
free me from this curse! Why did you not let me drown myself,
and end it? This cannot be happening! Ah, why did they not let
me drown myself? Nothing can ever be right in this evil world
until Airellen has forgiven me, until she has returned to me!"

"They're moving out, Sir!"

Vildern looked up, white teeth flashing in the black beard.

"They've broken at last?" Then he frowned at the distant figures.

"No, Sir . . . at least, not unless they're running the wrong way, Sir. . . ."

Vildern shaded his eyes against the glare. "They're going away from the mountains instead of toward them!" He swore angrily. "They're heading for the next pit! Boy! Get ahead of them! Ride to that next mine, and tell the officer in command to kill all his slaves! At once!"

Ingulf, muttering, brought up the rear as the slaves marched out.

"Now what are those evil animals up to?" he chattered to himself, as he saw the horse burst from the glittering enemy ranks and gallop past. "North, toward the pit!" he muttered. "They are evil, and everything they do is evil, so there is some evil or other that rider is up to. Something to hurt us. Toward the same pit we are marching to! Are they setting an ambush? Warning the guard?"

He had been without sleep for a long time, his weary eyelids told him. He looked north, across the harsh glaring rock, at the walls and towers of the city. He let his head drift to the right, to rest his eyes on the green of the trees.

"Sleep in the forest. Maybe water. Food and water for sure in the city. But can I take the city with two hundred? Three hundred after this next pit—if they leave the slaves in the pit. If that rider wasn't bringing word for them to take the slaves—No!" He straightened suddenly. "They won't take them away! They'll murder them!"

He began to run.

The holes in his soft-soled boots burned. The sunlight was warming the rock. The forests had already blistered his feet. The freed slaves he sprinted past were barefoot, many of them still naked. The waterskins of polluted, brackish water they had brought from the last pit would not last long. . . .

"Where are you going?" Rakmir's voice shouted at him.

"Hurry!" Ingulf called back. "Run! Or there'll be only corpses to save when we get there!" He pointed at the dwindling rider, and ran on.

He ran and they ran. And behind them, the glimmering ranks increased their pace, and slowly changed the angle of their line of march until they were no longer marching parallel, but marched directly in the tracks of the freed slaves.

Ingulf cursed as the horseman drew ahead, dwindling in the pitiless glare of the Twin Suns on stone. But then he was silent, as his lungs settled into a rhythm, breathing deeply, calmly.

His legs churned. Hard stone jarred his arches. His mind cleared as long deep breaths replaced the panicked panting that had gripped him at the sight of the dead woman's body.

The horse began to grow, emerging out of the haze of glare, and his teeth gritted in a grin.

Then he saw that the horse was still and riderless, standing at the edge of the pit.

And then the screams began.

Vildern, riding near the head of the column with the wolves, saw men in the rear of the marching enemy turning to look over their shoulders.

Panic setting in already! We'll drive them right over the pit's edge! he thought, and smiled a cruel smile.

By letting the enemy move ahead, he had totally changed the nature of the battle: instead of two shield-walls facing one another, they were now hunter and hunted; pursuer and pursued.

The sight of the enemies' backs was putting heart back into his own men. And soon panic in the foes' ranks would do most of his work for him.

Ingulf ran.

He reached the edge of the pit, and looked down into shrieking chaos.

Slashing swords flashed. Armed and armored men were butchering chained and naked slaves, who wailed and ran and pleaded for their lives. A very few were trying futilely to defend themselves with their chains, or with snatched-up picks and hammers.

The head of the ramp was too far away. Ingulf jumped for the narrow ledge below.

His feet shot out from under him. He rolled down the ramp, bruising his shoulders. But he gripped his flail tight in his hand.

At the ramp's foot he rolled up, his flail's head wheeling in the air.

Nearly half the slaves were already down. He sprang, the iron bar whirling, killing. And now the guards turned on him. There were more than a dozen, all in mail, but their shields lay stacked in a corner, and they were armed only with swords. The spinning bar smashed swords like glass, crushed helms and skulls, snapped bones like twigs.

To fight him they had to turn their backs on the slaves, and one, a man already bleeding from a flesh wound, stepped in with one of the miner's hammers raised high, and smashed it down with a shout on a gleaming steel helm, then ran back as the armored man slumped to the ground and the other guards turned.

That was enough. The iron bar looped out, its chain snapping up and down as its end writhed in a deft, bone-snapping scrawl across four men. Their screams brought the others around, and three more went down under vengeful hammers from behind.

From the ground above Ingulf heard battle-shouts and the clatter of shields. One of the men facing him turned back, and screamed as a pick drove into his face.

That left only three still standing. His flail snapped an arm and smashed a skull, and with wild screams the slaves surged forward, with picks and hammers, fists and shackles battering the living and the dead.

Ingulf jerked the whirling iron bar back behind him to keep it from crashing through the tangle of naked limbs. It struck sparks from the stone and scraped a fan of white powder where it hit, bouncing before settling.

Even above the slaves' savage wailing and the moans of the dying guards, Ingulf could hear sounds of battle from the ground above, the echoing rhythmic thunder of shields, the hoarse angry shouts. He shouted at the clawing mob before him, until they looked up.

"Find the keys to your chains!" he shouted. "Free yourselves! Arm yourselves! Come and help!"

He turned away and ran frantically up the ramp that led out of the pit.

When he knew the pit was near, Vildern sent the wolves forward and, spurring his horse, shouted the order that set his troops forward at a run, shifting out of their ranks to form a line. . . .

There was a shout from the enemy ranks, and suddenly the freed slaves wheeled in place, and shields faced his men.

While Vildern blinked at that, the enemy burst into a run, straight at the heart of his opening line.

Vildern opened his mouth to draw breath, to shout an order. . . .

Shields met with a crash like surf on a cliff. Men reeled. Hammers shattered wooden shields; splinters and spinning chips of layered wood flew up and fell. Vildern felt his heart twist as picks pecked out men's brains and hammers smashed skulls.

Spurring his horse, he shouted to rally his men, racing along the back of his wavering line.

His own life was likely forfeit, he knew: the Lords of Sarlow forgive no failures.

Men died. Other men staggered back, shield-arms broken by the heavy metal hammers. Vildern tried to fight the pain that wrung him. *His* men were suffering and dying!

He should not care. It was weakness to care. . . .

He raced his horse from end to end of the line, shouting encouragement, roaring above the crashing of drummed shields.

They still outnumbered their enemies, he reminded them. They could still use their massed weight to push the enemy over the edge, into the pit. He got them into line, got the wounded men back, sent the wolves around to harry the enemy flanks, distracting them with well-timed nips to bring their shields down. But the weight was the crucial thing. All they had to do was push the slave line far enough back. . . .

Ten men screamed at once and pitched forward on their faces. A whole section of his shield-wall was suddenly down.

Vildern wheeled his horse and spurred it toward the gap. Picks and hammers were murdering his men where they lay screaming and thrashing under the blows, and Vildern felt himself wrenched inside.

Before he got there another ten men went down. But this time Vildern saw the long iron bar surging up at the end of its stroke, and knew what had happened. He had forgotten the Islander, and the terrible flail he carried.

"Wings, fall back!" Vildern bellowed over the booming of the battle. "Regroup in a second line behind the Center! Front rank—*kneel!"*

The fallen men screamed and whimpered. Vildern wished he could take each blow truly on his own cringing flesh.

Frantic, Ingulf lashed his flail in a cruel arc under the shields and across the shins of the evil, murdering enemy animals who tortured and maimed their slaves. Shinbones shattered and man after man toppled forward, screaming. He tried to feel satisfaction rather than pity and disgust as the freed slaves swarmed over them with hammers and picks.

"Evil murderers!" he screamed as he struck. "Evil enemy monsters! You are trying to trap me in your evil world! But you'll not keep me from her!"

It was such an evil world into which Airellen had trapped him! He knew there was justice in the hate of the slaves, yet he cringed at the cruelty, at the whimpers of the fallen men as they writhed under the blows.

He knew that the Laws of Hastur were being broken, that he was being drawn into an evil as savage as that he fought. Yet he knew that the writhing creatures were themselves without pity—

"How can you be so evil?" He screamed, lashing out with his great flail. *"How can you be so cruel and uncaring? How can you be such monsters?"* But even in his own mind he was not at all sure whether he was screaming at the enemy, or at the slaves who fought beside him, or at Fate, or the Elves, or even at Airellen, whom he loved more than life, but whose indifference had driven him insane.

Vildern heard the madman's shriek, without understanding. Weakness, he thought, weakness of the *Ligtik*. No wonder they could never stand against the Real Men!

And yet something in the wild senseless shrieking tore at
him with guilt, for he had always to struggle against this same
weakness, and was torn by it now; for although every precept
of his people told him to put himself first, and let others suffer,
each blow that fell upon the flesh of men under his command
made his heart flinch.

The solid double wall of shields bristled with steel. Wood chips
whirled and danced as Ingulf and the freed men battered at the
foe. The thin shields shook: the layered wood shattering.

Ingulf smelled blood and death and fear. On each side men
died, as unruled hate snarled and hit. The stone grew slick with
blood.

"Evil animals!" Ingulf screamed, lashing the chained iron
bar across the shields. "Go away and die! Murderers! Vicious
evil things! Die! Die and go away!" The wood boomed and
buckled. Swords cut at him, flashing in sunlight; sometimes an
arm reached too far, and the whirling chained bar would whip
across it, and there would be a cry of pain and a new sword
lying on the stone.

Vildern heard a hysterical cry from somewhere in his ranks.

"No! Look! There are more of them!" And looking over the
heads of his men, Vildern saw grimy shapes climb from the pit,
blades and hammers in their hands.

Suddenly a man at the far end of his line bolted, and as
Vildern whirled his horse, shouting, a dozen others followed.

Sword raised to scythe them down, he raced toward them,—
then heard feet pound all around him as the whole second line
broke and ran. . . .

"Fools!" he shouted. "Stand your ground! They'll chop you
down as you run!"

But they were past hearing. They were not used to slaves
that fought back: they had been trained to trick their foes, and
catch them unaware, and smother them with numbers. They
were not trained to share the danger of their comrades, and
defend them to the last. They were trained to think of their own
skins first.

The end came fast. The first line, trapped kneeling, wa-

vered, and the armed slaves surged over them, shattered them,
heavy hammers battering. Many were slain as they tried to turn
and run. Those that held their ground had better luck, but were
surrounded and cut off as the slaves raced after the fleeing men
and dragged them down. Wolves fled yelping. Horsemen
galloped away.

Vildern saw the ragged Islander with his flail, and for a
moment considered rushing him, facing him. He was the
source of all this trouble. If he were killed, things would be
under control soon enough.

But no, others swarmed in his tracks, and Vildern could not
fight the whole lot of them, and a skilled Island Swordsman as
well!

Then he saw a group of his men, a remnant of the front line,
who had held together, and were cutting their way out of the
press. Heedless of danger, Vildern rushed to their aid.

Ingulf strode through ruin, following the fast road made by the
flail's flying rod.

"So many to free!" he moaned, his fury worn sullen.
Weariness lay on him. He knew he must sleep. He knew he
must leave some slaves. He could not conquer Sarlow single-
handed.

"So some must be left to be tortured and maimed!" he raged
to himself, and anger burned away his weariness. He sprang
among the fleeing foe, his flying flail breaking backs, tossing
bodies about as if they were straw, to pile them in drifts to mark
his path.

"Evil animals!" he shrieked at the soldiers who screamed
and fled before him. "You deserve to die! And where are the
poor women you've taken? You put men in pits to mine, but
where have you hidden the women? What must they suffer? I
must find them, free them!" Then that brought Airellen to his
mind, and his renewed fury piled more corpses high. "Where
are they? It's in the city they must be! We'll soon—" Then he
fell silent, thoughtful. He slowed, and let the foe run.

"In the city," he said again, after a moment. "So I must take
the city! But can I take a city with little more than two hundred
men?"

"*Keep together!*" Rakmir was roaring in his sea-captain's voice. "Don't scatter. Stand together! What if this were a trap, you fools?"

Looking up, Ingulf saw his freed slaves scattering, hate driving them in pursuit of the fugitives.

"*Back to the pit!*" he shouted. "*Gather at the pit's edge!*" Rakmir and Torvar took up the cry. Each had been gang boss in his pit, each had a number of men used to obeying him. Even so, it was some time before the men would leave the chase.

Slowly authority overcame hate. A small group of foemen backed slowly past Ingulf and out of the fight, swords flickering above their linked shields. A black-bearded man on a horse was in their midst: those that rushed them died.

Men came running to Ingulf and Rakmir, begging to attack that moving wall. But Ingulf had other plans.

"We'll kill more later," he said, "but we'll fight better if we sleep sometime! And eat, if there are any rations left in the pit! But we cannot sleep here. We'll make for those woods." He pointed to the green trees off to the northeast.

"That's the hunting preserve!" a fear-filled voice protested.

"The wolves hunt there!" cried another. "The Hounds of Sarlow, and the werewolves!"

"We have killed both wolves and werewolves," Ingulf answered, "and we'll kill more before we leave. But we are no safer here. If you know a better place, then take us there! But there we can at least sleep out of the sun. . . ."

Vildern and his men retreated slowly, backing away until they were sure that the pursuit had ceased. Then they made for the end of the stone, and the hill.

They overtook many who had fled. Most of these were wounded, many in the back, and they wilted under Vildern's baleful glare, but he had no words for them, not even curses, which frightened them more.

The planed stone ahead was dotted with running figures, but Vildern disdained to try to catch up with them. He and the men who had stood marched together at a steady pace.

As they drew near the hills, he saw troops stationed all

across the road. Near their center a handful of black-robed Sorcerers stood, and in front of them Eisvlu waited, blond-bearded and elegant, Sekthrig's most highly born lieutenant.

"So the great Vildern sneaks home with his tail between his legs!" Eisvlu's thin face was bright with joy at his rival's discomfort. "Your men tell me that you hesitated to attack the slaves, and let *them* attack *you*. That you bolted like a rabbit when Sekthrig was killed."

Vildern hesitated. Men said it never paid to tell the truth, yet it had not occurred to him to make up any lies to have ready. How stupid! And some of his own men must be Eisvlu's creatures. . . .

The thought stiffened him. Eisvlu was trying to assert command, by acting as though he had a right to judge Vildern already.

"Did you pay the man to tell you the truth?" he asked.

There was laughter, and Eisvlu's face darkened.

"That won't help you, slave-get! Now that I'm in command—"

"You are not in command." Vildern drew his sword. "I am." He slid from his horse, and took a shield that one of his men held out to him. "Now shut your mouth!"

Slave-gotten he might be, but he had fought his way to the rank that Eisvlu's kin had bought for him. And all the army knew it.

Eisvlu paled, and turned in appeal to the Sorcerers behind him. This was the dangerous moment. Ondrute and Ramaukin were both members of the Council, and Kelldule, though a *Ligtalp*-trained renegade *Ligskrat*, was so powerful that the Council heeded his words.

"Stop him!" Eisvlu whispered.

Ondrute laughed.

"Show us your strength!" he said. "Men were made to suffer for the pleasure of the Cruel Gods."

Eisvlu turned back, blue eyes icy and dangerous. Vildern strode toward him.

"Either kneel, and accept me as commander," he said, "or draw your sword."

Eisvlu pulled his sword out, and snatched up a shield. He

had lost face already, he knew, by appealing to the Sorcerers for help.

"Reikil! Gleipmoth!" he shouted. "Back me!"

Once there had been a rule requiring a combat between chiefs to be a single combat—but that had been long ago laughed out of existence. Vildern bared his teeth.

The two men whose names Eisvlu had called stood eyeing each other hesitantly. Vildern's skill as a swordsman was well known. . . .

"Vildern!" someone shouted from the men who had marched back with him.

"We'll fight with you, Vildern!" That was Ulvard's voice.

Gleipmoth slammed his sword back in its sheath and sat down. A moment later, Reikil did the same. Eisvlu's shoulders slumped.

Eisvlu leaped at Vildern, sword arching high.

It sank quivering into the thin wood of Vildern's shield just above his head, while Vildern's blade lashed under his own shield in a low, vicious slash. He twisted the shield, hoping to pull Eisvlu's sword from his hand, but Eisvlu was too quick for that. Vildern felt his edge hiss harmlessly in air, and whirled his arm, turning hip and shoulder to whip arm and sword around above his head in a cut that sheared away the top of Eisvlu's shield, and grated across the steel of his helmet. Eisvlu staggered back.

Vildern laughed. Slave-get he might be, but he had trained under Grom Beardless, and under old Bodvar the Killer before that!

He moved slowly toward the other. Eisvlu would have expected him to rush. He saw fear building in Eisvlu's face.

Eisvlu stuck his jaw out, and Vildern saw his lower teeth. He grinned back grimly, and stepped into the reach of the other's sword.

Eisvlu slashed, sword-edge shrill in the air. It thundered on Vildern's lifted shield, while Vildern's blade whipped under the shield to jingle on loose-hanging mail. He felt rings bunch against the thigh, and slung the blade back and up around above his head, lashing at Eisvlu's temple.

Eisvlu, frantic, aimed a second blow, but his sword clashed

against Vildern's steel, and Eisvlu staggered back, white-faced, then sprang again, edge chopping at Vildern's eyes. Vildern's shield came up. . . .

Vildern felt the other's sword scrape lightly across the face of his shield: warned, he sprang back as the stabbing point cleared his shield-edge. His own blade lashed down as he writhed his body away from the steel.

He felt mail-rings part under his edge. There was a choked gurgle.

He lowered his shield, and saw that his blade was wedged tightly in the mail that covered the side of Eisvlu's neck: blood welled up through broken rings, and Eisvlu collapsed, almost tugging the blade out of his hand.

He wrenched it free. The head flopped oddly, half-severed. A river of blood poured over his boots.

"Well, struck, *Captain*," Ondrute's voice was tinged with malice. But it was nearly drowned in sudden wild cheering from the men.

"Good work, Captain!" someone shouted, as Vildern wiped his sword.

Suddenly Vildern remembered his father, sitting with old Bodvar Killer by the fire. *"They call Captains who are kind to their men weak now!"* his Father had said. *"And do men love their Commanders as in the old days? No! The fools!"*

"Old Valgarth could have ordered me to follow him into a dragon's mouth, and I'd have gone," Bodvar had answered.

He turned toward the watching men.

"Men!" His voice rolled out strongly. "Those of you who have served under me know how I treat my troops! You'll have served under others as well. You can judge for yourselves what kind of a man is likely to replace me, if anything . . . happens." He was silent a moment, to let that sink in.

"There are always plots. If you want another commander—" But then his voice was drowned out, roared down by shouting. Fists and swords were waving in the air. After a few moments the roaring of words that drowned each other out turned into a chant, and it was his name they were chanting.

He turned to face the Sorcerers.

"Very clever," said Ondrute. "But I don't think it will save you. It will certainly not save you if you fail here. Now, you must tell *me* why you could not crush a handful of slaves."

"There are more than a handful," said Vildern. "Three pits have revolted and joined together, and they are led by an outlander with a sword of fire, the fire-magic of the Nameless One. And the outlander is a Swordsman of the Isles, and very skilled. I will make no excuses; I think any other officer in the army would have done much as I did, and with the same result. Sekthrig sent for you before he died. Will you not help us?"

"When night comes," said Ondrute, "my night-walkers will finish them!"

"Perhaps," said Kelldule. His voice was very deep. "But there are defenses against such night-walkers as you can raise. We do not know the power of this sword."

"Is it an Adept of Elthar that we face, then?" asked Ramaukin.

"I do not know," Vildern answered.

"*I* will know," said Kelldule. "Meanwhile. . . ." The renegade looked thoughtful, and Vildern's blood chilled. ". . . the chains and whips from the pits will have the blood of these slaves—some of them, at least. Get me those, and I will make a magic for you."

The newly freed slaves from the last pit had slept through the night, and now they stood guard while others lay like leaves over the grassy floor of a green glade. If there were wolves, they stayed far away.

Ingulf dreamed.

He ran, unarmed, helpless, a werewolf at his heels. He could feel its breath, hear its feet, as he fled through fields and streets.

He ran beside the river, feeling the beast's breath hot behind him. Heart pounding, he tried to hide. In the darkness he saw before him a flimsy riverside shack, and slid through the sagging door and pulled it shut. . . .

But there was light in the shack; light, and rich carpet, and beautiful, well-carved furniture—

And Airellen was there.

He stood frozen, staring, his throat clenched tight, unable to call her name. She did not look at him, but sat with her long hair flowing down her back, beautiful in her earth-brown gown, drinking from a silver goblet. . . .

The flimsy wall behind him buckled and caved in as the werewolf smashed through.

She turned, perfectly calm, and threw the goblet.

It struck the wolf's forehead. There was a flash of light. The werewolf screamed, staggered up in man-shape, reeled and fell on his face.

Ingulf stared, looking from her to the wolf. Still she would not look at him. She rose, still silent, stepped to the wall, pushed one of the loose, rotting boards aside, and was gone. The light went with her.

Ingulf woke, throat still clenched tight, face wet with tears. He lay shivering in sunlight. Men snored all around him. Nearby, someone spoke in an urgent whisper.

Suddenly Rakmir's voice spoke over the other.

"Don't be a fool!" the sea-captain snapped. "Just knowing which end of the sword goes in the hand doesn't make a swordsman. You saw him fight! Man, *that* is a Swordsman of the Isles! You'd only get yourself killed!" The other voice answered in a whisper.

Ingulf heard the words, but they meant nothing to him; his mind was still haunted by his dream.

Airellen! His eyes flooded with tears. What was the use of life? What reason to live if she would not look at him, not speak to him, not love him?

If he freed all the slaves, and led them against their masters, and destroyed the evil of Sarlow for all time, would that make Airellen love him? Would that bring her back to him? Would it set him free from this evil world?

Dorialith had bidden him to hope, to make his deeds deeds of song. That Dorialith would see that *she* heard the songs. . . .

Would this be enough for a song? If he took these slaves he had freed successfully over the mountains, that would be worth a song surely. . . .

One song. But would any song serve to move Airellen's heart? What more must he do?

Or was the Elf only mocking him? Was this some new, cruel game? Was he being led hither and thither, dancing out his part for the Elves' enjoyment?

Or was this all a dream wrought by Elf-magic? How could he tell? Would he wake to find himself back in the City of the Sea-Elves, listening to the illusion-weaving harps? Were they playing with him again, tearing his heart and mind apart for some cruel purpose of their own?

If Dorialith had lied, if no song would move Airellen, then there was nothing to live for, and he was destroyed and trapped in the evil world forever. . . . *Airellen! Airellen! Come back to me! Come back to me!*

At last exhaustion claimed him; he slept, dreaming of his love.

While slaves slept in the woods, Ondrute and Vildern kept vigil on the slope.

Messengers came to them through the afternoon. Orders had gone out to slaughter the slaves in the five pits nearest the three that had rebelled. The slaves in the rest had been chained and taken away, for safety, to the town of Kirgiff. Slaves were costly, and the Lords of Kirgiff, who owned the slaves, already had denounced Vildern and called for his removal. Fortunately Ondrute owned more than they, but there would be trouble for him later, he thought.

But the messages that came were disturbing—although, Vildern thought, they would serve to defend his action.

In two of the five pits, all had gone as ordered, and the slaves had been butchered like sheep. In the third they had fought, and gone down after killing four of their guards.

It was a long wait before word came of the other two.

One pit was found filled with bodies of slaves and guards. One or two of the slaves looked as though they had fallen on their own weapons. The man who told of it guessed that the few slaves who survived had killed themselves out of fear of the tortures that awaited them. But some might have escaped, Vildern thought.

Then word came that the slaves of the last pit had murdered their guards and escaped, but instead of moving to join the other slaves, were moving toward the mountains in a body, hunting for a path out of the land.

But these had no deadly swordsman with a sword of flame. Vildern sent his werewolves and the wolf-pack after them. The Hounds of Sarlow surged off in high fettle, and werewolves on horseback in their midst. They would trail the slaves until they changed at nightfall, and then attack and slay.

Vildern winced as the wolf-woman waved at him gaily from her saddle.

Ondrute had sent messages to the half-human Irioch savages who lived in the mountains, and men from their tribes were already gathering while Vildern mustered his men. The wolf-scouts had tracked the freed slaves to their lair in the wood.

Vildern wanted to set off as soon as enough men could be gathered, set fire to the woods, and attack while it was still day. If in the confusion, they could separate the Islander from the rest, surround him with a shield-wall, and kill him and take the fiery sword, then the rest would be easy, once night came.

But Ondrute overruled him. They would march just before sunset, and demons, not fire, would destroy the wood. Fire, after all, was the weapon of the enemy, and hard to control. The essence of the Nameless One was in it—had not the first fire been made when the Nameless One had twined one of his red hairs about the flaming gold hair of tSarl, the First Man? Demons obeyed orders, and fire did not.

So they waited, while Vildern fretted and wondered if he had, even now, enough men, and Ondrute, sure of his Demons' power, laughed at him. Kelldule had gone with servants to the pits; Ramaukin had returned to the fort. A galloper raced down from the fort with news that a chain of a thousand slaves had just been brought in by a huge raiding party of two hundred men, with Grom Beardless himself at their head.

The Twin Suns crawled down the sky, and Vildern mustered his marching order, while a rabble of twisted Irioch tribesmen swarmed around.

Ingulf woke with the sound of men stirring all around him, and a vision of Airellen in his mind. Bright dreams of her had cheered him, although he still remembered the nightmare that

wakened him before. Despair waited like a pit in the back of
his mind, but this was not the time. For he also woke with
burning hunger.

Hunger gnawed at them all. The slaves were often starved;
their shrunken stomachs were used to hunger, but the scant bit
from the last pit had not gone far among so many.

Many of the men, the deep-forest tribesmen, were on their
hands and knees looking through the bushes for berries and
roots. The sailors sat and griped.

Rakmir came and knelt by Ingulf's side.

"So now that we are rested, what do you want us to do?" he
asked. Ingulf did not answer at once, but sat up slowly.

"These monsters take women as slaves as well as men," he
said slowly. "What becomes of them?" Rakmir started as
though stung, and then looked at him pityingly.

"Is that what you are doing here, then?" He sighed, and
shook his head. "Best not to know. If you have a sister or a
lover or a mother who was taken, best to hope she is dead,
and—"

"No, no," said Ingulf, "that is not what I mean, and that is
not why I came. But—"

"They rape them, of course," said Rakmir. "Get children on
them. Eat them. Some they torture to death, out of sheer
cruelty. Best not to think about it. I was lucky. All that were in
my crew were men. That was bad enough. But I've seen men
brood over what happened to their women until they went mad
and attacked the guards. And then the guards skinned them,
and rubbed salt over them, and . . . best not to know. Best
not to think about it."

Ingulf stared at the man in exasperation, then waved a hand
at the walls and towers that could be seen through the trees.

"What is that city, there?"

"Do you call that a city?" Rakmir grinned. "No, Kirgiff is
only a little town, and most of it is the Castle of Ulvrat, its lord.
It has a slave market—a small one, almost a private one for
Ulvrat's use. He owns most of the pits, and the slaves in them,
and most of the slaves in Kirgiff."

"So there are slaves there?" said Ingulf.

"Except for Ulvrat and his guards and a bare handful of lords

near his own rank, who own a part of the pits and the fields
here, the people are all slaves. Most of those in the city are
born into slavery, the descendants of the folk who lived in this
land before the Sarló came out of the north."

Ingulf rolled up to his feet, yawned, and stretched. Men
began watching him, warily, fear and hope struggling in their
expressions. He drew a deep breath.

"Listen, men!" he shouted. "Are you hungry?"

A roar of affirmation made leaves dance.

"There is food behind those walls!" he shouted, waving an
arm at the curtain of leaves through which the walls and towers
of Kirgiff showed. "They think we are running and hiding!
They will not expect an attack! And there are slaves inside that
city, slaves that need to be freed!"

He saw some faces light with wonder and enthusiasm; in
other faces he saw hunger struggle with fear. But many faces
were sullen and angry.

"Are we *your* slaves now?" someone muttered.

Ingulf felt rage building, building; his fist knotted on the
shaft of his flail. He had not seen which face had spoken. He
fought to keep his voice steady.

"No, you are free. If you wish to run for the mountains, go
ahead."

"And be wolf food," a voice sneered from the crowd.

"Give me your sword and I'll try it," another voice
muttered.

"That's enough!" roared Rakmir, his deep voice throbbing.
"This is no time for—blethering! You cannot go back to the
pits. If we all fight together, some of us may get through this
alive. We must *act* as though we were all of one will, whatever
our private thoughts! There is no way to leave without a fight.

"Those Demon-feeders are waiting for us to run for the
mountains. They're expecting us, and we'd not get far. But if
we sack Kirgiff—they'll not expect that! And there'll be more
of us to fight them when we do try to move."

Ingulf drew a deep breath, swallowing back the rage and
despair which built up in him. He wanted to scream at these
men who might keep him from Airellen, who might force him,
through pity for them, to fail in his bid for a fame that might

make him worthy of her—if it mattered to her at all, if she
cared how many slaves he freed or what hardships he endured
for her sake. . . .

"Make ready to march," was all he said. "You can fill your
bellies in Kirgiff." Had his voice trembled? He wanted to rage
and cry and throw things.

"Perhaps," said Rakmir softly, beside him, "we should not
try the southern passes at all, but should go west, into the wild
country beyond the Alak, and try for the western range. The
passes there are guarded too, but if we can break through them
we'll be in Galinor, in civilized country." Ingulf shook his
head.

"No. That is wild country, near the Sea-Elves' city," he
said. Rakmir's face fell.

All around hungry men were shouldering hammers, picks
and swords. The sunbeams slanted through the branches. It
was late. Ingulf gave the signal and they hurried toward the
road. Wolves scattered from the wood's edge as they marched.

Mailed men glittered under a spiked hedge of moving spears.
Vildern peered straight down the roadway's long line through
the haze, seeking slaves.

Boots, drumming on the hard stone, beat steadily behind
him. Steel glimmered in the sun, shimmering on mail and on
sharp spear-points swaying overhead.

With the spears, Vildern thought, they could keep the slaves
from closing in; keep the heavy hammers back. . . .

And Kelldule had said that his spell would create spreading
doubt and treachery among the slaves. . . .

Ramaukin came bounding up in werewolf-form; unlike a
true werewolf, the Sorcerer could take beast-shape even in
daylight, and he retained his own mind and nature.

He saw dim dots racing over gray stone. Wolves running
from the forest, scouts coming with news. . . .

Vildern straightened in the saddle with a curse.

In the road, between the trees and the city wall, figures
swarmed, and he knew the freed slaves were hurrying through
the gate and into the city of Kirgiff.

*   *   *

Ingulf stared at the wall before them. Human hands, surely, had never reared that wall.

It looked like wet black mud. A single, massive block of blackness, smooth as if sliced by a razor, and set on edge on the stone plain.

But there was an arched gate in the center, where a single sleepy sentry lounged.

He looked up to see Ingulf halfway across the road, and yelped a warning as he scrambled to close the gate. Torvar's thrown spear took him in the chest, driving through burst mail-rings.

A second appeared, but by then Ingulf was across the road, and the whirling iron bar hurled the warrior sprawling, broken, and the way was clear. Freed slaves swarmed through the gate.

Beyond were cobbled streets and humble, quaint houses of wood and quarried stone that were dwarfed by massive palaces—but they were so old! Shabbier, newer huts were crowded between the walls of older buildings.

Little dark people cringed in fear, staring at the outlanders. Some wore simple tunics, and others were naked except for slave-collars.

"Get that gate closed!" Rakmir shouted, behind Ingulf.

The big Islander stepped toward the people of the city. He towered over them; the tallest barely topped his shoulder. Their black eyes were like the eyes of wild things poised to run.

"Do not be afraid," he said, soft-voiced. "I've come to set you free."

Black eyes stared at him uncomprehending. A sudden fear raged in him that they truly could not hear. Perhaps the Elves had not pulled him from the water after all, and he was a ghost now who did not realize that he was dead, and only went through the motions of living.

Or perhaps it was a spell that the Elves had put upon him. . . .

"Do you not understand me?" Ingulf shouted, voice suddenly shrill. "You are free! Join us! Take up weapons! Kill the jailors who rule you!" They cringed back from his voice, to cower against the old stone of their walls. "What is the matter with you? Do you not *want* to be free?"

There was a sudden scream from down the street. A slender, beautiful woman, clad only in jeweled chains, turned and fled, her long dark hair streaming.

No one turned to see her go. The black eyes watched Ingulf, silent, from beside the walls of the houses. Then a slow surge moved them out into the street, until a crowd blocked it.

"Look at his hair," a woman's voice whispered. *"Red as the sunset!"*

"Red as heated iron!" whispered another.

"That is only legend!" A man's voice whispered angrily, somewhere in the crowd. *"Legends lead down werewolves' throats!"*

"The Twin Suns are sinking!"

"Soon it will be night!" Other whispers stirred the crowd. The sea of black eyes watched him, waiting. . . .

A young man—a boy, really, Ingulf thought—pushed his way to the front of the crowd. His head would not quite reach Ingulf's shoulder. He wore a loincloth and a slave-collar—and scars. He tilted his head back to look into the Islander's eyes.

"Are you . . . ?" His whispered question failed on his lips, as though he feared to speak. "Are you . . . the . . . " Again the boy's voice quailed, as though there were some one word he dared not say aloud, barely dared to think. He licked his lips, and tried again. "What . . . is your name?"

"Ingulf."

A sigh—almost a sob—swept through the crowd. They began to drift away; whispers murmured through the street. The boy's face fell, and he shook his head.

"Then—"

Shouts and screaming from behind drowned his voice.

Larger figures were pushing through the rear of the crowd, throwing people roughly aside—mailed men, blond men, soldiers of Sarlow!

Torches were being lit all through the city, as the sunset glared in the west. Now the torchlight glittered on clean, new-drawn swords.

The crowd parted before them, as the little dark people scrambled from their path, into the shelter of nearby houses or alleyways. Some were not quick enough, and were hurled sprawling.

Ingulf let his flail's iron bar fall free on its chain. Behind him Rakmir shouted, and feet rushed. The freed slaves surged to his aid.

Ingulf sprang, the iron bar a sudden wheel in the torchlight. A sword snapped like glass as the bar glided in a long whirring flight. Bones shattered; men shrieked. Arrogant sneering faces filled with terror.

Vildern peered at the slick black wall with a baffled curse, as he listened to the shouting and the steel. Ondrute laughed harshly.

"Now we have them in a trap!" the Sorcerer crowed. Another voice joined his laughter, and one among the were-wolves suddenly reared up into man-shape, even though it was now dark. Vildern started. Only Ramaukin could do this. . . .

"There'll be feasting soon," Ramaukin cackled, still stooping, voice still harsh with growls. "We have them now!"

"Bring me the prisoner!" Ondrute shouted, and Vildern turned away, heart twisting. He did not like to watch sacrifice, even when it was only a slave. This was one of his own men!

"Remember the sword!" Ramaukin cried, in his shrill old voice. He had changed fully now, into a bald-headed, cherub-cheeked gnome of a man, wolf-gray hair fringing his shining dome. His little blue eyes flashed merrily. "You'll need more blood than that to call up a *Thyole!* Are you sure that—?"

"Even a lesser *Yothungr* can break a *ligzgirt!* Ondrute sneered. "No need to raise a *Grusthul!* They will not escape!"

"Unless it is one of the Great Swords of Power," said Kelldule sardonically. Ondrute glared at him, but did not answer.

A bound, sullen figure was dragged forward. Vildern could not resist one glance. At least the fool was behaving like a Real Man, and would not disgrace the Sarló before the Losvik. Ondrute raised a long knife, and Vildern turned away.

Well, this would teach the fool to hold his tongue before the Sorcerers! He would not profit by the lesson, but perhaps others would. . . .

There was a wild scream that slowly died to a girlish whimper as Ondrute wielded his knife. The whimpering went on and on.

"Eight are the Dark Lords and mighty are their names," Ondrute intoned above the victim's sobs. *"First the Three, Ancients of the Void . . . Eldest of all, the Dweller in the Gulf. . . ."*

Vildern shuddered as Ondrute strained his throat to pronounce the inhuman Names of Power. He could feel space twisting in his bones as the strange tones throbbed, out beyond the world. . . .

The whimper suddenly changed to a sharp rhythmic shrieking like that of a wounded baby, and once the tortured voice shrieked, "Don't! Don't!" But above the screaming, Ondrute's harsh voice went on, and the other Sorcerers' voices joined in at intervals, to chime the names. . . .

"Esch'kazoth'au'c'rhymvzhyl—come! Blood is poured and pain is loud! Come from out the Gulfs of Dark, from the poisoned void of murk where your hungry parents lurk! Pass through woven nets of Flame. Enter in this Fiery World, you that hunger in the Dark! Follow this thread of blood and pain; you shall have the food you need! Tarry not upon the way: Cthuggda hunts upon your trail, and all the Eight will hunt you now, and S'Bowith great and fell, now hungers for your taste! But by the Names of all the Eight: By Lyughoth proud and great, by Yijzoth's hungry maw, and by Yaddoth's ancient—"

Even that voice was drowned in the terrible scream of agony that burst from the victim's tortured throat—such a scream that Vildern turned, startled.

Blood flowed *up* from the screaming body, and twisted in air that shifted in sharp-angled patterns. . . .

Wolves and even werewolves cowered, whimpering, bellies to the stone; horses screamed wildly, mad with fear, and there were sudden thunders of hammering hooves. The wind was tainted with a smell that twisted Vildern's stomach and doubled him over.

"Pass now through this wall of stone, follow threads of blood and pain, seek out those who fight and slay, and eat the creatures there!" Ondrute cried, black staff raised.

Vildern's ears and bones throbbed with a note he could not quite hear: stone trembled underfoot. He looked up, and saw the darkness twist and ripple in jagged lines as the invisible creature crawled toward the city, clawing strange markings in the stone.

Old stone walls rang with echoes of the fighting.

Freed slaves raged through the town's dark streets, dealing death with their hammers and their picks. Ingulf led them, with his wheeling flail breaking bones as it lashed to and fro. Shields boomed. Men died. Battle-clamor roared. Hammers shattered shields.

Ingulf's flail snapped swords. Soldiers floundered on the cobbled streets as they slipped in the blood of the dead.

Dark-haired folk hid, crouching in dark doorways, watching from the windows of their homes. Ingulf felt their eyes on him, felt pain and pride and hate in them. Yet the people of the city gave no aid to either side.

And they were silent: still as statues, soundless. . . .

"What are you? What evil spell is on you?" Ingulf shrieked, like a mountain cat. *"Is it human you are at all? Will nothing stir you?"*

The stone walls echoed with shouting and with screams and the clattering of battle, but the people of the city made no sound.

Blood flowed. Blades flashed; flesh bled. Mail-clad men reeled. Hammers battered down their shields.

Then the earth trembled.

The walls of the city shook. There was a rumbling crash, somewhere in the night, that drowned all the sounds of battle.

Both sides fell back, staring across a blood-soaked space of stone.

More crashing sounds. And through them, human voices screamed.

Then, beyond the enemy line, Ingulf saw the house at the corner of the street collapse. Screams inside were cut off, and beams and stones were swept out into the street, and rolled along as though before a tide.

And the walls and roof of the building beyond seemed to

ripple as though reflected in a pond—except that the ripples were not curves, but jagged, pointed angles. A tiny moon seemed to flick wildly back and forth in the sky.

Inaudible moaning throbbed from the stone into the bones of Ingulf's legs. Torches down the street flickered and went out.

A wave of rubble was rolling down the street, thinning in the middle and leaving beams and squared stone piled in front of the houses. An awful, stomach-wrenching smell shocked Ingulf's nose.

The line of soldiers broke and scattered left and right, hammering on the doors of the houses, shouting to be let in.

Feet behind him told Ingulf his own men were beginning to run.

He shifted the flail to his left hand, and drew *Frostfire*.

From the darkened, silent houses came a breathless gasp that welled to a wordless keen of wonder. Opal light lit the street as *Frostfire* flared from its sheath.

"See!" a woman's voice cried.

"It *is* true!" gasped another.

The thinning of rubble parted in the center of the street.

"We *are* free!" a voice cried, and a thousand other voices echoed, *"Free!"*

Cobblestones were twisted from their settings and sent spinning; the pooling blood suddenly was rising up, thin red threads weaving in a cloudy net.

A tangle of interlacing lines hesitated a moment in *Frostfire's* light, then came on. Screaming soldiers were bolting past Ingulf, screaming with terror, but he paid them no heed. A foul stench choked him.

A running soldier slipped in blood and went down, and suddenly the cloudy lace surged forward.

Threads of blood leaped out of every mail-ring, weaving upward while its owner screamed.

Twisting and shrieking, the soldier was lifted into the air. Strange jagged ripples distorted the man's shape. All at once, the rings of his mail shirt burst and fell away.

"Evil animal!" Ingulf shouted, his voices hoarse and shrill. "You've come to destroy me! I defy you! Evil, murdering enemy animal! Go away, or I'll destroy you!"

The body of the soldier shrank and twisted, and broke into writhing fragments that vanished one by one.

Ingulf sprang, his arm tipped with opal flame.

He felt *Frostfire* sink into something like a wall of writhing snakes. He shuddered at the foulness, and then pain like the stinging of a thousand nettles burned through his arm.

Stone was ripped from under his feet.

An ill-smelling wind hurled him through the air, while he clung to *Frostfire's* hilt, deafened by a roar that buzzed in his bones.

He crashed against flesh and bone. A crush of bare soft bodies fell in a tangled pile. He heard Rakmir curse. The wave of stench buffeted them.

Suddenly the smell was gone. Another wind—a clean wind—whipped violently from the opposite direction, making them all stagger as they tried to rise.

"Hastur!" a voice shouted, and a dozen others echoed, in a wild, exultant keen, *"Hastur! It is Hastur! We are free!"* and then swelling throughout the street, louder and louder, *"Hastur has come! Rise, slaves! Rise, slaves!"*

Ondrute staggered, and fell to the stone; all the Sorcerers reeled. The sudden wind nearly plucked Vildern from his feet.

"What—?" From within the wall came shouting and cheers.

"It *was* a great blade," said Kelldule. "I tried to warn him. But he would not listen."

Ramaukin chuckled malignly.

"Listen!" he said, his bald dome bobbing. "Hear what they shout in the city!" Vildern listened, and his heart clenched.

"Rise, slaves! Rise, slaves!" Fear filled him as that chilling cry came, borne faintly on the wind. But Ramaukin still laughed.

"There will be much blood in the streets of the city," he said, bright blue eyes beaming, twinkling as at a secret jest. "Much blood. Enough blood to open a Gate for one of the Great Ones!"

"Rise, slaves! Rise, slaves!" Every alley echoed the ear-piercing cry. In a riot of red vengeance the people of the city held a carnival of death.

They swarmed out of their houses, men and women alike, armed with stones, kitchen knives, cooking ladles—whatever they could lay hands on. They swarmed over the soldiers, heedlessly falling under the swords until sheer numbers hemmed in the mailed men and crushed them.

Heads rolled on the cobbles. Blood streamed through the streets. Through the mad night of death and shadowy struggles, Ingulf ran with the rest.

A womans' screams brought him into a palace, and he saw that dark-haired girl who had screamed and run away in the street strapped spread-eagled against the wall, her jeweled chains smeared with blood. New whip-scars crossed her long-healed ones.

A thin blond man was slowly drawing a line down her body, from breast to belly, with a knife, when Ingulf and those with him burst into the room. Other women had been chained up to watch, though many had covered their faces with their hands. Guards started forward, but the great flail whirled, and they went down.

The thin-faced blond man turned then, as the chained women burst into hysterical shrieks of joy: he screamed once before the iron bar split his skull.

"He wouldn't believe me!" the woman on the wall sobbed over and over as they took her down. *"He wouldn't believe me!"*

Some of the other women cuffed her as she was taken down.

There was food. Ingulf stuffed it into his mouth and chewed as he ran on with the others, into the blood-mad night.

In the slave market at the city's heart, the blood of slave and soldier alike made cobbles slick and slippery, under a nightmare of thrashing bodies, tossing blades, and flailing chains. Ingulf saw a little girl slit a soldier's throat.

Here a handful of soldiers had stood guard over long chains of slaves—the miners from the pits, and fresh-caught, unsold slaves brought through the pass. These had surged upon their guards when they heard the cry of *"Rise, slaves!"* echoing down the city streets, and reinforcements had rushed here, and the little dark people had poured from their houses to throw themselves onto the soldiers' backs.

Ingulf sprang into the surging press. He could not use his flail in this crowd without killing the little naked men and women who fought beside him: *Frostfire* slid flaming from its scabbard as he raced toward the lapped wooden shields of the embattled soldiers.

Blades rang: blood ran. He saw the chained slaves struggling, weighted down by the dead still shackled beside them, as they fought with shields and swords snatched from their dead foes. Nearby, a group of the women of the city swarmed over a fallen soldier, stabbing with carving knives. A single soldier drove back a mob of slaves who lashed at him with axes and shovels.

Sharp edges lashed at Ingulf's eyes. Dancing and swaying, he guarded and dodged, then felt the jolt of the hilt in his hand as the edge chopped flesh.

"Rise, slaves! Rise, slaves!" Savage voices screamed all around them, and then again, *"Hastur has come! Free! We are free!"*

Hastur? What could it mean?

Torchlight rippled on mail-rings. Red blades lashed back and forth, and the hot blood ran. Blood was everywhere, blood in rivers.

Frostfire flew left and right, shearing away great chunks of the wooden shields. Rakmir's men came pushing through the press, and the shields roared under heavy hammers.

And the blood poured onto the street, streaming in rivers underfoot, while shrill voices screamed, over and over, *"Rise, slaves! Hastur has come! Rise, slaves! Rise, slaves!"*

IV

The Piping of Ciallglind

VILDERN AND HIS men marched into the madness of the city, with the war-cry of the slaves ringing all round them. The gates had been unbarred before they had come, by trapped soldiers fleeing the mobs that roamed the city: mobs that hurled themselves upon the soldiers as they marched through the gate.

The shield-wall hurled the slaves back, and swords slashed them down. Irioch swarmed in behind the mailed men. They marched to the slave-market at the city's heart, hearing the sounds of fighting grow louder and louder before them.

They saw torches, then, and the surging, screaming mob.

"*Plenty* blood," Ramaukin purred, beaming. He rubbed his hands together, gleefully. "Help me, Kelldule!"

The Irioch went loping into the city, a misshapen nightmare horde, but Vildern and his soldiers formed a shield-wall around the Sorcerers, at the edge of the market square, while the mob surged against them.

Vildern was frightened. If the two called up one of the Great Ones *here*, in the middle of his soldiers, it would likely eat them all, as well as the slaves. Yet he had no choice but to follow orders. . . .

Irioch returned, dragging wounded men, slaves and soldiers alike, and threw them inside the shield-wall.

The Sorcerers, chanting, collected the blood into little black jars.

The golden moons of the dawn were rising above the bone-white City of the Sea-Elves. The sea-surge boomed in the streets; the tower where the Council of Seven gathered throbbed with the crash and suck of the waves against its base.

"So long as it remains in the Maze," said Kandol, "I fear there is little my kin can do. Narsil the Younger wrought a Stone which could pierce the Shadow of the Ancients, but that secret was lost five thousand years ago, when Nardis fell."

"If the Stone of Tirorilorn is destroyed, and its flame goes out," said Ethellin the Wise, "then the barriers will fail, and we will have a new Age of Terror."

"The only comfort I have," said Kandol, "is that our most skilled seers have seen no such danger in all the tangled paths of the future. But this does not mean we should relax our vigilance. Even the wisest cannot see all paths."

Swanwhite stirred.

"It is good to know," she said, her voice bitter, "that all the world is not in danger. Yet still my people, and my kin, vanish."

In the silence that followed, the surf boomed through the streets of the city, and plucked at the tower like a harpstring.

"It may be that the Sons of Awan may accomplish what neither the Elves nor the Sons of Hastur can." The giant, Balian, who had been king over the mortal Kingdom of Handor in his time, three hundred years before, rose from the huge chair and stood towering above them all. "We do not depend upon the Powers of the Mind as you do, and so the Shadow of the Ancients should not affect us."

"What if it affects those powers you do have?" asked Dorialith. "What if you lose control of your size? Will you not be crushed by your own weight?"

"Have any of your kin ever entered the Shadow of the Ancients?" Ethellin asked. The giant frowned.

"*I* have not—or rather, not since I achieved full growth. In my youth I explored the ruins of Rinanthigo, but I might as well have been a Mortal Man then." He frowned. "Yet, certainly, one of our younger folk would be safe enough."

"Until he met whatever lurks in the Maze," said Swanwhite.

"Indeed," said Falmoran, the brown-bearded Captain of the Ship from Beyond the World. "Whatever this thing is, it has great power—"

"We do not know that," said Kandol.

"It had power enough to conquer Arnim Finn and his son!" Falmoran exclaimed.

"In the Maze," said Kandol, "that might not take power. A mortal, there, or a band of Mortal Men, or even a wild beast, might overcome the mightiest of us here. Without your powers, Falmoran, if you could see with only your eyes and hear only with your ears, if you could cast no illusions or change shape, how would you fare, against a band of robbers, say, or a lion?"

"I would still have my wits and my sword, I hope!" snapped Falmoran. "But Arnim Finn had traversed the Maze for centuries, and Culnaron had grown up in it! And Arnim Finn was *not* powerless; he told me that he could focus the Power of Tirorilorn even within the Maze!"

"I think that good proof he was taken by surprise," said Ethellin. "Certainly, if there is anything that can face the full power of Tirorilorn unscathed, it has no need to hide in the Maze!"

"Perhaps," said Kandol. "But this is much talk, and little to the point, and I cannot blame the princess if she is angry with us. I think the answer here is much the same as that we discussed earlier, about Rath Tintallain. You need a mortal—a hero."

"Well, if we indeed raise an army of heroes," said Ciall-glind, the Immortal Piper, Lord of Elthar, Eldest of the Elves, "perhaps we should take *them* to Tirorilorn."

"That would be a long voyage for Mortal Men," said Ethellin.

"I still think that my kin may be of use here," said Balian, sinking back into the huge seat that had been made for him. "If nothing else, certainly, a fleet of our mortal allies can clear the

seas and drive off those mortals who have besieged your city!
And I am not afraid to dare the Maze—and I will speak with
elders on this matter, and find out what we know about the
Shadow of the Ancients."

"I thank you, for my people," said Swanwhite. The giant
bowed and smiled.

"It would still be wise," said Kandol, "to find some other
power site and source which can hold the barrier-spell together
should Tirorilorn fall, and to adjust our net so it is not so
fragile. But that, I think, is a matter for our next meeting."

"Where shall we meet?" asked Dorialith. "Here again, or at
Caer Nodens?" For it was at Caer Nodens in the Golden Isles
that Mananan had called the first meeting of the Council of
Seven, nine thousand years before, when the Seven had first
laid out the net of spells that barred the Dark Lords from the
world, and brought the Age of Terror to an end.

"I move that we meet at Tirorilorn," said Ciallglind.

"What? And expose you all to the dangers of the Maze?"
Swanwhite exclaimed. "Bravely said, Eldest, but who will
replace you, if you vanish into the Maze, as my grandfather
did?"

"Riarbind," said Ciallglind, smiling. "He is little younger
than I. And *you* had to dare the Maze—and much else—on
your way here. Who will replace *you*, Lady, if you never return
to Tirorilorn?"

"Ocloqaran of the Mystic Shield, who rules in my name
now, and—"

"But no, Lady, if you were to vanish," said Ethellin,
"Ocloqaran of the Mystic Shield will also vanish in the Maze,
searching for you!"

"It—may be so," said Swanwhite, with a blush. "But there
is still my cousin, Prince Ilbiron, and my grandfather's trusted
advisor, Vorisquil. But who could replace Dorialith, or
Ethellin the Wise, or Kandol Hastur-Lord?"

"All of us here are replacements," said Kandol. "Dorialith
speaks for Mananawn his father, Ethellin for Nuadan, while I
try to fill the place of Hastur's grandson, Narsil the Elder. And
so with each of us. And I think Ciallglind's suggestion good."

"And I," said Dorialith, and the others all murmured assent. Tears glimmered on Swanwhite's lashes.

"And *when* shall we meet again?" Kandol asked, as Swanwhite opened her mouth to try to thank them. "In recent centuries we have met every twenty years, but in earlier ages we met more often. And our seers see a period of great danger eight years from now."

"We are the Council of Seven," said Ciallglind. "Let us meet each seven years!"

"Thus we did long ago, in the years before Nardis fell," said Dorialith. "Seven years from today, then, in Tirorilorn!"

"Good," said Kandol. "I shall leave it to you, Ethellin, to find Tuarim."

"I saw him in the Elfwoods, less than thirty years ago," said Ciallglind.

"Aye, he comes and he goes, wandering on odd quests," said Dorialith. "Fifty years ago he rode in here and put into my hands the great Crystal of Sullathon—a wonder I had never thought to see again! It is in the next room, there. Then he was off again— looking for the Horn of Ranarun, I think he said."

"Perhaps you can use Sullathon's crystal to find him," said Kandol. "So! We shall meet again, in Tirorilorn."

"Ah, you are all true friends!" Swanwhite's lashes were wet; her voice was choked. "I have no words fit to thank you! Yet I truly fear for you all."

"Well, then," said Balion, rising and striding to the door, "let us hope that the Maze is clear seven years from now! I shall speak to my kin, as I have said, and either I myself, or another of the Children of Awan, will come within the year with ships and men enough to drive the raiders from the seas about your city, and to search the Maze until we know what lurks there. Until then, farewell, bright-haired maiden!" He bowed, and bent down to pass stooping under the high arch. Swanwhite watched him go with a slight frown.

The meeting now was breaking up in truth: Kandol and Falmoran conferred in low voices: Ciallglind lifted the bag-pipes he carried always with him, and fingered the holes of the chanter thoughtfully. Ethellin had unrolled a map and, frowning, traced a road with his finger.

"Dorialith," said Swanwhite, "you said that you would show me this mortal of Airellen's. If it is a mortal hero that I need, to find Father and the others who have vanished in the Maze, this may be a good time. Or do you think him enough for such a quest?"

"Indeed," said Dorialith, "it is some such deed as this I have been hoping for him to do. And it is on me to look at him again. Would you like to see Sullathon's crystal?"

As they turned, there came a soft rustle of air, and the Hastur-Lord vanished like a blown-out flame.

Through a window they saw the dawn, and Balian wading out into the sea. He had grown in height now, to at least twice the size he had worn in the chamber, and the waves swirled around his thighs as he waded out to his waiting ship.

"You do not plan, then, to wait for help from the Children of Awan?" asked Dorialith.

"His gallantries are such," she said slowly, "that I wish to be no more in his debt than I must." As they watched, the giant waded up to his ship and stood looming above it, then suddenly vanished. Watching, they saw a smaller man-shape rise from the water and float to the deck.

Sullathon's crystal was filled with odd flecks of jeweled fire in the darkened room, but as Dorialith approached, an opal glow grew within it, slowly lighting the chamber.

The plains and woods of Galinor glowed green in the crystal as Dorialith's mind ranged across them, seeking Ingulf's trail.

Frowning, he deepened his concentration, forgetting the white-haired girl at his side. He reached out, searching a wider and wider area. . . .

"He must be far indeed," he muttered. "But the sword I gave him was forged by Govanan, in the Living Land. Perhaps . . ."

His frown deepened. Suddenly the crystal was crowded with reeling shapes.

"*Sarlow!*" Dorialith exclaimed. "What—?"

"What is it?" asked Swanwhite.

"It is a mortal man driven mad by a careless woman's magic!" Dorialith snarled, his mind plunging through to Ingulf's. "I told him to do great deeds, but *this*—!"

"I can see that!" she snapped. "What is that . . . throb-bing?"

Dorialith started.

Screaming filled the city.

Ingulf looked up into the dawn sky. The paling moons and stars and the brightening patch of eastern sky were blotted by a shadow that thickened into dense clots of darkness above the city.

The clots thickened into a writhing cloud.

Dorialith shifted the focus of the globe, and they could see the soldiers surrounding the chanting Sorcerers, and sense the twisting of space as it parted before the *Dyole*. . . .

From the jewel at Swanwhite's throat a twig-thin beam of intense, blinding flame lanced into the crystal globe, and into the flaming sword. . . .

The writhing cloud twisted, and began to assume shape, a mind-wrenching shape of horror on which the mind refused to focus. Jointed claws and interlacing tentacles writhed amidst tossing eyes and mouths. Ingulf's mind shuddered, and he raised *Frostfire*, trying to shield himself from that shape, while his mind twisted trying to compare this with something it knew—centipedes, spiders, insects, scorpions—all seemed beautiful and pleasant now, compared to this. Snakes, worms, crabs, eels—his mind turned helplessly back on itself.

Frostfire's flame forced his eyes shut as it flared sun-bright.

Blinking, he saw light leap from *Frostfire's* point to a nearby roof, and gather there like a mist of flame.

Out of the fire-mist a form took shape—a man's shape, he thought at first . . .

A *woman's* shape: a ghost-woman forming from the light.

"Airellen!" he screamed. But as his throat strained with the cry, he saw it was not so. The beautiful wraith raised her arms, and from between her hands lanced a blinding, burning beam of light that forced Ingulf's eyes closed, and still burned through his eyelids: a radiant torrent that raged into the sky, churning into the blackness there, to shatter the clotted dark. . . .

A deep throbbing note of pain boomed in stone and ached in bone. Ingulf reeled, weightless, feeling the world twist from under his feet in an instant of nausea. . . .

The ghost-woman turned on the rooftop.

Her hand dropped, and then spread out swooping over the crowd, and Ingulf felt a soothing calm like inaudible music singing through his nerves, driving the nightmare madness of the thing in the sky from his memory; and at the same time something stroked the inside of his eyes, and the streaks and blotches in his vision faded. . . .

Then, suddenly, the ghostly shape was gone.

And, miles away, Swanwhite reeled fainting into Dorialith's arms, while Falmoran, Ciallglind, and Ethellin the Wise burst with pallid faces into the room.

Ingulf stared at the spot where she had stood, eyes blurred with tears, wanting Airellen, wondering where she was, and if she ever thought of him. . . .

Or was he forgotten as well as alone? Tears welled in his eyes.

Did she hate him? Was it *her* curse that had trapped him in this evil world, where everything betrayed him and struggled to destroy everything he tried to do?

"Hastur, save us," voices were chanting. *"Hastur, aid us!"* his mind chanted with them. *"Drive this curse from us: Hastur, free us!"* Suddenly he realized the voices were in his ears and not only in his mind.

Only then did he realize that he stood on solid stone, surrounded by ranks and rows of kneeling folk, who chanted Hastur's name, but knelt to *him*. . . .

Vildern's stunned mind wandered through endless strands of doom looming overhead, not understanding the blaze that dazed his eyes, or the massed voices that chanted the Forbidden Name. . . .

* * *

Ingulf blinked at the kneeling ranks around him. Beyond them the enemy shield-wall still reeled like drunken men.

And scattered among the kneeling ranks around him, some of the mailed soldiers of Sarlow still lived, and as he watched he saw them stagger to their feet and lurch toward the shelter of the shield-wall, casually stabbing those nearest them.

"What are you doing?" Ingulf shrieked. "Wake up, you fools! Your enemies are among you! Get up! Kill those bloody-handed Demon-feeders!"

"Vildern!"

The sound of his name evoked him from the endless interlacing strands of madness, called him back to sunlight. . . .

"Captain Vildern!"

Could that shaken stutter conceal the calm tones of Kelldule? He turned his head. It did not feel as though it belonged to him, or as though it really connected to the body beneath it.

Ramaukin had fallen into Kelldule's arms.

"Captain, rouse your men. Retreat! Get out of here!" Kelldule said. He reeled as Ramaukin moved in his arms. The bald head lifted; the usually ruddy cheeks were gray.

"What . . . was . . . that?" the Sorcerer's croaking voice whispered. "An Adept? Is . . . it . . . blue-robed?"

"An Adept, yes," said Kelldule. "One more powerful than I had thought possible. That was no power of the Blue-Robes he summoned to his aid. That was"—he gasped for breath— "that was the power of Tirorilorn. And with that power aroused, I want—*away*—from here! Curse you, Captain, rouse your men!"

"What was that?" exclaimed Ciallglind. Ethellin and Falmoran echoed him before Dorialith could speak.

"A *Dyole*," he said. "We found—we were using the Stone of Sullathon—" He gestured at the crystal, now blank and dull. "—and we . . . chanced across a Gate just as it opened, a Gate into the Dark World, with one of the lesser *Dyoles* breaking through. The Princess used the Sullathon-crystal to focus the Tirorilon-fire, and closed the Gate again, before the *Dyole* could pass."

"Splendid!" Ciallglind exclaimed, "If only all the *Dyoles* could be stopped so easily! Let her take the Crystal to Tirorilorn with her! None of us could put it to such fine use!"

"She has saved many lives, indeed," said Ethellin. "But how is the Lady?"

Swanwhite straightened in Dorialith's arms, swaying a little on her feet.

"The room is whirling still," she said, "and I think someone has used my head for a bell, but that will pass."

"I do not understand these things," said Falmoran, "but it seems that you have done a brave deed, Daughter, and—"

"I am *not* your daughter!" Swanwhite's tone was sharp. "I will answer to my name in any of three languages, and 'Princess' is acceptable, but only my father, Culnaron, may call me 'Daughter.' Or were you speaking to someone else, Lord Falmoran?" Even leaning on Dorialith's shoulder her manner was regal, and her eyes sought and held his own.

He did not flinch; he met her glare calmly.

"I owe you no apology," he answered. "Even if you have indeed saved this world, you are far from the first to do so! Yet you know well I meant no disrespect, *Princess* Ealafinn, but only affection for the *grand*daughter of an old friend, and one who is a friend as well as cousin to my own beloved daughter. And you have been dear to me since you were a child indeed!"

"But I am *not* a child now." Her steady gaze did not waver. Neither did his, but his beard twitched to a smile.

"Age is not precious to those who have it," he said, and humor danced in his eyes. "But come, Princess! I meant only that you are dear to me as my daughter—"

"If your daughter is so dear to you, why are you not seeking her, instead of bothering your friends' daughters?"

That touched him. His eyes set with rage. He stiffened.

"I will, then!" He turned and was gone from the room.

"That was harsh," said Ethellin, staring after him.

Ciallglind said nothing, but set the blow-pipe between his teeth, and filled the bag.

Drones roared, and his fingers danced on the chanter as he turned and strode from the room, playing a tune that was called *"The Heart is Not a Toy."*

Shaking his head, Ethellin followed, and Swanwhite turned back to the crystal.

"Now, Dorialith," she said, "show me Ingulf again!"

The shield-wall fell back before the mob. The great shields thundered under stones and swords and hammers.

Yet little harm was done on either side.

Ingulf found himself short of breath, and strengthless. The heavy iron bar of his flail dragged on the ground: he could not understand how he had ever gotten that weight aloft and whirling.

He stood leaning on the long shaft, ashamed of himself and his weakness. But as he watched, he saw that they all seemed weak.

"Did that evil creature steal my strength from me?" he asked himself aloud. He slumped wearily, watching the fighting.

"It has stolen it from all of us!" he exclaimed. "Look at the enemy. They move like broken things! Surely, if they had their strength, the evil murderers would murder us all. The slaves can barely lift their stones!" And indeed, the mob was beginning to drift back, weary and drooping, while the shield-wall backed away from them. Thrown stones struck their shields: some fell short in the street.

"Indeed," said Ingulf, shaking his head, "they are so weak that the stones thrown by the women would knock them down, if the women had their strength! What did you do to us, you evil murdering animal? Why do you hate us so?

"Did it steal my memory, too? I cannot remember what it looked like. Was it like a slug, or a skull? Hatred twisted round and round itself, drooling hunger and lust! It made the whole world ugly." He shut his eyes, shivering in the bleakness of the cold and evil world. "All foulness! No beauty anywhere. For a moment it even stole Airellen's eyes from me! I could not even remember your beauty! And then the world was dark indeed, until I thought of you again! Oh, Lady, help me! I am alone!

"They all steal my mind! Did the monster steal my memory, or was it that witch, that ghost-witch?" He shook his head, confused, and watched the retreating shield-wall. Some of the

city's soldiers had reached its shelter, and were falling back
with it. Others had been borne down under the weight of
numbers, and their corpses lay now in pools of blood. Many of
the people of the city lay there with them.

"It makes no sense!" he muttered to himself. "They all steal
from me, enemies and friends alike! Airellen took something
from me too! But what was it?" He stared around him like a
trapped beast. The people of the city were gathering, in little
timid clumps.

"What do they want of me?" he murmured, under his
breath. A small, dark-haired girl stared worshipfully up at him
with wide blue eyes. Blood dripped from the fish-knife in her
hand, and her arms were red to the elbows. He remembered,
suddenly, seeing her—or another as young—slitting a soldier's
throat. . . .

"I am lost," he sobbed, with a little shiver. "What did that
creature do to us? Was it our humanity that it stole from us? I
cannot remember it—it was like briars—or like writhing
worms—but spiked—all poison and passion—all spikes and
slime. . . .

"Did the evil murdering creature steal my memory, or did
the witch do it, that witch-ghost made of light? She came out
of my sword!" He stared at *Frostfire,* and almost cast the
sword from him. Instead he wiped the blade clean and sheathed
it. His boots were soaked with blood. And all around him,
bloody-handed people were gathering, kneeling on the wet red
stones.

"Ah, Airellen, what a cruel, evil world you have sent me
into!" he whispered. "Why do you hate me so? Am I a monster
to you? An evil creature, a beast, all lust and hunger?" He
shuddered, and then became aware of the voices of the people
around him.

"Heal me!" one was saying, stretching out a maimed hand.
"Heal me, Hastur!"

"Help me," a woman whimpered, holding a bleeding,
wounded child. *"See my son! He is badly hurt!"*

"See my blood, where the sword cut deep!" another voice
called.

More and more voices clamored.

"Hastur help me, and heal me now!"
"Heal the pain of my broken bones!"
"Heal my daughter and make her whole!"
"Heal my wife! She was hurt for you!"
"Won't you touch me and heal me now?"
"Help my son! He will bleed to death!"

And now through the crowding wounded came others, twisted broken shapes clad in rags—cripples, lepers, beggars, all crying for him to heal them, to have mercy. . . .

"Have mercy on *me!*" Ingulf cried. "Why do you call me Hastur?"

"Who else can you be?" The little girl cried at his side, near enough that her clear voice carried even above the frantic voices that clamored and clashed above one another. "You have come to free us, with your hair red as sunset, and the sword of light in your hand! Were not those the signs by which we were to know you? We have waited for you so long!"

"What do you mean?" Ingulf cried. "Waiting for me? How can that be?"

A boy stepped up beside the girl, their faces so alike Ingulf was sure they must be brother and sister.

"A thousand years or more ago," the boy said, "the tribes of the Sarló swept down from Noria, to conquer the lands of Treethclith and Arvorclos and Tircladoc, and we have been slaves ever since. But in all that time, there has always been a legend that someday Hastur would return to free us, with a sword of flame which would slay even the greatest of the Demons that serve the Dark Sorcerers. And now that you have come, all the cities will rise, all across the old land of Treethclith!"

Ingulf's head whirled, and a thrill ran through him like a splendor of trumpets. He saw himself, suddenly, at the head of a victorious host of freed slaves, storming across all the land of Sarlow, and the people of the cities opening the gates before him, and the armies of Sarlow fleeing in confusion.

No need, then to abandon any to slavery, and as conqueror of Sarlow, surely, Airellen must pay him heed. . . .

Or would that matter to her? Would anything he could do matter to her?

What better hope had he? These people were willing to
follow him—indeed, they depended on him to save them.
What would happen if he turned away from them now?

They depended on him to free them, and these wounded
around him depended on him to heal them. He was no healer,
but perhaps, he thought, that ghost-witch that had leaped from
his sword could heal as well as destroy. But could he draw her
forth from his sword again?

As he hesitated, he saw Rakmir and Torvar pushing their
way through the crowd, and he saw with surprise a dark-
haired, scarred woman holding tight to Torvar's arm.

Beyond the crowd that begged for his touch, he heard wild
shouts of joy, and saw folk embracing. Women were weeping,
and he realized that many must be finding lovers and brothers
and fathers they had thought long dead marching in his army.

It was good what he was doing, he decided, bringing joy
back to lives that had been ruined. Surely Airellen would see
that?

Yet, even if she did not, even though it brought him only
suffering, it was still something that *should* be done—something that he should do. . . .

Ah, but what value virtue if Airellen did not care: if there
was no hope, if her eyes never glowed on him again? If this
soul-ugly world punished his virtues the same as his faults,
then why should he struggle?

But then, if the punishment for good was the same as for
evil, then it did not matter either way, and with good there was
always hope. . . .

He saw through the crowd the men he had rescued from the
pits moving toward him, behind Torvar and Rakmir, and then,
wondering, he recognized the girl who clung to Torvar so
tightly as the woman he had saved from torture in the
palace . . . when? Not long ago.

The great Crystal of Sullathon throbbed, lit with life, and
Swanwhite and Dorialith beheld in that eerie light the wildly
joyous crowds that surrounded Ingulf.

"What did I tell you?" Dorialith exclaimed. "It is a great
hero that is in him!"

"What is it they are saying?" asked Swanwhite, silently, and the two Sea-Elves fixed their minds upon the globe, hearing through the ears of the Crowd, and watching the fiery, swirling patterns of love and hate, of vengeance and sorrow and hope, as they flitted from mind to mind in the crowd. . . .

Freed slaves wept in hysterical joy as parted lovers, sons, mothers, daughters, fathers, sisters, brothers, wives, and husbands found each other in the crowd. Women's voices keened and sobbed, as they embraced those they had long ago given up for dead.

The dark little people of the city danced with a frantic joy, and made a pounding music with dusty, ill-tuned harps and viols and flutes and drums that they pulled out of hiding-places in the ancient houses. There was more enthusiasm than skill in the playing, and it was clear that it had been rare indeed for the instruments to be touched by fingers.

The two Sea-Elves, wincing a little at the music, watched and listened as naked, scarred men with swords or shields and hammers, and mailed men with picks moved through the crowd that knelt in adoration around Ingulf, and gathered around the ragged Islander. They could see fear and desperation spark from mind to mind.

Despair ebbed from Ingulf's mind, and a spirit, bright, exultant, took its place. A thrill of certainty surged up inside him: at last it all made sense!

There were no accidents; fate was *not* cruel! It was for *this* that Airellen had been placed in the path of his boat, it was for *this* that he had been forced to wound her and had fallen in love! All so that he would be brought here, to be the deliverer of Sarlow, that a great evil might be destroyed! At last his suffering had meaning!

He smiled at the men gathered about him, his comrades, his brothers-in-arms, the men from the pits. Two days ago they had been laboring under the whip. Now his love for Airellen had freed them. And that dark-haired girl who clung to Torvar so tightly—only last night she had been a plaything of the man from whose palace he had taken her—

"You saved her," Torvar said to him. "All these years we

had thought each other dead, all these years of suffering and sorrows best forgotten. Now we can go home."

"You saved me," she said. "Please take us home."

"No," said Ingulf. "We are marching on."

"But—that's madness," said Torvar. "Think of the women! We've got to use our numbers, and fight our way over the mountains before word of this reaches Kithmar or Bluzig, and they gather an army against us!"

Ingulf laughed. Again he felt the wonder of the secret he had stumbled across surge through him, filling his heart.

"No!" he said, joyous glory bubbling up inside him, swelling and building inside him like music. "We shall leave no slave in all the Land of Sarlow! We are marching on!"

He filled his lungs with the breath of glory, to explain how, in each city, the enslaved waited for the coming of Hastur, to throw open the gates to a red-haired man with a bright sword.

The dark-haired woman threw herself to the ground at his feet, in a storm of sobbing.

"Please!" she cried, kneeling before him, bathing his feet in tears, reaching up to touch his knees, sweeping the dust with her long hair. "Oh, please, *please!* Take us away from here! Please!"

Ingulf hesitated. From above her, he could see only the long dark hair that made him think of Airellen.

Was it an omen? Should he turn from this course, as though it were Airellen herself who asked him?

But no, this course surely led to her. It was an omen indeed, but one to harden his resolve, for just so, surely, would Airellen kneel before him, to beg forgiveness of the liberator of Sarlow!

"No!" he said. "I will leave no slave in chains; we shall—"

Something came down on the back of his head. Light flared at the back of his skull, and the ground rushed to meet him.

And he was lost in the darkness of Airellen's long hair.

Tiny in Sullathon's crystal, the watching Sea-Elves saw Torvar heave his pick high above his head.

Swanwhite gasped, and the jewel flared at her throat as the pick flew at Ingulf's back.

She checked the white beam that lanced the stone as the iron head passed harmlessly above Ingulf's head, and the wood haft rapped the back of his skull.

The Islander slumped and fell atop the kneeling girl.

She wriggled from under his limp body with a little cry.

"Is he dead?" They heard Rakmir ask. The girl stared, then tore open the tattered robe and pressed an ear against his naked chest.

"No," she said, after a moment, "not yet, at least! Small thanks to you!" She glared at Torvar. "The crowd will tear us apart."

"That was why," he gestured at the men standing around them, "I thought it better no one saw. But he left me no choice. If he'd agreed to lead us home, I'd have had no need to strike him!" He bent down, and pulled *Frostfire's* scabbard from Ingulf's belt.

Far off in the Sea-Elves' city, Dorialith groaned.

"Tie him up," he heard Torvar say. "There are ropes and chains enough." He saw how those around stared at him. "Well, what do you expect me to do?" he growled. "Leave him for the wolves? We'll have to carry him, that's all! Why are you all staring at me like that?"

"You may wish you'd left him," said Rakmir somberly. "When he wakes, he'll want your blood."

"By that time, we'll be safe in the mountains," answered Torvar. "I'll give him his sword back, and he can come down and try to conquer Sarlow all by himself if he still wants to."

"Unless he dies," the girl said. "That was quite a knock on the head."

"He won't die," scoffed Torvar. "Why, that poor lunatic! Anything that happened to that head would make it better!" He belted *Frostfire* about his hips, and lifted his pick to his shoulder.

Suddenly he gave a startled cry.

He held the pick out at arm's length, and reached a finger toward the metal. He stopped without touching it.

"It's *hot*!" he exclaimed. "As though it had been sitting in a forge."

Far away, Swanwhite laughed.

* * *

Hard stone bruised sore feet as Vildern's stumbling, stunned men marched on, lurching over barren rock. In his numbed brain, Vildern wondered wearily how many men had survived.

But then, the great *Dyole* could have eaten all of them. Not so bad, then, to feel so sick and miserable!

His head throbbed. Pain stirred his anger at the Sorcerers who had nearly killed all his men.

He heard Ondrute's weak voice close behind him.

"What was—that . . . that . . . ghost—that fire-witch?"

"That was the Power of Tirorilorn," growled Kelldule, his voice stronger.

"I heard you say that—that name before," said Ramaukin, weakly. "What is this—turalor—whatever it is?"

"It is a secret city of the Elves," said Kelldule, "far away, far over the sea. It was there, thousands of years ago, that the Sea-Elf Arnim Finn, with the aid of Narsil Hastur"—Vildern trembled to hear that naked Name; one of the Sorcerers cried out in shrill fear—"forged the great Stone to harness the fires of Tirorilorn, and with it wove the spell of the Barriers that hold the Eight from the world. It is hidden by that mystery that is called the Shadow of the Ancients, which is like a mist to the mind, that no sight can pierce."

"But how the Power of Tirorilorn could be loosed *here* I cannot understand, unless—" Kelldule's voice faltered. "Unless," he went on, as though to himself, "Arnim Finn or his son Culnaron has escaped from the Maze, and has come hunting me—but that makes no sense; he never saw me, nor knew the role I played—" Was that, Vildern wondered, fear in Kelldule's voice?

"But what has all this to do with that Islander?" Ramaukin asked, pettishly.

"I do not know," said Kelldule. "But that sword he carries is a Sea-Elf's sword. It may be—Arnim Finn *might* have forged such a blade—some of the great Swords of Power are said to have been forged by him—and he might have put a spell on it like the ones the Hast—the Blue-Robes are said to put upon the blades that they forge; a spell to draw on the Power of the Stone—"

"But what is an Islander doing with such a sword?"

"I do not know," said Kelldule, "unless Tirorilorn has fallen at last, or unless this Islander is more than he seems. If he is—Arnim Finn in disguise, or some other among the Sea-Elves—"

"We have fought off attacks by Elves before," snarled Ondrute. "We have even fought off the Blue-Robes!"

"You have not fought off Elves with Arnim Finn's Power before!" said Kelldule. "Do not judge by comparison with the Immortal King of Galinor, or even by Ciallglind and the other Lords of Elthar."

Vildern's head was throbbing, and he found it harder and harder to make sense of what he was overhearing. The sun beat down on his head. How long had they been marching?

Through the Great Crystal, Swanwhite and Dorialith watched rumor and panic dart from mind to mind in the streets of Kirgiff.

Wildly gesticulating people gathered in little knots on every corner, shouting and waving their arms.

The Sea-Elves listened through the minds of one person after another. Some were refusing to leave their homes, saying that now Hastur had come, the city would be free once more. Others said that Hastur had come to take them away to the lands where everyone was free and there was no evil.

A few repeated the curious rumor that Hastur had been killed, murdered by his own men, but no one believed them.

Yet still the story spread, and panic seized even those who believed it impossible. *"Legends lead down a wolf's throat,"* men muttered in the alleys.

"But I saw with my own eyes!" another insisted. *"Hastur! The flame from his sword drove the demon away!"*

"But if he is gone, if the masters return, what will you do?"

"We have a son in the army," one man said. *"He pretends to be one of them, but he loves us in secret. He will hide us."*

"I am a skilled worker," said another. *"I was sold for ten thousand golden Bloods. They will not kill me! I am too costly."*

"Hastur will not abandon us!" said some others. *"Our town*

has strong walls," so some said, refusing to leave; but by far the greater part ran to their houses, and began to gather their pitiful possessions. Some gathered others' possessions as well, and there was looting and riot and fighting.

The Sea-Elves watched the people of Kirgiff pour in panic through their city's gates, to scatter across the stony plain.

"Nothing unites them now," said Dorialith. *"See how they scatter, some to the south, some to the west? Fear rules them."* In the great glowing crystal they watched scurrying family after family, pushing and dragging piled carts. *"They have forgotten hope; they have forgotten love and kinship, save for the closest. You see that no family dares trust another? Now they have forgotten even hate!"*

"What makes men so weak?" asked Swanwhite. *"And why do you think that one would be of use to me?"*

"Ah! I had truly forgotten, Princess," said Dorialith, *"just how young you are! I forgot that you have never seen Elves at their worst! Think over the old tales of our people, and you will realize that elves can be just as greedy, vain, foolish, and vengeful as mortals can. But we live longer, and we learn. The oldest of these would still be children, by our reckoning."*

"You had forgot? Indeed, then, Elvish pride is vain!" she laughed. *"We shall see!"*

Before noon the plain crawled with clumps of refugees, and when Torvar and Rakmir marched out at the head of their more orderly army of slaves, they stared in open-mouthed awe at the sight.

Swanwhite reached for their minds, to hear through their ears.

"Where are they going?" they heard the dark-haired girl say.

"They don't know," said Rakmir, "except 'toward the hills.' They don't know which way to run. They don't know how to find the passes, or where the soldiers are."

"Well, where are *we* going?" she asked. "I know no more than they!"

"We take *that* road." Torvar pointed toward the west. "I marched there once on labor detail, long ago. A small guard fort blocks a pass so steep and treacherous that they hardly guard it at all. Built to stop whole armies from the outer world—not to keep slaves in! A high wall and an iron gate—but low stone walls on this side, with a flimsy door—and the garrison is small."

"Let us march on!" Rakmir said. "We've miles to go before dark yet, and a hard fight at the end."

"March, men!" Torvar shouted, and unsheathing *Frostfire* waved it high.

As the Elf-sword's frost-white steel glittered with sunlight in the crystal's heart, the jewel at Swanwhite's throat flared.

Almost at once she checked it, but a faint shimmer of fire burst from the blade, and a roar from the marching men showed that they took it as a good omen.

"I wanted to make it too hot for him to hold," said Swanwhite, bitterly, *but the Great Stone of Tirorilorn was not made for such tricks—as Father and Grandfather told me over and over again, before they would allow me ever to wear this key to its Power! And yes, Dorialith, I see that elves can be as bad as mortals; but if you lecture me about it, I will be angry."*

Outside their tower, the two Sea-Elves could hear harps chiming above the hoarse surf, weaving the sea-birds' wailing magically into their song.

In the glowing crystal they watched the slaves march out of the city. They saw Ingulf, still senseless, bound and slung over the broad shoulders of a brawny man, who laughed and joked with his comrades, his aura swirling brightly against Ingulf's duller color. But the Elves saw that the Islander was alive, and although his brain was bruised, it would heal if allowed to, and the injury itself would not kill him.

Rakmir's trained shield-wall moved as a unit, splendid now in bright mail looted from the dead. Behind them the men and women they had freed in the slave-market marched, and they too were newly armed.

As they strode across the stone, the scattering families fleeing from the city turned from their aimless flight to follow.

"Dorialith?" asked Swanwhite. *"Can they escape? Will they be able to fight their way out? Was Torvar right to strike Airellen's lover down?"*

In answer Dorialith shifted the scene in the crystal, sweeping rapidly across rivers and checkered landscape, to Bluzig, the City of Blood, Sarlow's dark capital.

All roads west out of Bluzig were clouded with swirling dust. Through it, metal glinted as a multitude marched, mail-shirts and spear-points swaying with their stride.

At the head of the choking columns rode a figure like a statue of black steel: a man in smooth plate-armor that fitted close to his body. While they watched, he removed his helmet, revealing blond hair and a strong-jawed, cruelly sneering face, and wiped dust from the eyeslits.

"That must be the armor stolen from the Dwarves," said Dorialith. *"And the one who wears it has been named to me as Svaran the Black. The Dwarves say that that armor will resist even a Hastur-Blade."*

"It is a great army," said Swanwhite, *"but it has far to march."*

"Had Ingulf continued to lead the slaves," said Dorialith, *"they would have met that army. But, since there are other old cities between Kirgiff and Bluzig, each with great numbers of slaves to rise and rally to Ingulf's aid, it might be that he could have matched their numbers."*

Outside the tower now, voices joined the harping, rising in wordless song. In the great crystal the scene changed, and moved back to the square plain of stone.

For a moment they watched the shifting pattern of tiny shapes as the freed slaves swarmed like ants, and scattered groups slowly drew inward toward the orderly block of men led by Rakmir and Torvar; then that view vanished, and Torvar's face appeared.

"There are enough of us to swamp the garrison even without this rabble!" They heard Torvar's scornful voice through the ears of those around him. "Now that there is a weapon against the werewolves—"

"Now that *you* have a weapon against werewolves," the girl's voice said. "The rest of us are just as—listen! There they are again!"

Wolves howled eerily, faint with distance.

"But they are only plain wolves," said Rakmir from her side. "It is still broad daylight."

"Are we walking into a trap?" she cried, as though he had not spoken, hysteria tuning her voice.

Her face vanished from the crystal. The stone plain blurred as Swanwhite and Dorialith sought the origin of the howls.

Beyond the stone square's edge, across the green pasture land: here they saw cattle scattering, fleeing, and then they saw the wolves—ten weary, drooping wolves, some wounded, and in their midst, four horses, with naked, blood-caked figures swaying in the saddles. One of them was a tall, blond-haired woman.

"*And who are these?*" Swanwhite asked. "*More prisoners?*"

"*I think not,*" Dorialith answered. "*It is not the wolves that their horses fear. Werewolves, I think.*"

Curious, Swanwhite looked closer. She glimpsed an image in the blond girl's mind, of a bright sword flaming in the night. . . .

Men and wolves fought. She tasted blood on her tongue; her teeth tore meat that screamed. A dark shape leaped from a rock: steel flaring bright in its hand, lighting blond hair and a handsome face. . . .

A sledge-hammer fell on her skull. She felt the savage pain of breaking bone: her brain invaded, the sky ripped open, the taste of salty music burned her eyes. . . .

Then the bone was rolled back: blended taste and sight and scent and scream shifted and twisted apart, until a recognizable world emerged. She could feel her skull still healing. . . .

With a fastidious shudder, Swanwhite pulled herself free from the other mind.

"*Werewolves indeed,*" she said, still tasting blood. "*But whose sword is that I saw in her mind?*"

"*Hard to say, from so brief a glimpse,*" said Dorialith, "*but it could have been the Sword of Eruir, Athnacru, that Eruir gave to Cadoc, or it might be Sulivel, the sun-bright sword that Nuadan gave to Kenual, the king of ancient Treethclith. Duinon, too, had such a sword, but I do not know what became of it.*

"*Of course, it might be a Hastur-Blade, and so outside my*

knowledge; or one of the swords wrought by Lanno or by Ruro Halfbreed, or even by some Adept of Elthar. But the light of a Hastur-Blade has most often a different quality than that. We know it is not Nuadan's own Klaivsolas, and not my father's blade. . . ."

"It was a Mortal Man that held it," Swanwhite interrupted.

"It was indeed," agreed Dorialith. *"Now, what have we here?"*

In the glass the whole side of the mountain was bright with mail. A great mass of men moved down the road, from Klufbirk, glittering like a river in the Twin Suns' light.

The eye of the crystal turned across the plain. The soldiers who had marched out of the city were advancing to meet the newcomers.

Beyond them, on the far edge of the plain, the swarming, scattered groups of rebel slaves from the city were gathering around the marching ranks of the freed slaves from outside.

The Sea-Elves could see fear in the furiously pulsing sea of auras, ripples of fear spreading to wash over the calm of the ordered ranks that marched in the middle.

Outside the tower where Swanwhite and Dorialith watched, a flute had joined the wordless singing of the elves, and the ringing chime of harpstrings.

Now above the splashing hiss of the waves a bagpipe joined, and then another. The music rose, surging in a mystic shimmering of magic that caught the ear and the mind, swelling in a wonder of heartbreaking beauty.

And then, as the skin prickled, and the tears rose to the eyes, and the heart swelled until it seemed it could bear no more, a new sound entered weaving in and out, through the others, with uncanny skill, blending with harp and flute and the other bagpipes—yet marked off from all by the clarity and sharpness of tone, the skill of fingers that had practiced for thousands upon thousands of years, the unmistakable piping of Ciall-glind, that caught up all other sound to weave into a net of music that wound caressing around the soul.

A Mortal Man, hearing that music, would have gone mad from its unbearable longing. Then, frozen, listening longer, he would have grown sane again, and his mind lifted to a wisdom far beyond his kind. And for the rest of his life he would bear in his eyes a touch of mystery and wonder, to say that he had heard the piping of Ciallglind.

But there were no Mortal Men in the City of the Sea-Elves. Swanwhite and Dorialith listened with all the city, unmoving, still as stone, save for those whose fingers were a part of Ciallglind's spell, moved to pluck the strings of harps, or dance over the holes of flute and chanter, while strange, liquid visions washed behind their eyes, and flooded their hearts with the glory of the world.

One by one, those fingers, too, stilled, and the throats that had thrilled with wordless song settled into the peaceful breathing of a calm unknown to mortals, content to sit and listen while the music of the Immortal Piper flooded their eyes and their hearts with tears of unbearable joy.

Vildern's men marched toward the mail-glinting mountain road, while Vildern wondered at the numbers waiting there. Had help come from the nearby forts? But that was impossible, for they would have had to march on the road. . . .

He recognized Grom Beardless, flanked by the chief officer left in charge at Klufbirk, and another man Vildern did not know. This was Grom's doing, then. But where had Grom found so many? The message last night had said that Grom had two hundred men (and a chain of a thousand slaves) but there was certainly more than three times that here. . . .

Grom came down the hill to meet him, the bright blue eyes, usually so cold, beaming like a boy's. He grinned.

"I hear you're in command now," Grom's soft voice murmured, "and I'm glad. It's time. And I'd much rather deal with you than with any of these rear-licking wellborns." Their slave-black hair had always been a bond between them, although Grom shaved his beard and kept his hair cut short enough to hide under helm and coif. "I'll not try to steal it from you."

Vildern would have looked sharply at any other man who had said that, suspecting a lie to put him off guard. Grom he trusted, alone among all the men he knew, except, perhaps, for Ulvard.

"Take the command," he said, quickly. "I've not done that well with it, and perhaps you can find a way to strip the bones that I've missed. So far, I've been stopped at every step."

Grom's eyes turned cold, watchful; the boyish grin died.

"What are you trying to do? Cover yourself by putting the blame on me?"

"No!" Vildern felt despair well up in his throat, choking him. Trust between men was so fragile! "No. . . ." He shook his head. "I only hoped . . . I don't know if even you can handle this, but—if you can't . . ." His voice dried up in his throat. He heard the wolves again, closer now. They had been calling for hours, and at first he had rejoiced to hear them. "If you can't, I certainly can't! No one can. And I would rather serve you than lead."

Grom's eyes softened, though they did not return to the happy candor which had first met Vildern. Instead, there was a sadness now.

"I think I understand. Though many a man would mock you—mock us both."

The wolves called again. Vildern chewed his lower lip. Though he was no Beast-Speaker, and had no Beast-Speaker with him, he could still feel the fear and urgency of those calls.

What could have gone wrong? It made no sense! He felt himself entangled in an invisible net of ill-luck whose webbing ran everywhere, though centered on the Islander. . . .

Looking up, he saw the Beast-Speaker Rothgalin, whom he left behind in Klufbirk, listening to the wolf-calls with an incredulous frown.

Indeed, all the officers and men of Klufbirk seemed to be here. . . .

"Who—who's left in Klufbirk to hold the pass? You *can't* have left it empty, but who—?"

"A handful of wounded men, too weak to march," Grom answered, "and a young Sorcerer, Sturgarl—and something that Sturgarl called up out of the forest. I don't know what the Sorcerers call it, and I hope I never see it or anything like it again; but while it hunkers in the pass before the gate, I do not fear that anything will come up from beyond the mountains. And, oh yes, there is a chain of nearly two thousand slaves under guard in the courtyard, and though there are only a few men to guard them, they have seen what is waiting outside the gate, and I do not think they will try to go anywhere." He laughed. "From what men have been telling me, the price of slaves will be going up, and a thousand of those slaves are mine! I will soon be too rich to sneer at!"

"But where did you get so many men?" Vildern asked, trying to count those above him on the slope.

"I had two hundred with me, and three other raiding parties were close by, and came in this morning. But here come your wolves. You'd best find out what happened to them, and then tell me what it is that has so—so well—what has allowed these slaves to defy you."

Vildern, turning, saw the wolves coming, the remnants of the combined packs he had sent after the escaping slaves—but so few? There seemed to be only—he tried to estimate the milling shapes and his mind reeled. Surely there must be more! It was not possible that less than fifty would return from such a fight. He must be miscounting somehow!

And the horses running in among the bounding bodies—the pitiful handful of horses, with naked men—and one woman— on their backs, all bleeding from wounds. . . .

They had been attacked on their way back, then, he thought with relief, just after dawn, before they had time to dress themselves. For with the fire-sword still in Kirgiff, there was no weapon that could wound them when they were in wolf-shape. . . .

Then the wolves were swarming into the space between the two bodies of men, and the horse-hooves pounding on rock. The wolf-smell rose around him, and the blond bitch-wolf was pulling up her horse beside him, and he could see blood caked on a long cut across her ribs, just below her round, red-nippled breasts. . . .

A long, firm-fleshed leg flashed in the air, as she slid from the horse's back and sprang at Vildern, and before he knew what was happening, her arms were locked around his neck.

"*It was a trap!*" she shrieked, almost in his ear. "The fire-sword was waiting, hidden, in the mountains!"

He got his hands up between them and pushed her away, and

felt his loins throb and tremble as his fingers sank into tender
flesh. He heard her gasp with pain and was glad.

"*Another* fire-sword?" he gasped, trying to fight off the
effects of her spell on him, to keep his mind on important
things.

"Yes," she answered, "Bright as the sun! He came out of the
hills, a bare-legged forest savage, but blond, like a Real
Man—" She hesitated suddenly, and flinched, as though
expecting him to strike her, then went on.

"We caught up with them a little before dark, and hung back
keeping them just in sight—playing with them, herding them.
They were making for—for the Haunted Pass. I remember
laughing, and wondering how they thought they would get out
there—"

"*Darmurung!*" Ramaukin exclaimed. "You see, Ondrute! I
tried to warn the Council, I told them—"

"*Hush!*" Kelldule's deadly voice hissed.

"I—I stripped to wait for the change, and—" She hesitated.
"Sunset came. I changed. We charged them, and they scattered, screaming, running for the mouth of the pass. I pulled
three of them down, and then—"

Vildern felt her shiver, and her hands clutched convulsively
at his mailed shoulders. He was suddenly aware of the
Sorcerers gathered around listening, and felt his ears
burning. . . .

"Sudden light flared in the rocks. It hurt my eyes, and lit the
mouth of the pass, as though it were dawn—turned grass and
leaves green—and then the savage came running down the
gorge, the fire-sword over his head . . . and"—she knotted
her brows—"and—several of the slaves, shouted something all
at once—some word I didn't understand. . . ."

"*Madok?*" Ramaukin asked. She turned startled eyes on
him.

"Why . . . almost. Something very much like that."

"I warned them," the gray-haired little man muttered,
shaking his head. "You heard me, Ondrute. I warned them that
the guardians were gone, and that Elves had been there. He *did*
come back!"

"Go on with your story, woman!" said Kelldule.

"The slaves—turned and fought, then. They killed many of the common wolves and—" she shuddered.

"One of them crushed my head with a hammer," she whispered. "It *hurt*! It would have killed me if—" She shivered in Vildern's arms, and suddenly pulled herself up against him. Vildern felt his ear hot. What was she trying to do to him?

"It took— a terrible time to heal." She pushed herself away. "But it *did* heal! And I saw—" She closed her eyes. "I ran at him, and he tried to stab me. I ducked, but it cut me—" She lifted her left arm, to show the long cut that crossed her ribs. Its crust had broken open when Vildern had pushed her away, and was slowly oozing blood.

But Vildern found his eyes drawn inevitably up from the cut, to stare at the round breast. Its nipple stared back.

Why is she doing this to me? Women were always using their power to torment men, the spell that He Who is Not Named taught the First Woman. . . .

"I ran away then," she said. Vildern forced himself to look away from her breasts, only to find himself staring at her long legs, and the tiny triangle of fine blond hair. "We all ran. Those of us who are still alive . . ."

He felt himself trembling. The throbbing in his loins was stealing his mind. Why was she doing this thing to him?

It must be true what men said, that women really wanted it. He remembered the man who had claimed he had had to kill two of his women because he had caught them trying to rape each other!

And men said that once a woman's spell was on you, only the greatest of Sorcerers could resist. And if men *could* resist, then the other spell Hastur had taught the First Woman, the spell of mortality that dragged all men down at last would prevail, and the Seed of tSarl perish, so tSarl could never be reborn. . . .

But women were alien: evil animals who could never be trusted. They turned on you without warning. . . .

Suddenly he realized that Ramaukin was speaking—and he'd not heard a word! This witch would kill him if he didn't control himself somehow!

He brought his hand around in a hard slap across the face that knocked her sprawling. Hurt eyes looked up into his, shocked tears gleaming.

She was trying to make him run to her, trying to steal his manhood and make him a weakling who could not hurt her. But he had never tried to hurt her! Why was she doing this?

Ramaukin laughed.

"That's right, Lad! Don't let her own you!"

It was Dorialith who first loosed himself from the spell of Ciallglind's piping, and turned his mind to the Stone of Sullathon, to look upon Ingulf.

It was longer before Swanwhite freed herself. The suns were falling toward the west: the enchantment of Ciallglind's piping still wrapped the city in a magic mist of music.

But she saw in the crystal globe a different scene; the spikes and wedges of a constantly shifting pattern of dots that she suddenly realized were tiny human figures, swarming like ants in their hundreds, all surging inward.

Wolves dashed from the plain to right and left, darting in to snap at children, and out again.

Beyond the wolves, ring-mail shimmered with sunset colors where blocks of men moved further out, like shepherds herding sheep into a tighter flock.

"There will be blood and terror come nightfall," Dorialith's deep thought spoke in the depths of her mind. *"Do you not see how so few werewolves can put fear in so numerous a crowd of people? Before long, since they all flee inwards, toward the center, they will crush the ranks of Torvar's host."*

The freed slaves fled toward the rainbow sunset's flames. The Sea-Elves watched them in Sullathon's Crystal. Outside their rose-bright tower they could hear the Immortal Piper, piping down the suns.

"I am troubled," said Swanwhite. *"Is there nothing we can do?"* They saw the land in the glass grow dark as night flooded over the world.

In the dusk the piping of Ciallglind mourned the fading of the light.

"There is nothing I can do," answered Dorialith. *"But*

perhaps you can. The Power of Tirorilorn is with you. If you loose the fire of Tirorilorn, then—"

"*No!*" Swanwhite cried, aloud, then again, "*No!*" still more shrilly, and the images flickered in Sullathon's Crystal. "*I dare not! Twice already now, my anger has nearly loosed the flame wrongly in these foolish quarrels among mortals!*

"*Do you not understand? I am no Hastur, nor am I Grandfather! Had the flame escaped me: had I allowed even a portion of its full power to fall upon Torvar's pick, nothing would remain of Ingulf or Torvar, or of any who stood near them—save burnt bones. And much of the city would have been destroyed. Had I not been able to use Ingulf's sword to direct the power, I would not have been able to drive the Dyole from the world and close the Gate to the Dark World without destroying the city.*

"*But that is the task for which the Stone of Tirorilorn was wrought—not for venting my anger, not for helping one mortal against other mortals, however evil. And not even for use against lesser night-things, such as these werewolves. Think! Even if I could control the flame, striking through Ingulf's sword, closely enough that I strike only the single werewolf, the beam will drive on into the ground where the wolf had stood. Can you not see what would happen then?*

"*I can do nothing—I would destroy more than I would save!*"

Dorialith was silent. As the last light of sunset faded from the sky, the piping of Ciallglind ceased. Yet the music of his spell lingered, for he had woven into it the wailing of gulls and the throbbing of the waves of the shore, and these still mourned the passing of the light.

In the Crystal of Sullathon the night had fallen, and the watching Elves saw the werewolves change.

Ingulf awoke in the darkness of Airellen's hair.

This cannot be happening, he thought. He could hear snarls, and frightened screams; he glimpsed dim shapes moving in the night, and occasional stars.

He was bouncing up and down; his hands were bound and he was bouncing on a bear's shoulder. His head was a bell, ringing with pain. His mind was mazed with memories and mysteries. . . .

This made no sense. He was tied up, and confused, borne on a bare shoulder through noisy night. Where was he bound?

The last thing he remembered was the dark hair of Airellen at his feet. . . .

The pain throbbed in his head as under him the shoulder rose and fell, like a drill in his skull's bone.

A snarl, a scream, a snap of breaking bone behind! Ingulf tried to look, but could not bear the pain, and slumped over the heaving shoulder, helpless. Even with his hands unbound, he could not fight. . . .

And through the haze of pain, he knew that death was near him in the dark.

"The end comes," Dorialith said, as dark werewolf shapes came rushing into view.

Bone-white Elf-towers thrummed with the high tide's paean as waves surged through streets.

The two watched bearlike werewolf jaws crush screaming slaves. The bound Islander hampered the man from whose shoulders he hung: They fell behind.

Steel-clad soldiers came charging, swords swinging, out of the dark.

Dorialith tensed, eyes fixed on the bound, helpless, living bundle, all skin and bone. But Swanwhite turned away.

"I cannot bear to see more," she said, her voice filled with pain.

A sad end it seemed to Ingulf's mad campaign. Rakmir's ranks broke as frightened slaves shouldered them aside, while the man appointed to bear Ingulf, now far behind, turned in the dark to fight, throwing Ingulf to the ground with bone-jarring force.

Steel-clad men ran with the bounding wolves: one slashed him down, and turned to the bound man, sword raised to stab—

But out of the pain-filled night another rushed. Above the bony ribs the stabbing wrist was caught: a shoulder pushed the killer back.

"Fool!" bellowed a dark-bearded man. "That's the Islander who bears the fire-sword!" Bound, Ingulf lay still, his shoulders painfully twisted, his robe, blood-stained and dark, half-torn from bony limbs and chest left bare.

"I want him alive." Dorialith heard the dark-bearded man's voice. *"He* knows who sent him, and the other fire-sword! We've got to make him talk!"

The crystal globe went dark as Dorialith bounded from his chair.

"I must go to him!" he exclaimed. "Swanwhite—"

But she was gone.

Stepping to the window, Dorialith saw her bare body flash into the sea, and then the head and shoulders of a white seal rose from the waves, swimming outward, away from shore, to the north.

The White Seal

VILDERN WAS GLAD he had chosen to take the lead, running close behind the wolf-pack: otherwise he would surely have missed the bundle in the torn tartan robe.

A moment later, and he would have been too late. Barely able to believe his eyes, he had been running toward the slave who had borne the bound Islander, when the man had thrown his burden down and turned to face Reikil.

But he had caught Reikil's arm in time, and now the Islander lay at his feet. He bent down to look at the face closely.

No, there was no mistake. This was the man he had seen waving the fire-sword.

But the sword was gone, the man unconscious, and his hands were fettered. What could have happened? If he had been betrayed by one of his lieutenants, why had he not been killed? If he had passed the sword on to some subordinate himself, because of injury or illness, why the fetters? It made no sense.

At least it explained the ease of this victory. Women and children were screaming all around as wolves and werewolves pulled them down. Had this Islander still commanded, Vildern was sure, there would be real fighting going on, instead. But as it was, the fighting-men were hemmed in by the fleeing crowd, and seemed utterly helpless.

He would be happy enough to leave this slaughter to Grom and the others, who enjoyed it. He knew it was a sign of weakness, but this might give him the excuse he needed . . .

"Pick him up!" he snapped, coming to a decision. This *was* important, after all. The two soldiers who had followed him most closely blinked and then stepped to the crumpled body and lifted it. Other soldiers stared. "Ulvard!" he barked. "Take command here! I'm taking this prisoner back to Kirgiff."

Turning, he found himself face to face with Ramaukin, with Kelldule standing at his shoulder.

"Leaving so soon, Captain?" The bent, gray-haired Sorcerer purred. "Hungry? There will be plenty of corpses—why that one?"

"He is still alive," said Kelldule, frowning.

"Alive?" Ramaukin was startled. He reached out and pinched the Islander. "Not much meat on him! Looks as though he has been starving for months!"

Vildern swallowed the urge to shout *fool* at the sorcerer—men had died for less . . .

"This is the man who carried the fire-sword," he said instead. "He knows who sent him, and may know what their plans are. He must be made to talk. We must find out what two—at least two—fire-swords are doing here." *You fool*, his mind shouted after his mouth closed.

"Ah, I understand," Ramaukin chuckled, nodding his gray-fringed bald head. "Well, I'm glad to see you combining business with pleasure, and pleased to see you have better things to do than fondling bitch-wolves. But you are a good officer." He bared white teeth in a smile. "You've shown yourself to be a good officer. You should be very glad of that—and glad that more of us on the Council cannot read minds."

The round face beamed with cruel laughter as Vildern's blood ran suddenly cold.

The bent gnomish figure turned away, still chuckling, and trotted off. The chuckling changed in pitch; the back stooped even more, until the hands dropped to the ground, and the Sorcerer darted off on all fours, a wolf among wolves, into the screaming madness of the hunt.

Kelldule laughed.

"Fortunately," the renegade said, "Ramaukin does not read minds very well, and even though he felt it best, both for his dignity and for your safety, to frighten you, he is too intelligent to kill good men for petty slights. As am I."

The two soldiers holding the limp form of the Islander had stood frozen, frightened out of their wits, while the Sorcerers had spoken with Vildern. Kelldule touched the Islander's tangled red hair lightly, then nodded his head.

"The spell I made to breed treachery among the men whose blood was on the chains I found is working, I perceive," the deep voice purred. "The sickness I sent should have struck by now, too, and that will be slowing them down." Vildern, not understanding, only stared at the renegade.

"So you plan to torture him, to find out what he knows," said Kelldule. "A good plan, but one that will take time. There may be an easier way."

Kelldule lifted his hand to the Islander's lolling head once more, and stretched it across his brow, thumb and fingers on temples. The renegade's eyes grew remote.

After a moment he shook his head with a sigh, and his hand dropped away . . .

"Well, see what you can find out under torture," said Kelldule. "Nothing I see is clear or makes sense. Does the name *A—erellen* mean anything to you?"

"No." Vildern shook his head: the renegade wizard frowned.

"It is the only name I can find in his mind—almost the only word—and is part of some strange confusion, with a woman's dark hair, towards which he falls and falls. I can see little past that, but what I do see makes me fear."

"What else do you—" Vildern stopped, breathlessly aware of Kelldule's rank. But the Sorcerer answered him.

"Nothing clear—but I thought I saw the faces of several Sea-Elves, including one I recognized. The face of Arnim Finn's granddaughter. And if the Elves of Tirorilorn are a part

of this, we may be in such danger as you cannot imagine. I fear
the Power of Tirorilorn, and most of all do I dread Arnim Finn.
I myself helped to trap and bind him in the Maze, and if he is
loose—I fear him far more than I fear the Hasturs—the
Blue-Robes, as you call them. And it was the Power of
Tirorilorn that drove the *Dyole* back out of the world—and as
far as I know, only Arnim Finn or his son could have loosed it.
So there is some great danger here."

Kelldule fell silent. All around them slaves wailed and
wolves howled . . .

"I think, indeed," said Kelldule, "that I shall come back to
Kirgiff with you. That we have been allowed to pursue as far
as we have is strange enough, and remembering what happened
to your werewolves makes me wonder. I have no wish to come
face to face with Arnim Finn this night!"

Away from the screaming of the slaves they all marched,
leaving behind death and terror and the wolf-pack's bloody
fangs. And that tall blond girl, Vildern realized, would be one
of those behind, a wolf-furred shadow running through the
fleeing, helpless slaves, tasting hot, red blood in an orgiastic
flood as she killed.

Kelldule, marching at his side, said no more. They stepped
over the corpses of the slain, wolf-torn slaves. Piled bloodied
bodies stiffened in the icy air of night, while behind them in the
distance others were screaming in their flight as they died.

Wide strides took them through piled dead, while behind the
ululation of the hunting-howl swelled, as the skilled wolves
killed and killed and killed.

Vildern and Kelldule trotted on. Moonlight silvered iron
rings on a corpse: Vildern saw a face he knew stare up above
a bloodied throat. He stopped to look as always—this was one
of his own men. It took him a moment to remember. Then he
recalled the face.

It was this man who had refused to give the wolf-girl her
clothes. And the throat was not cut, as he had thought at first.
It had been torn by fangs—wolf fangs.

They marched all night. It was a full day's march back to
Kirgiff: the slaves in their terror had run fast and far.

In the darkness before them Vildern saw flaring orange light that pulsed and throbbed, and in the dim dawn dusk turned to a great reek of smoke that reared above Kirgiff.

An army was encamped about the town, and dying slaves wailed from stakes and crosses that lined the road all the way to the city. Vildern stared.

"What—?"

"Sekthrig called for help," said Kelldule. "It has come."

Ingulf woke out of the dark of Airellen's hair into a nightmare confusion of frantic screaming. Acrid smoke burned his eyes.

He was still chained, still being carried. Stinging dark smoke swirled in the sunlight, and beyond was madness where naked figures screamed on stakes; old men and old women writhing in obscene agony while blood poured down wood between their legs . . .

Smoke swirled in a merciful veil to hide the figures, while Ingulf sank back into the comforting dark inside his throbbing head . . .

Svaran looked down from his horse as from a throne. He had removed the bald steel ball of his helm, and arrogant blue eyes bullied them from the clean-shaven aristocratic face, under the blond stubble of his close-cropped hair.

"Vildern," he said, through his teeth. "You were the officer in command, were you not? You have brought a prisoner, I see. Good! We have a stake for him. Right beside yours."

"*Fool!*" boomed Kelldule. The soldiers stepping toward them froze; Svaran stiffened on his horse. "This prisoner is the only man who can tell us the truth of dangers that can destroy us all!"

"Who are you, to dare use such a tone?" asked Svaran. Then, without waiting for an answer, he snapped, "*Seize him!*"

Over his shoulder, Vildern saw Kelldule's eyes change. Suddenly there was neither white nor pupil between the slitted eyelids, but only the deep, shining blue of a summer sky.

He threw his arms wide, and the soldiers that reached for him stopped, staring at their hands—

—at where their hands had been—

Where their hands had been, the heads of vipers hissed as they turned on wrists twisted back toward the guards' faces. Arms writhed boneless, looping, twisting—lunging as serpents strike. Long fangs sank into flesh below staring eyes.

Two voices screamed as one; two dead soldiers swayed and fell, their fingers clawing in the scratched skin of their cheeks.

The blue plates of Kelldule's eyes rose to Svaran.

"I am Kelldule." The deep voice softened, dangerous as a silken noose. "The Council has accepted me as a member. Vildern and his prisoner are under my protection. Defy me at your peril!"

Svaran's face was very white. But now from the ranks of the soldiers behind him there came a low laugh, and soldiers scrambled to make way for one in the dull-black robes that so many of the Council of Sorcerers affected.

"Very good, Kelldule, but Svaran and this army are under *my* protection! Do you think to try your silly outer-world mind-tricks on *me*? If I—"

The ends of the long, hanging sleeves of his black robe burst into sudden flame as he spoke. He broke off with a short, sharp word, and, ripping the burning cloth from his robe, threw it on the cobbles at his feet, where it blazed up under a cloud of smoke. He snatched a glass globe from his breast and raised it high, as if to throw it: a twisting shadow showed dimly through the glass. But Kelldule laughed.

"Come, Raekind!" he mocked. "The fire at your feet will burn your *Nisugon* if you try to loose it against me now, and even were that not so, you saw my testing by the Council! You know I can banish it easily—or anything else you can summon without the blood of many men! Will you squander your power so foolishly?" Raekind did not answer but stood weighing the glass in his hand, measuring with his eyes the distance between himself and Kelldule.

"While you waste my time in this foolish test of power," said Kelldule, "an enemy draws near with power enough to destroy us all. Ramaukin, Ondrute and I raised a *Grusthul* against these slaves, Raekind—and upon the very threshold of this world it was hurled back, and the Gate closed, by a power of which you have probably never heard, and which I never expected to see loosed upon this continent! This prisoner may be our only hope of understanding the danger before it is too late—and *you* would put him on a stake, without questioning him?

As for Vildern, he bears no blame for the disaster here. Svaran himself would have fared no better." Vildern drew a shaky breath, feeling his heart pounding furiously. "And we shall soon see," added Kelldule, "how Grom Beardless has fared."

Vildern saw Svaran stiffen in the saddle at the sound of his rival's hated name.

Then the black steel armor clambered awkwardly down from the horse, and knelt before Kelldule.

"Master, forgive me," Svaran began, "for I—"

"You are forgiven," snapped Kelldule, cutting short the ritual of abasement the other had begun. "This is no time for ceremony! If this is the danger I fear it to be—I tricked and trapped Arnim Finn once before, but that was in the Maze, and unaware. If he is loose—!"

"Give Vildern whatever he needs." The renegade whirled, and walked away. "My own equipment is in Klufbirk. There is no more time to waste!"

Cold water shocked across Ingulf's face.

The dim, numbed brain in the throbbing skull stirred. Eyelids twitched.

Another cold slap splashed. Some trickled into his mouth, some soaked his eyelashes, some flooded his nostrils. He sneezed. His sticky eyelids began to pry apart. Smoke stung his eyes.

"*He's waking!*" A loud voice in his aching ears made the bone in his skull ring like a struck bell with pain. He winced, clenching his eyes shut again.

They opened just as another cold wave broke across his face.

His body hung between tearing, stretching shoulder joints: metal bit into his wrists. The tip of one toe grazed the floor.

The light only dazzled his eyes: he could not see clearly. But fingers gripped his chin, and pushed up his head. He found himself staring into blue eyes in a black-bearded face. The whiskered mouth moved.

"Who sent you?" a gruff voice growled, an earthquake in his skull that made him shut his eyes with pain. *"How many of you are there? How many fire-swords?"*

The voice crashed through his skull: pain pressed his eyes shut and gritted his teeth.

Fingers let go his chin and let his head fall. His weight dragged against aching shoulders and wrists.

Something came whistling out of the light, wrapped around his naked hips like a belt, stinging like a tree branch, and something slashed his thigh like a knife. His whole body was rocked by the impact: the air was hurled from his lungs in a sound that was half a scream and half a grunt . . .

The coiled leather slithered off his skin, and only then did the spiraling line of pain between his waist and knees really begin to hurt.

He tried to breathe, but his belly was stuck to his backbone and the air would not come. Then, just as a cool trickle of air began to steal down his throat, the whip hissed back and drove it out of him.

Darkness closed around him: dimly he felt his body jerk and sway while the whip bit again and again.

Then it stopped, and he hung in blood-streaked darkness, his skin laced with stinging spirals of pain.

He hung there forever, and then cold water splashed across his face.

Fingers locked in his hair and pulled. His eyes came open, and he was looking again into that black-bearded face that he remembered.

Through the stinging on his skin he felt heat. There was a familiar smell in the air. His mind puzzled at it for a moment, and then flew back to happy childhood memories, of days when he and the other children of the village would run down to the blacksmith's forge, to watch the massive figure as he pulled bright flowing iron from the deep bed of coals . . .

"See this?" the gruff voice snarled. *"Talk! How did you sneak in? How many of you are there? What are your plans?"*

Just below the face something glowed dull red, and his lash-laced skin cringed from its heat.

"Why did you come here?" The black-bearded man shouted. Hair shriveled on Ingulf's chest as the red glow came closer. *"Who sent you?"* Ingulf's confused mind struggled to remember, to understand. Why *was* he here? Who *had* sent him?

"Airellen!" he muttered, to himself, not aware he was speaking aloud.

"Who is Airellen?" The rough voice roared, and the fingers in his hair tightened, jerking his head up. *"Why did she send you here? Where is this Airellen now? Talk, or it will be worse for you!"*

The voice throbbed in his aching skull. What was happening? Who was this, and what did he want? What was he talking about?

"What are you talking about?" He struggled to gather his wits. "Why are you doing this?"

"Where is Airellen?"

"I—do not know?" The tragedy of his life hurt worse than the pain of the whip. *"She is a seal on the ocean! She is gone from me, gone!"*

"What—?" The black-bearded man hesitated, plainly puzzled by the answer, then snarled. "How many others did—she?—send with you? Where are they hiding?"

"I am alone!" he cried. *"No others came with me! I am as alone and as—"*

He screamed as the hot iron seared his chest. The pain was too great: he fell from it into nothingness.

When he came to himself again he was hanging from aching shoulders in the dark behind his eyelids, and no one was touching him. The skin of his chest was a constant, unbearable stinging.

Voices were murmuring somewhere, too low for him to hear words even if he had been listening. Every so often they were drowned by a loud whimper whose source he could not guess.

He hung there a long, long time. The voices grew louder, but the pain in his chest was much more real than the voices.

". . . just die on you! Look at his ribs!" It was an old man's shrill voice, hoarse and wheezing. *"Once they get that*

thin, they don't last long! If y' don't feed him, ye'll get no answers, nor even any sport!" Another voice, deeper, murmured in answer, but it was only a low, wordless rumble.

Ingulf hung in darkness, while deep voices murmured, and his burnt skin blared in his nerves.

Sudden shouting and a babble of voices roused Ingulf from stupor, although after a brief jerk of his head, he lay still. His wits had returned enough to realize that they would begin again if they knew he was awake.

At first there was only great confusion of voices, and then one rose clear above the others—

"*. . . was right! Two fire-swords at least!"*

"Two that I saw," said another voice. *"But that was enough. All the werewolves broke and ran. I think we should skin the lot of them! If we weren't so short-handed . . ."*

"You can skin a werewolf more than once, remember," said a third voice, amused. *"Very good discipline! They do tend to become arrogant, because of their invulnerability, and it is good to remind them of its limits, every so often. . . ."*

"And where were you?" asked the second voice, hotly.

"Would you like to be reminded of your limits, Grom Beardless?" said the third voice, no longer amused. *"You can only be skinned once—unless we have one of the werewolves bite you first, perhaps—"*

"Kill him and be done with it," said the first voice. *"He'd be too dangerous a werewolf. . . ."*

"Too powerful for your liking, no doubt!" the third voice sneered.

"Master, forgive me, for my life lies in your hands," the second voice said. *"I know that I am but dirt beneath your feet, meat for your table, blood for your . . ."* The voice sank, and above it now, the third voice was laughing.

"Take off his mail and flog him!" said the third voice, after a moment. *"But, now, Vildern, tell us what you have learned from this precious prisoner of yours!"*

"Not much yet," said the rough voice Ingulf remembered. *"He passed out too quickly. Old Raverlok says he'll die if we aren't careful. But so far, just a name—Eorling, or Iarolim,*

something like that—and—he said it was a seal, and they come from the sea."

"The Sea-Elves," said the third voice. *"That is very bad. If the Were-Seals are in it, then we are facing power indeed! But why should they strike so far inland? That makes no sense!"*

"Is this not a matter for the Council?" a new voice asked. *"We should take him to Bluzig!"*

"You may be right," said the third voice. Beneath it, Ingulf heard a frightening, familiar sound, a hiss followed by a crack, but his brain was too dull to try to make sense of it. It was not until a man's voice cried out in hoarse pain that he realized that someone was being whipped, just as he had been. . . .

The voices were drawing away now, and the groans of the man being whipped were too loud for Ingulf to understand what was said, until a voice—a third voice—shouted.

"That's enough!" The sound of the whip stopped, and the voice went on more quietly. *"Not only is this a bad time to cripple the best swordsman in Sarlow, but you are enjoying it far too much, Svaran! You should remember that once your armor is off, the lash will bite you just as deeply!"* The voice chuckled cruelly.

The pain of the burn forced a low whimper from Ingulf's throat.

"Awake, are you?" said the old man's voice, close to his ear. A hand in his hair jerked his head up; water poured into his mouth. He gulped thirstily while some trickled down his chest, onto the burnt skin. All too soon the water was taken away, and something else was shoved roughly into his mouth. *"Chew that and swallow it,"* the shrill voice said, *"or I'll shove it down your throat!"*

But Ingulf needed no urging.

The sound of hinges woke Vildern in the darkness before dawn, and his hand found his sword-hilt even as his eyes opened, and he slashed out blindly in the dark. . . .

He felt his edge catch and rip in flesh even as he was hurled back onto the wildly swaying bed. The air was driven out of his lungs before he could shout, and his sword flew from his hand.

A heavy, hairy body pinned him down, even as hot wet blood gushed over his hand. . . .

Two red eyes like glowing coals glared down into his own. He tried to scream, but there was hardly any breath in his lungs, and only a choked gasp came from his suddenly dry throat.

The dull claws he had heard clicking in that sudden rush of feet that had guided his cut, ripped the cloth of his tunic from his shoulder. His eyes closed. In a moment those massive jaws would close. . . .

Something rough and wet slimed across his face.

It was a long moment before he realized that he was still alive, and even longer before he tried to understand why. Then reaction set in, and he laughed hysterically while the were-wolf's rough tongue licked his face and beard.

He felt the cold beast nose touch his neck, and suddenly cloth shredded as the great fangs ripped his tunic down the front.

The faintest light of dawn filtered through the barred window, and he saw then the beast's back, shaggy shoulders, the upthrust, hairy ears. The rough tongue caressed his chest.

Slowly, the dusk lightened, and she began to change. A bird chirped somewhere outside. He watched the black fur on top of the head as it began to crawl, to pale, to lengthen. Another bird called, and then another. Her ears began to shrink and crawl apart as the skull between them swelled.

As the shoulders and forelegs changed shape, the dark fur shortened, and pink skin showed through the stubble. He felt the tongue changing as it licked lower and lower on his belly, where his pulse was gathering as his flesh stirred.

Dawn brightened. He felt her breasts swell against his thighs. Her tongue tickled: he laughed. Lengthening blond hair flowed down her back.

But not until it was full sunlight, and the change was complete, did she lift her own face to him, bright blue eyes crinkling in a mocking laugh.

"You tried to stick me with a *sword*!" she said. "You *do* have something better, after all." He stared at her in consternation, and she suddenly launched herself up his body, her breasts sliding from his thighs all the way to his chest.

"Rape me, you fool!"

It was very different from his usual experience of women grabbed and thrown down in a raid, terrified and fighting for all they were worth. It was not even like the passive slaves you could rent from their owners for a low fee in some of the larger cities, like Kithmar, where the Sorcerer-priests were lax, and the laws enforced badly. He was not sure who was raping whom, and it confused him badly, and frightened him more than a little.

Even though at the end she did scream and thrash, she did not seem convincingly afraid, and afterward she smiled and snuggled up against him like a child.

"My name is Eluvorg," she said.

"You're of—good blood, then," he said, astonished. "Why are you in the army?" She laughed.

"I was born to hunt and kill—and the army seemed better than a dull life with nothing to look forward to except being raped by Father—or whoever he sold me to. So I tricked my brother into biting me, when we were still very young. My father was furious. He would have killed me, I think, if he had not been afraid of my brother. As it was"—her voice had become cold and deadly—"he had me whipped, and then to punish me further, he burned my old nurse alive, and made me watch.

"But I never regretted it. I can hunt, I can kill, I can be raped when I want to be—and I can punish anyone who rapes me when I don't want them to—don't be afraid," she said, seeing him shrink away from her. "I *chose* you, because you are kind, and strong, and always think about all of your men. I know men say these are signs of weakness, but they are fools! And you came to defend me, when no one else would have. And besides"—she smiled at him wickedly— "I wanted you."

"So, it's true, then," he asked, "what they say, that women really do want it?" Her brow furrowed.

"Once, I think, there was another word besides rape. I think the slaves know what it is. But—sometimes I want it and sometimes I don't, but even when I *do* want it, I want it from some man I want, and not just any man who has the strength to throw me down, or the rank to have me butchered if I refuse!"

"But," he asked, honestly puzzled, "if it isn't strength or rank you want in a man, what worth *can* a man have?" She stared at him, then laughed.

"You don't listen very well, do you?" she teased, but he only stared at her. Fear was beginning to build up in him again.

It was true what men said: women were alien, unpredictable beings whose motives could not be understood. What did she really want of him? Why had she turned the power of her body at him, and then, when that had not worked, come in and raped him like this?

That she was a werewolf made it worse. He had lived and fought beside werewolves for years, and had lost much of his fear of them, but the other werewolves he had known had all been men, whose motives, if a little crueler and bloodier than other men's, were still understandable. But how could he tell what a female werewolf might want or do?

And yet there was no denying that her body was very sweet, and the effects of her power on him far more pleasant than any of the things men were *supposed* to enjoy. . . .

Before he realized what he was doing, his hand had moved, caressing her soft body, and he felt the trembling of desire again. She was controlling him with her power! Why was she doing this?

This could ruin his career in the army if it got out; if the Sorcerers, or even the men, guessed that he had fallen under the spell of a bitch-wolf witch. . . .

And he did not care! She had even conquered his fear, even though he was in bed with a creature that combined the powers of a werewolf with those of a woman. . . .

She sighed and stretched and pushed against him, and he rolled over on top of her. This was a little more familiar, at least, even if she was not afraid of him or fighting. . . .

Afterward she held him tightly, and her power over him was such that he enjoyed it, even aware that she could have reached his throat with her teeth, or held him while an enemy came in to murder him.

"I feel so much safer with you," she said. He turned his head, to stare into her eyes.

"What do you mean?" he asked, tensing slightly.

"After my brother was killed . . ." Her eyes suddenly filled with tears, and her voice caught. After a moment, she went on. "He always protected me. The other men knew, and knew that between the two of us . . . but after the Islander killed him—well, you saw! You stopped it." Suddenly she was holding him even more tightly, while she sobbed and her tears were spilling onto his shoulder.

But suddenly Vildern understood. So *that* was what she wanted of him! There was an understandable reason for her behavior after all: she wanted him to protect her against other men!

Curiously, under his relief, he found himself oddly disappointed, as though he had wanted there to be some other reason—but he could not imagine what it could be.

"Who was your brother?" he asked. "Did I know him?"

"My brother was Vludric Vladricsin," she answered. "He always spoke well of you. Said you were the best officer . . ." Her voice caught again. "But then that—outsider came, with his fire-sword and—how I *hate* him!"

Suddenly, he straightened.

"I—should be down in the dungeons torturing him, now!" he said. "Svaran would love to have an excuse to—" He did not finish, but started to scramble for his clothes. His tunic was ruined, of course. He'd have to get a new one out of the stores. And her clothes weren't here. She would almost certainly be seen leaving his quarters, and word would be all over before noon. . . .

"Let me come with you," she said. "Let me help!"

That would make it even worse, he thought. Enemies would carry the tale to the Sorcerers, and they would reprimand him, or worse, for his weakness. . . .

Yet she was pure-blood after all, he thought. Or nearly so. He could never afford such for a wife. . . .

That thought rocked him: he stopped, one leg in his breeches, and stared at her. Could her family stop him, if he decided to marry her? Then his sons would be higher rank, and his daughters worth money. . . .

When he rose to go down to the dungeon, she followed.

Light burned through Ingulf's eyelids. Voices rang in his aching head. He gasped in a deep lungful of foul-smelling air, and blinked at the glaring torchlight. He slitted his eyes, and his wrists tugged at rough, rusty iron that chafed his skin.

This was not the darkness of night, but some foul, enclosed space with stone walls. Echoes made his ears throb.

"He is awake," one of the painful voices shouted.

"Feed him!" boomed another.

A shadow moved against the torches: a hand grabbed his hair and pulled. Water was poured into his open mouth, over his chin and beard. He swallowed, but the water had stopped. He was still thirsty. He opened his mouth to call for water, and something was thrust into it. It tasted like mold. He started to spit it out, but a hand caught it, pushed it back, and jerked his chin up violently, cracking the back of his aching head into the stone of the wall to which he was chained.

Darkness in his brain. Rust-pitted steel cut into his wrists as he sagged there. He woke to a voice shouting at him, its echoes surrounding him, a shrill pain in his ears.

". . . stupid goblin-raper, swallow it!! Come on, chew!" His mouth was full of the taste of mold; but the stuff was hard and cut his tongue and gums. He blinked into the torchlight and smoky shadows, his eyes stinging.

After a while the stuff in his mouth seemed to be softening into a kind of paste, and obediently he began to chew, and got most of it down. Then a little more water—not enough—was poured into his mouth, but it could not wash the taste away. The smoke stung his eyes, but he could see a little. A black-bearded face swam into his sight: the face he had seen with the red-hot iron . . .

"Where were you going to go to meet the others?" the rough voice rasped. The question made no sense. What others?

"Where is your meeting place? How does Aralim give orders to you? Talk! How do you keep in touch with each other?" He shut his eyes, and shook his head, confused.

"I don't—know!" he gasped, voice a dry croak. "I don't understand—"

A whip whistled out of the darkness, across the torchlight, and sliced across his chest, setting new fire to the unhealed burn, and slamming his shoulders up against the wall, driving the air from his lungs. His body arched and small popping sounds came from his back.

The lash came in again across his belly. He jerked and sobbed, without air to scream. The weight of the strokes battered his back against the wall as the supple leather cut again and again across thighs, groin, belly. . . .

After a while the pain-wracked body began to seem unimportant, as though it belonged to someone else, and he floated above, watching it sag down limply into its chains. . . .

Then everything vanished—voices, whip and body—and he hung in aching blankness. . . .

Out of the dark that covered him, lost in a pit of pealing pain, he heard a woman's silvery laugh.

It singed his uncomprehending brain: it battered at his heart. The dark was charged with elemental hate; the laughing mystery a spark of joy the captive thought was fate. . . .

"Airellen!" he sobbed.

Silence, and then faint whispers. The silvery laugh again, but softer, and then gentle fingers stroked his face.

"Airellen?" he croaked.

"What is it?" a woman's voice crooned. "Why are you here?" Smoke and darkness shrouded his eyes, but he thought he saw the face he longed for, the face that had stared at him from so many trees and shadows, the eyes that haunted him whenever he closed his own. . . .

"I do not know where I am!" he cried. "I came to do great deeds, as Dorialith bade, and they hailed me as Hastur."

The hand dropped from his face a moment: faint whispers echoed. His dazzled eyes and dazed brain sought her in the shadow and the smoky torchlight glare, trying to make her face out of the darkness, hungry for the sight of her. Then her soft hand stroked his slashed flesh. He felt her tongue and lips trace his bleeding welts.

" Dor-eii-ol-lesh sent you? But why? What deeds?" Her

voice strained at the name, strange and hesitant. It seemed deeper, too, more like the voice of a Mortal Woman. *"Who hailed you by—that name? And why?"*

"To prove my love for you," Ingulf sobbed. "It was all for you! I came to free the slaves, and drive the evil animals away!" Again her hands left him, and he hung in whirling darkness while whispers echoed from the stone.

"But—why did they call you by—that name?" she persisted. Soft breasts and warm lips touched his naked flesh; his body stirred, throbbing.

"It—it was the Silver Witch," he murmured. *"Frostfire—* the White Witch sprang from her flame. The Ghost Witch. She burned the—that thing—" His voice stammered into silence. Looking he could see the top of her dear head as she caressed him with her lips, and her dear dark hair all around—but it was not dark in the torchlight, but threw back flame with a golden shimmer. . . .

"No!" he shrieked. "You are not she! Who are you?"

"Am I not?" She laughed. She raised a human face to him, licking his blood off her mocking lips. "How do you know? Have I always the same shape?"

"N—no," he stammered, "but—but—" Her lazy, mocking smile was replaced by a puzzled frown. "It was all for love of you!" he cried. "I have longed for your touch, longed for you to speak to me—and it is not you, Airellen! How can you be so cruel?"

Her hands found tender flesh, and gripped painfully tight.

"Cruel or no," she crooned, "you must tell me who else Dori-lees sent on this quest. And where do you expect to meet them, to—plan your next move?"

"I do not understand!" he whimpered. "Why are you doing this? What other do you mean?"

"The other that Dor-io-leeth sent—the other fire-sword! Answer me!"

"There are no others! It was myself alone that—"

He screamed as her hand squeezed, and the pain from his groin shot up through his body, so excruciating that he fell again into black darkness.

* * *

And far away in the northern seas, a white seal darted through white surf around a dark rock, tasting the waves, seeking the faint, elusive taint of a scent in the water. . . .

"I think that was—that that may have been the word. . . ." Eluvorg mused.

"What word?" asked Vildern. "What are you babbling about now?"

"The word we've forgotten," she said. "The other word, besides rape. Remember?"

"I don't know what you're talking about." He shook his head, frowning. "*Dorialith!* It sounds like Kelldule's worst fears are true!"

"You—know that name, then?"

"It is a name out of old legends," he growled. "A ruler or king of the Sea-Elves. They say that there is a city, west along the coast, all white towers, not really very far from here at all.

"They say that ships have gone—whole fleets have gone, over the centuries, to attack that city. Sometimes they just get lost in the fog. Sometimes ships that try to land find themselves—suddenly—somewhere else. Usually on a reef, or being driven up against a cliff. But there are some very old—and very frightening—stories about ships that actually came to shore. . . ." His voice died away, and for a moment he strode along in thoughtful silence.

"I told you I'd get information out of him," she trilled proudly after a moment. He smiled at her, indulgently.

"You did," he said with a nod, "but can we make any sense out of it? Dorialith, and this Silver Witch, Frostfire, that came out of a flame—and what did he mean when he said they hailed him as . . . the Nameless One?"

"He—he does have flame-colored hair. . . ." she murmured, sudden fright muting her voice.

"We could not hold one of the Children of the Nameless with mere steel chains!" He made his voice contemptuous, as he tried to fight the prickle of fear. They said that the Nameless One had made the first fire by wrapping one of his own red hairs around one of the brighter golden hairs of tSarl. . . .

The Nameless One had been the first Animal that the Dark

Gods had made to be food for tSarl, and tSarl had indeed eaten
him, but he had re-formed himself out of the dung of tSarl,
because the Dark Lords had not yet invented death. . . .

The hammering of running feet brought his head up. A
soldier came running down the long corridor, and skidded to a
halt in front of them, sketching a jerky salute.

"Commander Vildern? Come quickly! Prince Svaran sum-
mons you! There is trouble—disaster! Follow me." He turned
and dashed away.

"What is it?" asked Vildern, as he lengthened his stride to
follow.

"The fire-sword has struck again!"

They ran. Then, hearing soft feet behind him, Vildern
stopped and whirled, catching Eluvorg by the shoulders. He
shook her.

"Are you mad?" he hissed. "Remember your place! Don't
follow me like that! There'll be enough gossip to ruin me as it
is!"

He ran after the guard, leaving her standing flame-faced in
the corridor behind. The guard had looked back and seen, but
he had said nothing. He would have enough to say later,
though. *Captain Vildern is weak. He's under that bitch-wolf's
spell!* Perhaps he should have the man murdered. Ulvard
would do it. . . .

Svaran had found himself a throne—the dead lord's, Vildern
supposed—and before the dais Grom Beardless stood, his face
a mask of grief, staring down at the handful of wounded men
who knelt in the clear space before the throne. The room was
crowded with soldiers, staring and milling.

". . . through the chain, as if it were made—of— *wool!*—
instead of iron!" a hysterical voice was saying. "The slaves
were just as stunned as I was. They nearly fell over—"

"Not the one I was next to!" a voice interrupted, from one
of the kneeling figures. "And the chain that took me down
didn't feel like wool to me!" A wordless grunting of agreement
came from a muffled figure beside him, a man with a broken
jaw.

"Two werewolves died on that blade," the first speaker went
on. "Then the rest panicked, and—"

"It was almost dawn!" another kneeling man protested. "The sunlight was about to change us! We always run away at sunrise. We have to!"

"We're helpless in the dawn!" another man shouted. "You know that well! You're only trying to shift blame off your own shoulders!"

"When the werewolves ran away," the first man went on, implacably, "their panic spread to the other wolves. And then there were a handful of us, against a dozen or more in the attacking party, and a thousand freed slaves. All of us are wounded."

"We have not yet heard what Sturgarl has to say." That was Ondrute's voice. Vildern's eyes found the skull-faced Sorcerer in the crowd that stood to the left of the dais, along with Raekind and Ramaukin. Kelldule he did not see.

A young man in Sorcerer's robes stepped out of the crowd behind the kneeling men.

"You told me yourself, Uncle, that I had no power to match a fire-sword! But surely you cannot mean to have me judged with these others! I claim privilege!"

"Yes, of course," said Ondrute, and hissed something under his breath, then added, "Svaran, Sturgarl is above your authority, and can be judged only by the Council."

"Of course," said Svaran, with an ill grace. "May I humbly beg that my masters will take the matter before the Council?"

Grom Beardless stirred, and turned toward the Sorcerers.

"Masters." His voice was sharp with desperation. "Would it be possible to raise a Demon to pursue the slaves, and bring them—"

His voice was cut short by a scream from the far side of the chamber.

Vildern, turning, saw a knot of milling men where soldiers scrambled away from the wall, where in the air a ghost-white figure hovered.

And then, not in his ears, but his mind, he heard laughter that rang like trumpets, and then a voice:

"Aye, ye fools, fly from doom! Flee, for the doom of Sarlow is upon you!"

A soldier sprang, slashing with his sword, and sprawled as

the blade passed through the white shape harmlessly, as though through empty air. Again soundless laughter rang loud in all their minds.

The white shape moved out from the wall. Men scrambled aside from its path. To Vildern it looked like an old man with a long white beard—but the cheeks above the beard were smooth and unwrinkled as a baby's face, and the eyes were bright and wise.

"So it is a Demon you would conjure up!! Do you forget so soon? Or perhaps you believe that that power which banished the Great Dyole from Kirgiff is now swimming away through the Great North Sea? That could well be true, but will you dare believe it? What do you know of the powers that move now against your land? Will you believe that your prisoner is no more than an unfortunate madman? Dare you believe that he acted alone?

"Fools! I am coming now! I know how many men wander your land with swords of flame, and you do not! I know why your city was not destroyed, and what power could have destroyed it. I know why the Sons of Awan journeyed to the City of the Sea-Elves, and who the Hastur-Lord met with there!"

"Who are you?" shouted Raekind.

"Ask of your prisoner." The silent voice throbbed. *"He knows me! Or will he not speak to such as you?"*

And the apparition was gone, as though it had never been.

Soldiers shouted in alarm. But the Sorcerers, gathered in their black robes, stood frowning, unmoved. Grom's teeth were bared in a snarl, but he stood firm. Svaran had donned his black helmet: his face could not be seen.

"Be still, you fools!" Ramaukin shouted. "That was only an illusion, a picture drawn in your minds for you to see! There was no one here, and there is no danger!"

"Vildern!" Svaran's voice boomed eerily from the closed helm. "Come forward! Have you learned enough from your prisoner to tell us who that was?"

Vildern walked down the center of the room, aware of the eyes upon him. He drew a deep breath before he spoke.

"Dorialith would be my guess." He saw Ramaukin start, and the other Sorcerers stared. "One of the Sea-Elves, certainly."

"If not Dorialith," said Ramaukin, "it was most likely Ethellin the Wise. So you have made him talk, then?"

"A little," said Vildern, "and much that he says does not make sense. Dorialith sent him here. There is also someone named Fire-frost, whom he called a silver witch, who sprang from the fire, and—another—woman, named—Iarellen, I think—"

"A *woman*?" Svaran asked. He took off his helm.

"The Elves and the savages are all ruled by their women," said Ondrute. "They have no manhood, and cannot resist women's magic, for they do not rescue man-children from their mothers as soon as they can bite, as we do, but leave them to have their manhood rotted away. That is why they are all such womanish weaklings. . . ."

"Was there more to what Commander Vildern was telling us?" asked Ramaukin, "or are we going to spend our time telling ourselves what we already know? Did the prisoner tell you where this army of fire-swords hides between attacks, or how large it is? Did he tell you his own name?"

"He *said*—" Frowning, Vildern stared them all down. "He *said* that—someone—had named him with the—the name—of the Nameless One." He watched as fear rose in every face. "I do not understand what he meant by that. He does have red hair, indeed, but many Islanders do. I do not see that can mean anything. Fire burns him. Whips cut him. Iron holds him. He cannot be one of the Blue-Robes, unless he has lost all power. . . ."

"He had power enough to drive out the Great One!" Ondrute exclaimed.

"He said that it was the witch—Frost-fire—that drove out the Great One. He says that she appeared out of flame."

"What are they trying to do to us?" cried young Sturgarl, terror in his voice.

"He says that he came here to drive us from the land," said Vildern, "by rousing our slaves against us."

"That is a matter for the Council!" growled Ondrute.

"In any case, we are in great danger here," Raekind exclaimed. "If fire-swords can strike at our very gates, and then vanish again with more than a thousand slaves, and—if

the Sea-Elves' power reaches into this very chamber, then—
perhaps it were best to question the slave behind the barrier
circles of Bluzig."

"There is a legend," said Ramaukin, slowly and thoughtfully, "that comes down from very old times, when our
ancestors still lived on Noria's icy plains. Then the Losvik
were the greatest of the allied tribes, and their Sorcerers built,
with aid of the Lords from Outside, a mighty citadel, whose
shell the Blue-Robes could not pierce.

"Then the Losvik and their allies prospered, raiding widely,
and building a rich trade in slaves and meat. Yet the Blue-
Robes overcame them at last, by a simple stratagem." Ramaukin paused, and looked dramatically around. "One of the
Blue-Robes so bespelled himself that he forgot his powers, and
who he was, so that any looking into his mind saw that he
believed himself only an ordinary man. Then he was taken
prisoner by raiders, and brought as a slave to the Citadel of the
Losvik. But the spell was so made that once he saw the inside
of the citadel his hidden memory returned, and striking from
inside the barriers, opened a way for his kin to enter.

"And that is how the mighty Losvik were broken, so that
only scattered remnants remained, to take refuge among the
Eythrol and the Sarló."

"You think, then, that this is—one of the Blue-Robes?"
asked Raekind. Ramaukin shook his head.

"I do not know that it is *not* one of the Blue-Robes. I do not
say that it is. But if it is, the Barriers of Bluzig would be its
goal. Wherever we take it, and whatever we do, we must *not*
take the prisoner there."

"Should we not just kill him, then?"

Not until we have answers to more questions," said Ramaukin, "or another prisoner that could answer them."

"Then"—Raekind looked nervously around— "what can we
do? Where *can* we take him? We can't stay here—"

A low cough from the dais cut him off.

"I own a castle in Kunzig." Svaran's voice was quiet.
"That's downriver, about half-way to Kithmar. The dungeons
under it are sunk very deep in the rock. If any of the members
of the Council wish to question the Islander themselves, Bluzig

is close, and there is a good straight road. I also keep some of the most skilled professional torturers in the country in my own personal employ, and they are of course at your service. They will be able to learn things no amateur"—he shot a quick, contemptuous glance at Vildern—"would *ever* be able to learn. The docks are still crowded with the barges we were going to use to transport the slaves, and I can carry almost the entire army if you will."

"The most skilled in the country, you say?" Ondrute smiled. "Interesting. But you have not yet judged these failures brought before you."

The group of wounded men before the dais, forgotten in the confusion, had risen, and some had begun to edge their way toward the crowd around them; suddenly all of them fell groveling on their knees again, mumbling incoherent pleas, while Svaran sneered down at them, enjoving his power.

"*Silence!*" he shouted suddenly, and grinned as they all looked up in terror.

"For myself," he said, very softly, "I am inclined to be merciful, seeing by your wounds that you did indeed, fight before you fled. But I am not the man who lost a thousand slaves because you dared not remain to fight. Your fate, therefore, I shall give into the keeping of Grom Beardless." He smiled, and his eyes twinkled with a boyish, happy look that made those who knew him tremble. Grom blinked up at him in startled surprise. Vildern felt a sinking in his chest. These were not his own men, but they could just as well have been. . . .

Grom turned, and his cold eyes looked down at the wounded men who whimpered and groveled at his feet.

"Do not whine like slaves!" he snapped. "You are men!" He looked at them, then said at last, "I am a ruined man, but you are not to blame for that. No man could have predicted that the fire-swords would strike again so quickly. Go back to your quarters. Your wounds are punishment enough."

Vildern nodded approval, but he heard faint whispers of "*weakling*" and "*womanish slave-get!*" from the crowd; some here had hoped for a show—Svaran among them: his disappointment was plain.

"Captain Vildern!" Svaran's voice startled him. He snapped

to attention. "I shall relieve you of your prisoner now. He will
go downriver with me to Kunzig, while you return to your
command at Klufbirk. I am leaving both men and werewolves
to replace those killed in the recent battle."

Vildern saw a half-smile on Svaran's face, and knew that the
other was hoping for some protest, for some excuse to punish
him.

If so, he was disappointed again. Vildern saluted formally.

"I thank you, Sir, for relieving me of this duty. Have I your
permission to go?" Svaran's smile faded.

"You may go."

Ingulf lay in dark dreams of pain.

"Airellen!" he cried into the dark. But she turned away, and
fled from him, while he followed, like a ghost. . . .

In his dreams, he was dimly aware of men taking him down
from his chains, and pouring water into his mouth. His hands
and arms were numb, like pieces of wood driven into his
aching shoulders. Pain gripped his groin and belly and chest,
and his legs collapsed under him as soon as his wrists were
freed. Moldy bread was shoved in his mouth, and he lay there
on slimy stone, swallowing now and then as the bread
dissolved. . . .

Then he awoke from nightmare in the green forest, sighing
with relief that it had only been a dream. Leaves rustled all
around; sunlight was dyed green. A bird called from the trees.

He tried to roll up, but his arms had been cut off at the
shoulders. . . .

He woke from that nightmare to find himself back home on
Tray Ithir, at the dinner table, a child again. His mother was
stirring the cauldron over the fire; his father sat opposite.
Greedily Ingulf attacked the food before him, cleaning his
plate. He drained his cup, but could not taste what it was. Still
thirsty, he called to his mother, and asked her to refill his cup,
but she never turned. It was then that he realized that he was
only a ghost, and that no one saw him or heard him. . . .

He awoke into another nightmare in which he lay in darkness
on slimy stone. Dorialith was in this dream, shining and
translucent, crying *Ingulf! Be strong, and hold to hope! I*

*am coming to you, and other help is near! But it will take time
for me to reach you.*

And beyond Ingulf could see, through the darkness, the
white towers of the City of the Sea-Elves, and then he knew
that all the torture he had gone through was but another illusion
that elves had put upon him with their harping, to keep him
from Airellen. But he had not been fooled; it had been too
sudden, and there was no reason for him to have been
transported into the hands of his enemies. . . .

He could not feel his hands or his arms: his shoulders ached
with cold as though wedges of ice had been driven through the
joints. He tried to lift his arm, but nothing moved.

What had happened? Had they cut off his arms? He tried to
look, but it was too dark to see. He tried to move again, and
this time felt, dimly, *something* moving. Something made of
wood or maybe sawdust-stuffed cloth rose and fell against the
stone with a muffled thud—but there was no sense of pain,
only a faint tremor in his aching shoulder. . . .

The effort exhausted him, and he lay stunned, his mind a
dull blank of suffering. . . .

Then he drifted from that dream into another, hearing
running water somewhere nearby. He was back in the forest,
under the green leaf roof, emerald in sunlight, with a terrible
thirst upon him. A brook gurgled nearby, and he rolled toward
it. He tried to push himself up to crawl, but he had no arms.
The blood from his shoulders ran into the stream, but he was
too thirsty to care. He tried to dip his head into the stream, but
someone gripped his hair, and held his head away. . . .

He woke, to find himself back in the Sea-Elves' city. Harps
played around him, and he knew that everything he had been
through was only an Elvish illusion. But there was a goblet in
front of him, filled with golden wine, and he snatched for it
thirstily.

But the carved hand at the end of his wooden arm only
tipped the goblet over, and the precious sunlight-golden liquor
spilled across the table.

He stared about in panic, his throat dry as sand, and saw
Airellen pouring golden wine into her own goblet. He called to
her, begging for a drink, but she did not seem to hear. He

called again, louder, but she looked past him, as though he
were not there, and drained the goblet with a gulp, and walked
quickly away, and he followed, a lonely ghost, calling,
calling. . . .

From that dream he woke into another, in which armored
men bearing glaring torches seized him. Water was poured into
his mouth, and he swallowed, thankfully, but there was not
enough, there was never enough. . . .

They jerked him up roughly from the floor, lifted him by
holding arms that might as well have been made of
wood. . . .

He woke again to the City of the Sea-Elves. Airellen handed
him a goblet filled with wine, and he drank and drank, but she
turned away from him, and he chased after her, a lonely ghost,
calling, calling. . . .

He woke from that nightmare to hear a werewolf's harsh
breathing as he ran through shabby streets, unarmed and
helpless. He dashed to a decaying shanty, pushing the door
open, planning to hide. . . .

But inside was light and music, and Airellen was there, a
cup halfway to her lips. . . .

He called to her, but she would not hear. Suddenly, the
fragile wall of the shack collapsed, and the werewolf burst
in. . . .

He woke from that dream into another, in which armored
men dragged him by his aching arms down long corridors, and
then at last through a sunlit arch into narrow streets where
mail-clad men jeered at him.

Face after sneering face he saw, and all of them laughing at
his pain. No, not all. There was the black-bearded man who
had tortured him; his face was sad and troubled. And another
face, clean-shaven under a steel cap, with one unruly lock of
blond hair escaping onto the forehead's top, stared at him with
sick pity. That face was familiar, somehow, and as Ingulf,
blinking, tried to remember where he had seen it before, the
man looked away, glaring at the men around him with a baffled
look. . . .

Then that face was gone, and as the dream went on, he was
dragged through the streets of Kirgiff into a part of town where

he had never been, to a gate that opened onto long wharves that ran out onto a little river, where flat-bottomed, shallow barges waited.

They dragged him on board one and chained him, while something like a black steel statue watched, flanked by black-robed men.

This dream had gone on for so long he almost believed it, but then he woke from that nightmare, to find himself back in the City of Sea-Elves. Elf-Women walked past, Airellen among them. He called to her, he stepped up to her and touched her hand, but she paid no heed. . . .

Meanwhile, far to the north, a white seal swam through the waves, following the faintest trace of a taste in the water. . . .

As Vildern watched the Islander being led onto the riverboat, he wondered, with a faint twinge of guilt, that he felt so little resentment at having his prisoner stolen from him like this. He should be enraged at having his rights trampled. . . .

He supposed it was mostly that he did not enjoy the torture itself, and was relieved to be able to stop. It was a dangerous weakness, he knew. It was too easy for him to imagine what his subject felt, even when torturing women, whose bodies, after all, were only caricatures of the body of tSarl. He had at least gotten used to that. But torturing a fellow man was worse. . . .

Such weakness had to be kept secret. If anyone guessed he was so different, so womanish, then he would indeed be in the victim's place. Officers, especially, had to be strong and cruel like Grom, or like that rear-raping butcher, Svaran. . . .

"*Rear-raping butchers!*" a low voice muttered nearby. Vildern started as though stung, and whirled. Hearing his own thought echoed so closely was unnerving.

"Rule your tongue, soldier," he snapped, "before someone cuts it out!"

The soldier—pure-bred and high-born, to judge from the blond hair that poked from the edge of his mail coif just under the steel cap, stared back insolently, his hand much too close to his sword. The fool! Was he going to *force* Vildern to kill him?

"I'm an officer, idiot!" Vildern snapped. "If you do kill me, after they skin you they'll pull out your nerves and scrape them with rock, and then they'll eat the flesh from your bones while you watch! You know that! How have you stayed alive this long?"

In the interests of discipline, Vildern knew, he should have the man flogged, here and now! But he did not want to. After torturing the Islander, he felt no need to cause pain to another man. . . .

Even though he knew he would be doing this fool a favor, and saving him from some worse fate. . . .

"What are you waiting for?" The man was staring at him, stupidly. Unless the fool asked for forgiveness, Vildern dared not let this pass. "Say it! If I have to raise my voice then there'll be nothing for it but . . ."

A hand plucked at his sleeve.

"Vildern!" It was the wolf-girl's voice.

"Not now!" he snapped, irritably. "This is important!" He fumed. What was wrong with her? If his weakness for her became known, it would surely cost him his rank, at the least, and might put him at the mercy of enemies who sought his death. "Well, do I *have* to have you flogged?" The man was still staring at him.

"Forgive me . . ." he began, stupidly. Vildern heaved a sigh of relief.

"All right, go on. You know the rest of it, surely? *One* of them, anyway?"

The man's brows knitted, then suddenly cleared.

"Master, forgive me, for I have—I have . . ." He hesitated, as though unsure of the wording. "I have— forgotten—!" There was a touch of panic on his features.

". . . Forgotten my place," Vildern prompted.

"Forgotten my place," the man went on. "I know my life is . . ."

"No, no, no!" Vildern whispered. "You're mixing two different rituals!" He shook his head. This man must be an extraordinary soldier indeed, to have gone without using the rites of abasement for so long that he forgot them. "Study the formulas, fool! They'll keep you alive." Suddenly he felt very tired, and did not want to bother with this any more. "All right, that will do! Get back to your . . ." He glanced at the insignia on the man's belt. "You should be on that boat! Hurry up and get aboard, before someone reports you missing!"

The man saluted—clumsily, Vildern thought—and dashed off, to join the men crowding onto the boats. Vildern rubbed his eyebrows, suddenly aware of the beginnings of a headache.

He turned toward Eluvorg. Her head was lifted, tilting curiously as she watched the departing soldier, her nostrils flaring, sniffing. . . .

"Well, what is it?" he snapped.

"I am . . ." She hesitated, then said, "I volunteered to carry the message that—the men of Klufbirk—that all companies are assembled and ready to march back to Klufbirk, Commander!" She blushed, her eyes, very wide, fixed on his as she saluted. She smiled, and a wave of desire throbbed through his groin. . . .

Her eyes became brighter, and he realized, belatedly, that his brows had relaxed; that his headache was gone, and the frown with it—that he was grinning at her like a fool!

He *was* a fool! Why did he let her have this power over him?

"Very good, soldier," he said, fighting the smile that he could feel tugging at his lips. "But," he said very softly, forcing the frown back to his face, "you *will* remember, in the future, to call me *Captain* or *Sir*—or Commander—in front of others—not 'Vildern'! Is that understood?"

"Yes, sir," she answered softly—but she smiled as she said it. He did not like that. He had meant to sound stern, and keep her properly chastened, but he did not think he had succeeded.

This was dangerous! He was commander now! How would he be able to keep discipline, and guard himself from treason from his officers, if he was going to turn into a simpering idiot every time she was around?

"Follow me, please, Sir," she said, and he fell into step behind her. Then, very softly, over her shoulder, she asked, "Who *was* that you were speaking to, Sir?"

"Why—" He blinked in sudden confusion. "I didn't take his

name." *I should have,* he thought, *and then reported him to his own commander for further punishment. . . .*

And that, he supposed, was why he had not taken the man's name. . . .

"All the time you were talking," she said, "I was trying to remember who he was and where I had met him before. He smelled very familiar, but—this nose doesn't work as well as—the other. His face was familiar too, but I cannot place it."

For two days, Ingulf passed from one uncomfortable dream to another, but now, at least, he was back on the ocean, where he belonged. . . .

Again he speared Airellen from his boat; again he sailed in haste from the Scurlmards in his search for the City of the Sea-Elves.

Sometimes he hunted for her in his boat, seeking her in the far islands where she hid as a seal. But he could not manage the boat very well, for he had no hands now. . . .

In one recurrent dream, he found himself chained in a barge filled with soldiers from Sarlow. During these dreams they gave him water and moldy bread. Sometimes the two hot suns beat down on his naked skin, and sometimes a clammy river mist floated in a thin veil between the rocking barge and the bright stars and moons above. In one of these dreams, he saw again a familiar, beardless face looking at him from among the guards. . . .

Vildern was wakened by great claws scratching at his door, in the darkness, but he lay still and pretended to sleep. Only when the sun had come up and a human hand knocked softly and a voice he recognized called did he open the door and let her in.

Afterward, she reproached him, but he pointed out that it would be very easy for some enemy to bribe one of the other werewolves to come to his door in the morning.

"I could bite you," she said with a smile. "Then you would be safe from all these things." His blood went cold. She rolled over in the bed, rolled on top. "And then we could run together in the night, hunting. We could cross the mountains and catch the savages in their villages at night, and tear them apart, and run down the deer. Then we could be together, always!!" Her eyes were bright, and she pressed close to him. He licked suddenly dry lips.

"I—I do not wish that," he said, lamely. She pouted.

"Can't you see that I want to share my life with you?" she whispered. "Remember the word I told you about? The word the Sorcerers have made us forget? The word your prisoner used? *Love*? That is what I want! I want to be loved!"

He shuddered. Already she had so much power over him. Now she wanted to make him into a womanish, helpless weakling like the Islander. . . .

"Do you never feel the need for more than just the raping," she cried, "for more than just power? The Sorcerers try to cut us all off from each other, to cut us off from the needs of our flesh, to make us cold spirits like those who dwell beyond the world. Don't you ever feel the need for a human touch, for someone you can trust to see your weaknesses, who can share your doubts and your worries? I need that!"

He did not answer. What was she trying to do to him? Wasn't the power she had over him enough? Now she wanted to change him still more!

That was what women were like, or so men said. That was how they gained control of you, stole your strength and manhood, to make you a sniveling weakling, like the men of the outer world—

But still, he thought—pure-bred, high-born! He would never, ever, have been able to buy such a wife! She could bear him sons who aspired to high rank, and daughters whose sale would bring in real money, to lift him out of the abysmal poverty in which he had always lived. . . .

"Can't you—don't you understand?" She pressed all her soft warmth against him. "I *need* you! And I need you to need me!" He felt his pulse mounting. He did need her, he thought, and was suddenly frightened. What was she doing to him? How had this wolf-witch gained so much power over him? Had she wormed her way so far into his weaknesses that she was already in a position to rule him with the magic of her body?

"I want to know all about you," she said, "all your sorrows and hopes and fears. I want to share all your troubles, dry your tears. . . ." She laid her head on his chest, not disturbed by the fearful pounding of his heart.

Bad enough that she obsessed his body, he thought, why did she have to possess his mind, too? He was lost. She would use her obscene power to ferret out the secrets that he dared not admit to his own mind, the secrets that would betray him as a coward and weakling, the rightful prey and sport of his fellows, deserving only torture and death. . . .

"I want your children," she said. He felt her breasts, her hands moving on his body, felt his own flesh stir and knew that he was lost. She would draw him back, again and again to these honey-sweet, forbidden joys. . . . "We can make a better life for our children," she said. Yes, women were always plotting against the Real Men, and this was their greatest weapon. For men could not get sons without them, and so the infants would be under their mother's control. If the boy-children were not taken from them as soon as they could chew, the women would poison their minds and turn them into weaklings, like the men of the outer world. . . .

He felt her touch, alluring, caressing. He was lost. He needed her, and was already in her power. She would rule him, with her words and her body, prying into his secret core, stripping away all his defenses. There was no way to protect yourself, except violence. And she was invulnerable—

At night.

He remembered the dagger he had hidden under the mattress, against assassins. . . .

But did he still have the strength to use it, or the will? Already he was sliding into her, even as his hand groped under the blankets. . . .

Sweet pleasures thrilled through him, and he saw delight in her bright eyes as she moved over him in mounting passion, and his body arched up. He was lost, his joy bursting into her, and she cried out with wonder. . . .

Then his groping hand found the dagger.

In the madness of his pleasure he almost let it go again, but then swift revulsion seized him, and he gripped it tightly and whipped it up with all his strength into the ribs below the wildly trembling breasts. . . .

Her eyes and mouth flew wide.

"No!" she shrieked. *"Why?"*—but then she choked on blood that flooded from her mouth; her eyes fixed and glazed. He jerked his head aside, to keep her blood from blinding him, and pushed her corpse off him.

But his vision was blurred. His eyes were filled with womanish tears, and his heart was twisting with regret.

Too late! He had killed her to save his manhood— but too late, and now, too late, he wanted her back—too late, too late!

He sat and wept beside her sprawled body.

The dream of the rocking boat grew more real, more distinct from the other dreams. Ingulf could think of no test to distinguish this nightmare from reality.

Yet he had no memories that could explain this captivity. He was not even sure that his invasion of Sarlow was real, but even if it were, his last memory was of someone—*Airellen?*—kneeling at his feet, begging him to turn back. . . .

He had been a victor then, a conqueror! How could he have come into this captivity?

It did not make sense! It could not be true. Yet tingling prickles of returning pain throbbed in the numb arms that dangled from his shoulder, and the suns burned his skin. . . .

Its vividness was maddening.

Now down the river ahead of them towers rose, on the right bank of the broadening river. A grim fortress on a rocky hill dominated a spreading town of ancient decaying houses and crude hovels. A town like Kirgiff, but bigger, and unwalled.

The men heaved at the sweeps, and the fortress loomed nearer, blocky and squat, and the hill under it higher and more steep. The soldiers laughed and shouted, and now from the banks answering shouts came back. Ingulf closed his aching eyes against the glare of sunlight, and huddled in the filth of the boat's bottom, hoping that he would wake up, or at least escape into some other dream. . . .

The barge shuddered with a thump of wood: feet clamored, voices laughed and jeered, and then hands seized him and jerked him roughly to his feet.

A key unlocked his chain from the boat, and then he was

being dragged over the side, onto a long wharf. It smelled real enough.

They dragged him up the cobbled streets toward the fortress looming on the hill. That steel statue strode ahead, robed figures on either side.

Ingulf closed his eyes, helplessly, and let himself be dragged. Then he felt the burning heat cut off. Opening his eyes, he glimpsed ponderous stone walls, the pulley for a heavy portcullis, monstrous gates.

Then he was dragged through and hustled roughly down stone steps, down and down, deep into the rock.

He was dragged into torchlight, and a long corridor, where steel doors shut off cells.

There were things in human shape behind the walls, things that screamed, and things that raved; things that beat the hard stone with iron chains. His captors laughed, as Ingulf's face showed pain.

"He'll scream like a woman!" one said, and grinned. The clammy dark closed in behind their torches. The screams and raving hinted at tortures ahead. Why could he not awake?

The walls' thick stone seemed real enough, the men who grinned and jeered as they dragged him seemed too depraved to be real.

But the most real thing was pain.

His arms were limp under the weight of chains. A door opened. They dragged him in and chained him. There he saw the light of hot torches reflected from the instruments of pain laid out and waiting. Solid granite walls surrounded them.

Behind him, wretches raved, and all around him cruel captors grinned.

He dimly understood they meant to grind away his will. He lay still in his chains, and closed his eyes: he shut his lips and raved inside his head.

At last the glare of torches slowly faded from the walls, and he was left alone, to dark and pain.

He rolled, and tried to sit, despite the pain. His teeth were grinding in a mirthless grin of anger as he fought to rise.

The wall was rough and clammy-cold. His heavy chains

were dragging down his helpless arms, and torturing his shoulder while his mad mind raved.

"Murdering evil monsters!" Ingulf raved aloud at last, his voice a scream of pain. *"This makes no sense, no sense! Why are you torturing me so, you evil Elves? You grinning liars! This cannot be real!"*

His chains rattled. His shrieking echoed from the walls.

His tortured mind imagined skulls that grinned and raved with him, and shook their iron chains. Then pain triumphed: he slumped against the wall.

A white seal's head rose from the waves.

Across the tossing surge of the salt waste of the Great Northern Ocean came a sweet wild singing, wordless as birdsong, haunting and lonely.

Then the high, faint voice shaped words. . . .

> *Why should beauty vanish in a day?*
> *Why should men, like flowers, fade away?*
> *O-hone-o-ro.*
> *Where do they go?*

But the white seal had not stopped to listen, but shot arrow-straight toward the sound, her supple body graceful as an eel in the water.

Wild waves lashed the rock where Airellen sat, her seal-shape laid aside; but she paid them no heed, her head thrown back as she sang to the stars and the bright wandering moons.

> *Centuries and Ages pass us by:*
> *Mountains fall and ancient forests die*
> *While Elves live on.*
> *While we live on . . .*

When the white seal surged up out of the surf, she looked down and the song ceased as she rolled up, poised for flight.

"Swanwhite!" she exclaimed. "I did not look to see you here!"

"I came to tell you that you can go home again," said Swanwhite, slipping out from her seal dress. "If the mortal who troubles you is not yet dead, he soon will be."

"What?" Airellen's face was suddenly as pale as Swan-white's. "You cannot mean—no, no, of course not! No, Swanwhite, Dorialith told me that—that man—would live for—many years yet, and it has only been a few months. So—the man will yet be living, and I will bide here—"

Swanwhite laughed.

"Men will live for many years only if they do be living peaceful and contented lives, not when they throw themselves into battles and mad adventures."

"Swanwhite! What do you mean?"

"Why, the mortal went off to do great deeds. He seemed to think that that would make you love him!"

"Where did he get such a foolish idea?" snorted Airellen, with a blush, and a toss of her head. "Why should I care for bloody-handed deeds? But—you have not said—what are you hinting at? Stop playing with me, Swanwhite."

"Why, the mortal, Ingulf, went into Sarlow, to try to free the slaves, and his magic sword has been taken from him," Swanwhite said. "Now the men of Sarlow have him prisoner, and will torture him to death, and then you can come home—"

"*No!*" cried Airellen. "Swanwhite, no! You cannot mean it! Ingulf—tortured? This is—where is he? I must go to him! *Where* in Sarlow?"

"Up the River Lumrof—" Swanwhite began—but already Airellen had taken the seal-shape about her, and was leaping into the sea.

Allowing herself at last the small, secret smile she had been hiding, Swanwhite followed.

VI

In the Mist

MEN WITH TORCHES woke Ingulf and fed him, and then dragged him up and fastened his numbed hands above his head to a chain that hung from the ceiling.

The manacles had sunk deep into the swollen, puffy flesh of his wrists. Suddenly he could feel his hands again, a sharp, intense pain, as though blood spurted from the tips of his fingers. The ache in his shoulders was still worse, and all through his chest and belly knots of pain tore at him.

Through the haze of pain he heard a voice, and opened his eyes to see a skull. . . .

He blinked, and saw that it was a bald man, whose face was only skin tight-stretched over bone.

"Where is Dorialith?" The high voice rasped again. *"Where did you last see Dorialith?"*

"In the Sea-Elves city, was it not?" he mumbled confused, as much to himself as to the other. "Or did I see him in Kirgiff, or was that but a dream?" He could not think. His hands hurt so. . . .

"And where is Frostfire?" The voice rasped, coldly.

"Frostfire?" His mind groped. "Gone! Vanished! I do not understand. . . ."

"And where is Err-Earil—Oralin?"

"*Airellen!*" he shrieked. "Why, oh why have you left me? Why have you turned from me and left me alone to this torment? Why must I—?" But then he had shrieked all the air out of his lungs, and he could not seem to fill them again. Everything was dark around him, and then quite suddenly he was lying on the ground, and someone was pouring water over his face.

He opened his mouth and swallowed gratefully, then choked and coughed and blinked water from his eyes. Out of the blurred torchlight above him the cold voice came again.

"Tell us what you know, now!" it snarled. "Or do you want us to hang you back up?"

"I don't understand," groaned Ingulf. "What do they want? This makes no sense. . . ."

"How many of you are there? Where do you meet?"

"Who?" Ingulf closed his eyes, trying dully to make sense of the question. "Where do *who* meet?"

"How many men in your army? How many men joined you to free the slaves?"

Ingulf frowned, trying to remember. How many men had he led? The first pit . . . the second pit . . .

"I don't remember," he said. "A hundred? Two hundred? Four hundred?"

That seemed to cause some excitement: several voices were raised at once, clamoring loudly. It made no sense. What was it all about?

"Where did you come through the mountains?" the voice hissed after the other voices had quieted.

"Why . . ." Ingulf knotted his brows, confused. "Up at—the pass up above there—the pass with the fort in it." That brought another jangle of voices.

"How did you get past Klufbirk?" the voice snarled. "And where are all the others hiding now?"

"I don't understand—what is—Cluvbirr—and where are—who?"

"How did you get past the fort without being seen?"

"I climbed—"

"And where are all the others who came with you?"

"What?"

"All your companions? The ones who crossed the mountains with you!"

"No one crossed the mountains with me. I came alone—"

A foot crashed into his face, blotting out the room with sparks of light.

"Hang him up again!" the harsh voice commanded.

Far to the north, a dark-clouded storm came striding over the ocean on wind-whipped legs of rain and burning feet of lightning, growling with thunder as it stepped from wave to wave.

And through that murderous wild ocean, diving through the mountainous swells, two shapes swam, a dark shape and a white, swimming south, toward the coast of Sarlow.

Again and again Ingulf was wakened from merciful unconsciousness and questioned, and the questions never seemed to make any sense, and the answers never seemed to satisfy them.

Sometimes it was the skull-face man, and sometimes a rosy-cheeked man with twinkling blue eyes and a fringe of wolf-gray hair around a pink dome, and once it was a handsome, beardless young man with dark hair and cold blue eyes. It made little difference: the questions were always the same, and the pain never stopped.

If it was a nightmare, it was interspersed with no other dreams; when he fainted from the pain, there was only blankness until they roused him again. At one point they unchained his hands—they were useless anyway—and he saw that the manacles had left deep furrows in his wrists, between puffy ridges of swollen flesh. Then they fed him, and they all went away, and the next time they roused him they asked him jokingly if he had had a restful night.

And indeed after he had eaten he realized that a peculiar clarity was settling over him. There were only two of his captors now, burly, short-haired men who whistled while they kindled a fire and tested various pulleys and the rack, and kept the fire burning merrily, roasting pieces of meat over it and eating them, and when the fire had built up a thick bed of coals, laying the irons into it to heat, while they chained Ingulf up to the wall.

The manacles brought feeling back to numb hands, and the men laughed when he cried out.

A short time later the door of the room opened, and the torchlight reflected from polished black steel. Ingulf stared, as what looked to be a black steel statue came striding through the door.

Behind came the dark, beardless man who had questioned Ingulf yesterday. Today Ingulf saw he was dressed as a soldier, in a knee-length hauberk of mail, with a sword at his side, though he bore no shield.

Behind came four other men in mail—a guard, it seemed. They carried shields, and ranged themselves along the wall, two on each side of the door.

One of those faces, too, was familiar.

The steel figure lifted its hands to its head, and after a moment lifted the metal skull off to reveal a human head underneath. Then Ingulf realized that it was a man wearing a black steel armor that fitted his body. He had never seen the like before—except in his dreams of the boat on the river. . . .

No dream, he thought.

The burly men bowed to the armored man.

"Is everything ready?" the armored man asked. His voice was arrogant.

"Almost, Prince Svaran," one said. "The irons are still heating."

"No hurry," he said, stepping toward Ingulf. "What do you think, Grom? Do you think Ramaukin is right, and he really does not know anything?"

"They do say the *Liktalp* are masters of illusion," the beardless man replied. His voice was softer. "It would be a clever plan, certainly, to send him without his—"

The slamming door cut through the words.

One of the guards, the one whose face was so unaccountably familiar, had slammed the door shut, and dropped the bolt across it.

Turning, he drew his sword—and the blade flamed in its own light, brighter than the torchlight.

And in the light of that drawn sword, Ingulf recognized the face of Carroll Mac Lir.

The other guards shouted, drawing their swords. One sprang at Carroll, sharp blade hissing high above his head.

It sank deep in the rim of Carroll's lifted shield while bright steel wheeled low, under the mail-shirt's metal hem.

A scream rang on stone: a foot and shin toppled, cut off at the knee. Blood poured in a sudden red flood: the dead guard fell.

Grom and Svaran whirled, blades flying free. Grom ran toward the fight. Svaran followed more slowly. The jailors ran for weapons.

Carroll rushed to meet the charge of the other two guards, his body drawn back compactly behind his shield. A leap like a cat's clapped his shield's flat against that of the nearest guard and hurled him reeling with an echo like deafening thunder. The dead guard's sword flew spinning, ripped from Carroll's shield-rim.

The guard staggered back against the other, his helmet rasping as the bright edge stroked it, leaving a long scratch in the steel.

Grom snatched the dead man's shield from the floor, and the two torturers rushed toward the fighting. One had an axe; the other had pulled a long iron bar out of the fire, its end white-hot, and drawn a long knife.

But Svaran had stopped, and was settling the round helmet down over his head.

Ingulf saw the two staggered guards steady, and their two swords whipped out as one.

Carroll's blade flashed out like lightning, and one guard toppled, sword clattering, face suddenly veiled in blood.

The other blade drummed on Carroll's shield, while Grom sprang at his back, sword raised high.

"Carroll!" Ingulf shouted. *"Look out!"*

Without turning, Carroll launched himself at the man before him, bright blade whirling in a lace of light. Long slivers flew from the wooden shield as the guard stumbled aside, turning as Carroll bounded past, spinning to face both foes.

Grom slowed. The guard was now between him and Carroll. The torturer with the hot iron was hurrying to take his place behind Grom. Svaran, sword on shoulder, helm on head, strode calmly up the center of the room.

But Ingulf saw the torturer with the axe creeping along the wall, toward Carroll's back.

Then he saw the guard's sword lash out in a cut, and the flaming blade soaring above it like a hawk.

Both struck at once: Carroll's shield boomed while his edge clove mail-rings and shattered bone. Blood burst from the guard's right eye.

Before the body fell Carroll had wheeled away, to spring at the man with the axe. Grom raced after him.

Taken by surprise, the axeman froze, then heaved his axe high. As it fell Carroll stretched his shield-arm up, and the disk's rim rammed the axe shaft with a loud *crack,* while the bright steel whistled in a half-circle to shear deep into the man's side.

And again he was running, Grom behind him, straight at Svaran's black-armored form.

Svaran's heavy blade flew from his shoulder, breaking a great wedge out of the thin wooden shield as Carroll struck. Ingulf saw the bright blade bend around the black helmet.

Svaran reeled, but did not fall: his arm drew back to his shoulder again, and lashed out once more. The power of the blow hurled another piece spinning from the thin shield, and knocked Carroll reeling back.

And now Grom Beardless was upon him.

Carroll leaped, spinning in the air, sword-edge skimming toward the eyes above Grom's shield.

The eyes disappeared behind the raised shield-edge, and a silvery shimmer of steel wheeled out from under the shield, slashing at Carroll's legs.

Both shields roared: wood chips flew. Carroll sprang past Grom, his sword's flame swirling in the gloom, while Svaran and the remaining torturer spread out to close in on him.

And as the long swords whistled and crashed between Carroll's shield and Grom's, Ingulf realized that the two men were closely matched.

Carroll circled, trying to keep Grom between him and Svaran, and nearly got the hot iron in his face. He flinched away, and Grom's sword came diving over his shield.

He dropped to one knee, and the sword glanced from the back of his helm. Grom loomed above him, sword raised to kill—

Carroll sprang suddenly in a long lunge out from under the falling sword, and whirled, slashing. . . .

Svaran's edge hissed toward his exposed arm. Mail-rings jangled and broke. Carroll staggered back, bright blood running down his shoulder.

As Ingulf watched in horror, the three closed in on the outnumbered, wounded Carroll.

Carroll backed away, keeping his shield at an angle from his body that kept the flat turned toward Grom, who was moving in cautiously from his left with the prudent torturer behind him, but its rim aimed at Svaran.

Svaran laughed, cruelly, and his blade lashed out in a lightning-fast blur.

Carroll's shield leaped to meet it, and Ingulf's heart lurched as he saw Grom's blade rising to whirl in an arc that would end at Carroll's head. . . .

Carroll's shield boomed, and then Carroll's elbow bent, rolling the shield up beside his head, brushing Grom's falling steel aside, while the sword which had dropped in Carroll's hand suddenly reared high, as the wounded right arm rose, curling over his head to spin the bright blade at Grom's eyes even as Svaran, laughing, cut again.

Grom's shield pushed the blade up, but it lashed on around, to drive Svaran's steel aside with a ringing rasp as Carroll's right foot stepped, and he launched himself in a long leap at Svaran's steel-clad form.

Grom's sword cut empty air as Carroll twisted to drive his shield, with all the weight of his body behind it, into the face-plate of Svaran's helmet.

The metal figure staggered back, and the bright sword flashed. Ingulf saw the steel wrap like a whiplash around Svaran's pealing armor, then spring back. Svaran reeled and the wooden shield slammed into his helmet again.

Svaran fell, clanging, to the stone, and Carroll jumped over him and swung around, in front of Ingulf, to face the charge of Grom Beardless.

Two wood shields crashed as one. The long blades swooped and soared: the room resounded to the drumming of shields.

Ingulf, watching, drew a deep breath. His father was Sword-Master to his clan, and even though this style of fighting was utterly different from his own, he could tell skill when he saw it.

And he saw it now: each of these men was utter master of his own style.

When he had served in the imperial forces, he had seen men who fought as Carroll fought: shield always steady before the left side while the sword arm moved in great swooping circles, which never moved the shoulder forward, with most of his cuts aimed at the enemy's right eye, and the thin bone of the temple.

Grom's cuts were more often straight down at the skull, and the mail at his shoulder would flash past the edge of his shield when he cut—then draw back quickly as Carroll's blade swept in.

The blood on Carroll's mail had caked, and his arm seemed to move as quickly as before, so the wound could not be deep.

Ingulf watched, helpless, while the long swords whined and whickered in the air. Behind Grom, the torturer circled, looking for an opening, and once stepped back to his brazier, dropping the long iron bar he held and pulling out another.

Svaran stirred, armor rasping on the stone, as he lifted himself slowly, shaking his head as though stunned.

The shields drummed as the swift swords flew back and forth. Suddenly the torturer sprang in from the right, thrusting white-hot metal at Carroll's face.

Carroll jerked his head back—and Grom's sword lashed over the edge of his shield, and glanced from the side of his helmet.

The glowing iron thrust in again, and Carroll knocked it away with his sword, while his shield crashed with Grom's blow.

Suddenly Carroll lunged to the right, and his sword's point drove into the torturer's unarmored body.

Grom's steel licked at the outstretched arm. Carroll's shield thundered as he caught it—but the falling man's body held his sword in its ribs, and he could not tear it free.

Heaving himself to a sitting position, Svaran laughed.

The hanging skirt of Carroll's mail rang as Grom's lashing blade drove up against his leg, but without the force to cut through. Then Grom's blade was whirling high at Carroll's right eye, and Ingulf glimpsed the mail-rings that covered Grom's shoulder.

Carroll spun to the right as he hurled up his shield, and with the force of his movement his point slid free.

He stabbed quickly past his shield's edge; Grom's driving arm came down upon the point. Mail-rings opened. Grom jerked back from the sharp spike; just above his elbow, blood ran.

And already Carroll's sword was whipping around, lashing at Grom's eyes. Grom guarded, reeling back: his return cut thumped weakly against Carroll's shield.

And then that shining sword bit down on Grom's shoulder, ripping through mail-rings, with a red spring rilling behind.

Grom reeled back with a cry: the bright steel crashed against his helm and glanced away as he fell under the stroke.

Svaran heaved himself to his feet.

Ingulf let his breath out in a long gasp, and as he breathed in became once more aware of the agony in his arms.

"So!" Svaran's voice rang hollow from his helmet. "The invincible Grom has fallen!" He laughed. "Well! so much the greater will my fame be when I have killed you, warrior!" He bent, and lifted Grom's shield from the ground.

"I suppose you will make me kill you quickly. A pity. I would like to spend a few months watching you die. . . ."

He strode toward Carroll, the hacked shield held before him.

Carroll leaned on his sword, watching the advancing metal shape, while he breathed in great, shuddering gasps. Only when the ponderous, striding armor was almost upon him did he raise his shield before him, drawing back his right arm and leg in a single smooth motion. Svaran laughed, his sword resting on his shoulder.

Suddenly his elbow jerked up, and then, as he stepped, the sword left his shoulder and came skimming round at Carroll's left ear.

A large chunk broke with a *crack!* from Carroll's shield: his sword belled loud on Svaran's shoulder-plate. Again Svaran laughed as his sword flew. Again came the crack of breaking wood and the tolling of steel as Carroll's sword sprang back from the armor.

Ingulf, watching, felt his senses swim. He would faint again! He bit his lip, fighting to stay conscious. . . .

The figures blurred before his eyes. He jerked his head up. It had fallen forward. Before him the long lines of light swayed back and forth between two figures—*Crack! Clang! Boom! Clang!*

He shook his head to clear it: forced it up.

Carroll was staggering as the heavy sword drove again and again into the shield.

He staggered back a step, then ran at his iron enemy, sword swirling round his head again and again and again, blurred into a crystal wheel that ground and rasped at the edge of the eyeslit. . . .

"Harder!" Svaran laughed, harshly. "Strike harder, warrior! If you strike hard enough, surely, you can cut through?" Again the booming laugh and then the flat shields clapped, and Carroll reeled back, his wheeling sword still battering the black steel helm.

Again Ingulf found himself jerking up his drooping head, and still vague figures fought there in the gray mist over his eyes. He shook his head, trying to see. The bright blade battered at the black steel.

Suddenly there came a loud cry. It startled him all the way awake. He saw a sword fly through the air. Svaran backed away, and the bright blade battered at the black helm.

"Curse you, Outlander!" Svaran's voice cried. "You'll suffer for that! You'll watch the maggots eating the flesh cut from your bones before you die! You'll—"

Carroll laughed.

The shield was almost cut away from his arm, but he still held his sword, and Svaran's steel gauntlet was empty.

Carroll stabbed at Svaran's eyeslits, but the shield brushed his point aside. The black steel figure backed away. . . .

Then Ingulf knew he must have fainted again, because when he jerked his head up, Carroll's face, dripping sweat, was in front of his, and his arms were raised as he fiddled with something above his head.

A sudden sharp pain in Ingulf's shoulder made him cry out. He turned his head, and saw that one arm had fallen to his side. He was slumped, still hanging from the other arm.

Another sharp pain, and he staggered, feeling his knees give under him as he fell against Carroll. . . .

". . . out of here!" a voice was saying, somewhere in the gray mist. "What am I going to do? I can't carry you! You've got to walk. They'll be hunting for us soon!" He tried to find his legs and make them move. After a while he felt himself stumbling through dimness, lurching against another body. His arms hung limp from his shoulder, his knees kept folding up, but an arm supported him. . . .

Then he found himself lying on the floor. There was a great babble of voices, screaming and shouting. Then an arm lifted him again, and he found himself staggering through a vague world of gray stone corridors, stumbling on stone steps.

Then he was lying on stone, in sunlight, hearing shouting and the sounds of steel. They were still fighting. He must have dreamed that they had stopped. . . .

Then he was staggering again, while an arm held him up. It was dark now, and he felt a water-smelling wind. He pulled his head up, and glimpsed roofs against a sky filled with stars and wandering moons.

"Carroll?" he croaked.

"Yes," said a voice near his ear. "Yes, Loon, it is Carroll. And I think there is a place we can hide, up ahead. I hope there is. I need sleep!"

Then everything was dark again.

* * *

As the sky lightened, and the moons turned gold, dark waters filled slowly with emerald light. Swarming shoals of fish darted through the green sea in great silver clouds.

They scattered, arrowing away in sudden flight in all directions.

Through the dawn sea came two shapes swimming, a black seal and a white, scattering the clouds of fish as they sped south, toward the mouth of the great river Lumrof.

The currents of the river guided them in toward the seaport. Wooden ships clustered thick in the great harbor of Kithmar, and voices shouted as the seals rose to breathe.

But before a javelin could be thrown, or a bow drawn, the two shapes were weaving through the muddy water, with the black hulls far above them.

Then they were entering the fresh-water current pouring into the great bay, and swimming between the anchor chains of ships moored there.

They were far upriver before they surfaced again, with the white water foaming about their shoulders, swimming against the tumbling current with a speed no mortal beast might have matched.

Ingulf awoke, aching in every limb.

He opened his eyes, and saw a stone wall.

Had it all been a dream, then? The rescue, Carroll fighting with Grom and with Svaran—all a dream? Was he still a prisoner?

Then he realized that he saw the stone before his eyes by diffused sunlight.

He tried to roll over. His arms were still dead, but after a moment he managed to flop awkwardly onto his back. A dusty sunbeam glowed between him and the dark roof.

Armless, it was hard to roll, but he turned his throbbing head on its aching neck, and saw Carroll lying a little way off, unconscious, bloody, pale. Red blood leaked through links of mail.

"Carroll?" Ingulf breathed, and the other stirred and rolled up on his elbow, groggy, but with one hand on his sword-hilt.

"Carroll? Is this real? Is it really you? Where are we?"

Ingulf babbled. Carroll blinked at him, confused; then a sad smile lifted the corners of his lips.

"Poor Loon!" he said. " 'tis I indeed, and real, but I cannot wonder that you doubt it."

"Where are we?" Ingulf asked.

"Well"—Carroll pushed himself up to a sitting position—"we're not out of the city, as I'd hoped to be. But I had picked this as a possible hiding-place. The noble who owns this palace is away, and there are only a pair of slaves left to—*Hush, now*!" He raised his hand sharply in warning. Something echoed far down the corridor, like a distant door closing, and then they heard the echo of the *clack* of feet.

Carroll crept close to Ingulf, and whispered in his ear.

"We should be safe until dark, but we dare not stay too long. When night comes again, the werewolves will be back on our trail."

"It is a wonder they did not catch us last night!" Ingulf whispered back.

"Oh, they did," said Carroll. "I killed three. But it was close to dawn by then. You were blind as a log, though. I'd tried to get to the wharves, to steal a boat, but—"

He fell silent as the corridor rang with the echo of a distant voice. Another answered it, and then distorted echoes of laughter shrilled somewhere in the empty pile of stone.

They heard footsteps, and then the ringing boom of a door, then silence again. Carroll heaved himself wearily to his feet, and peered out the window.

"Noon already," he whispered, dropping down beside Ingulf. "As I thought, the slaves don't bother much with these side corridors. When I've rested a bit, I'll clean off this mail, and go buy us a bite to eat. By sunset we must be ready to move. With luck, that should give us time to be well away before the werewolves come after us, and give us a chance to steal a boat—or even buy one! Across the river we should be able to hide—it is mostly wild country, except right on the shore. And it is not far to the mountains; and once we cross them, we'll be in Galinor."

"Carroll," said Ingulf, after a long silence, "why did you

come back for me?" With a twisted smile, Carroll shook his head.

"Why, I hardly know," he said, with a bitter laugh, and then his face sobered, and he stared at the Islander.

"I was ashamed," he said, at last, very slowly. "I started south, into the forest, like a sane man, but then—you made me remember something that happened—after I escaped from Sarlow . . . long years ago. You made me remember—this sword. . . ." He patted the sword's hilt, and sat silent for a long time.

"The Hasturs took—those of us who were alive—to—to the Elfwoods, down over the mountains there—along the marches of Tumbalia and Galinor—and left us with the Forest-Elves.

"I was—mad with hate. Maybe as mad as you, but in a different way. . . ." He was silent then, silent a long time. Ingulf said nothing, but only listened.

"There was a—a bard among the Elves," Carroll said at last, "who sang to us—healing songs, I think, but—he sang many old tales, and one—not a very old tale as *they* reckon things—one tale was of a hero of the folk who dwelt here before the Norian tribesmen—before there was a land of Sarlow.

"The song told of the fall of that kingdom—I think it was called Treethclith, or something like that, I cannot remember now. And after the last great battle, the last of the great heroes of that kingdom, wounded to the death, was borne away by Elves, and lay dying in a cave in the hills—the Cave of Garinvel was the name of the song. . . .

"And one among the Elves asked him to whom he would leave his great fiery sword. And that dying hero raised himself up, and drove the sword deep into the stone of the cavern where he lay, with his last strength, and with his dying breath he said— *'Let him take the sword who can draw it from the stone'*—and then he died.

"And the song told how the Sorcerers of Sarlow, fearing the Power of the Sword, had set Demons to watch over the cave, for it was foretold that whoever took the sword would do great harm to the Land of Sarlow." Carroll's lips quirked in a smile.

"Well, to do great harm to the Land of Sarlow was the

dearest desire of my heart just then." He laughed. "So I asked
how the cavern could be found, and after long argument, the
Elves consented to guide me. And more than that, with flaming
arrows and Elf-magic they drove aside and kept from my back
the guardians that had been placed over the cave—shadowy,
dog-headed things that could move about even by day. Without
the help of the Elves, I could never have gotten into the cave."

He fell silent as distant echoes of voices and of feet rang
hollowly; when he spoke again it was in a low whisper.

"Light filled the cave, for the sword flared in the stone.
Lumps of silver reflected the light—for the cavern had been a
mine, and it had been abandoned with silver scattered on the
floor, and some still in the walls. The nearness of the guardians
kept the need-fire burning. But they were strong enough to
enter the cave despite the need-fire.

"The sword was indeed driven very deep in the wall, and
when I laid my hand to its hilt, I kicked aside the bones of
others who had tried to draw that sword, and had been caught
by the guardians. I braced my feet against the wall and
pulled—but the sword seemed to be part of the wall. And at my
back the Elves were striving to hold the guardians away—but
despite all their magic, and the need-fire that filled the cave,
the things were coming closer.

"Fear gave me strength to try again—but I might as well
have been pulling at solid stone. The sword did not budge.
Then fury filled me, and I remembered the deaths of my
family, and all those I had seen die in the pits, and as I wrestled
with the hilt, I called out to the spirit of that long-dead
warrior—and then it seemed at last that I felt some movement,
and that the sword was not part of the wall, after all.

"But still it did not come free, although I tugged until I
thought my arms would break. My companions still held off
the guardians—but only barely, and slowly they were coming
closer.

"Then hate and fear alike left me. I drew a deep breath—
then, suddenly it seemed as though I saw a great light in my
mind, and in that instant, the sword flew free, and I turned with
it, and smote the guardians, and the sword's fire hurled them
out of the world. . . .

"The Elves made songs about me, and prophesied that I would do great deeds—and indeed, I have raided the slave caravans, and have helped many villages that would no doubt have been destroyed. And yet—I never dared to do what you have done."

Carroll lay quiet now. Ingulf felt exhaustion creeping over him again.

"So at last, I," Carroll said softly, "when I first left you, I went back into the woods, but I was ashamed that I had deserted you, and at last—I went back to the cave. I felt—that I had proved—unworthy of the sword. And then—I looked down from the mountains, and saw—men fleeing, escaped slaves being hunted, just as we were. . . . And I remembered well thinking that—you had done it, that you had succeeded in what I, who had won the sword from Garinvel, had never dared to try. So I ran to their aid—to *your* aid, I thought.

"It was dark before I reached them, and the werewolves had changed. But the sword killed many, and the rest fled, howling. But you were not there, and the slaves seemed to know nothing of you—and yet, from their story, I knew that something was happening. I guided them through the pass, and stayed.

"And then, late in the evening of another day, I looked from the mountains into the plain, and saw signs of many people moving, and after a time I realized that great numbers of fugitives were milling and fleeing, while blocks of soldiers followed. And again I came down from the mountain. It took time for me to get there. But I thought surely that this time there would be news of you, for it was plain that your coming had stirred up great events.

"It was dark by the time I reached them, and soldiers and werewolves were already closing in. But the werewolves scattered from the flame of my sword, and the slaves rallied to it—and indeed they outnumbered the soldiers, and it was only their panic that had kept them from crushing the soldiers before I arrived. Then I saw your sword flash—"

"My sword?" cried Ingulf. "What, *Frostfire?*"

"Indeed," said Carroll. "Do you not—? Torvar—talked as though—as though you had given it to him. He said that you

had been injured, and had had to be carried. When dawn came
I went looking for you, along with Rakmir and a few
others—two children, born into slavery—"

"I do not understand!" Ingulf shrieked, suddenly, his voice
echoing eerily. "This makes no sense! None of it makes sense.
We had won! Everything was going well. And then——" He
shook his head, and one shoulder twitched as he tried to lift his
limp hand. "And then Airellen came to me, and begged me to
stop. And then I fell into her hair. Why did she destroy me?
Why does she hate me so? What happened to me? I cannot
understand!"

Carroll stared at him, pityingly.

"Poor Loon!" he said, after a moment. "Rakmir did say, at
one point, that you'd been hit on the head. And your head
wasn't right before it happened. Ah well, at least you're alive.
I was sure you were dead, after we found the body of the man
they told me had been carrying you, and then your robe, all
bloody and torn. Torvar was destroyed with grief, when—
hush!"

A voice echoed down the corridor, its words lost in the shrill
of echoes. A door clashed, sending echoes ringing, and then
footsteps, and the voice again.

Footsteps and voice drew nearer, and Carroll rose, hand on
hilt. Again the voice, louder, and then again.

"My—yel—dov!" The distorted voice called, the echoes
adding music to its tone. "Where-air are you?" The footsteps
were coming closer and closer. . . .

"Wha-at-tar-you-do-oo-ing down here?" the voice called
again. Then from further away, a door boomed, and another
shrill echo of a voice called, too distorted to understand.

"There you are!" the first voice replied. "I thought it odd
you should be down here!"

Distorted echoes answered.

"A trick of the ears, I suppose!" the voice called back. "I
could have sworn I heard you down this—"

The answering echo shrilled even more sharply. The voice
laughed.

"That's true enough! Nothing down that way but empty
rooms and old tables! Nothing worth stealing, any more, and

only good for—" But now the words grew faint, and were twisted by the echoes into shrill tones. Carroll breathed out quietly, and then rose cautiously to his feet.

"There are safer places than the middle of this corridor," he whispered. "Lie still. I want to see these empty rooms they speak of. . . ."

He strode off, while Ingulf slumped wearily back to the floor. *Lie still*, Carroll had said! Ingulf angrily wondered what else Carroll thought he could do.

He tried to sort out the peculiar sequence of his memories but instead drifted into a tortured sleep, where Airellen drove great nails into his shoulder-joints. . . .

"Say you do not love me," she said. *"Hate me and I will set you free."*

But barely had he fallen asleep when Carroll, returning, woke him, and lifted him in his arms as though he had been a child.

"We are in luck, Loon," Ingulf heard him say. "One of these empty rooms has a bed in it! It must be a hundred years old, but it is soft, and no foe will trip over you there."

He was carried out of the corridor into a dimmer place and laid on something soft.

And then once again he was seeking Airellen through the shabby shacks by the river, with the hot breath of werewolves panting at his heels. . . .

The white foam of the river flew from the sleek coats of the two seals as they forged their way through the swiftest, thickest currents of the broad river Lumrof, fighting their way upstream.

Sometimes voices were raised from cities and settlements on the banks, and once a boat changed course to follow them. Then they dived, and darted sleek and silent above the silt, startling the otters, and terrorizing fresh-water fish.

By late afternoon they were far upstream. Something gleamed faintly in the murky waters of the bottom, and the white seal, diving, tugged it playfully clear of the mud, and found herself holding a silver goblet in her jaws.

The dark seal eyed her companion with astonishment when she rose, bearing the glittering object in her mouth.

Ahead of them, on the right bank, wild forest grew down to the water's edge, and toward this, the white seal made her way, sunlight flaring silver at the point of the broad wedge of ripples she carved across the water as she swam. The darker seal followed, mystified.

At the shore, Swanwhite set the cup on a log, and then slid from her seal-dress and stepped ashore. Airellen, still in seal-form, protested.

"We have to know where to look for him," Swanwhite pointed out, dipping the goblet in the river, filling it with clear water. "There are many places he might have been imprisoned! Let me look, now!"

Airellen was silent, watching. A bird called, far off in the green woodlands.

Swanwhite breathed on the water, and looked deeply into it. The dark seal drew herself up onto the bank.

"Not far now," Swanwhite said at last. "But something strange has happened. He is free, for the moment. But they are hunting him! I see a city that swarms with soldiers. When it is dark the werewolves will hunt!" She raised her white head, and the far-seeing eyes were misted as though blind. "Come! It will be sunset before we can reach the city."

She put the seal-shape about her again, and slid into the water.

A hand shook Ingulf's shoulder, then dust made him sneeze. He woke; Carroll stood above him.

"Time to go," said Carroll. "Do you think you can walk at all?"

"I think—" Ingulf tried to push himself up, but fell back when his arm collapsed under him. But the arm had moved— awkwardly, numbly.

"Lift me to my feet," Ingulf said. "I think my legs will work, but I cannot use my arms." Face troubled, Carroll lifted him to a sitting position, and swung his feet off the bed.

He heaved himself up; swayed on his feet a moment with Carroll's arm supporting him, and caught his breath as pain stabbed through his lower belly and groin. He felt his knees tremble, but they did not collapse. He took a tentative step, and then another. His numb arms twitched as he fought for balance.

"I can walk," he said, after a moment. "I don't know if I can run, and I'm sure I cannot dance, but I can walk." Carroll took his arm away and stepped back. Ingulf took another step, and then another. The trembling stopped, but pain continued.

"That is good," said Carroll, after a moment. "If I had to carry you, any fool could guess who we were. This gives us a better chance to reach the docks. Here, put this on." He held out a rough-woven pale brown tunic, then grunted as Ingulf looked at it helplessly. He lifted Ingulf's arms one at a time, and slid the sleeves over them, then pushed the thing over the Islander's head.

"This is a slave garment," said Carroll. "Walk a little behind me, as if you did not know me, and pretend that you do not, and—perhaps—they will think you just another slave, and me just one more soldier. For a time, at least." He loosened his sword in its scabbard, and then picked up a new, undamaged shield he had found somewhere, and strapped it across his back. Ingulf saw that his armor was cleaner, and the blood gone from the shoulder.

"Here, drink this." Carroll lifted a skin to Ingulf's lips, and Ingulf swallowed. Wine stung his sore mouth and throat. Then Carroll held bread and cheese to Ingulf's mouth, while the Islander bit and chewed.

Then they went out, through the long corridor, to emerge at last at an archway that looked out at the rainbow sunset. The street was nearly deserted.

Carroll waited until he was sure no one was watching, then told Ingulf to go ahead, and wait across the street.

Ingulf walked out boldly enough, but fear tore at him.

Several minutes passed before Carroll slid from the building, and then swaggered out into the street, and went walking down the middle as though he owned it.

Ingulf watched the slaves sweeping, down the street, and tried to imitate their stooping walk as he followed Carroll.

The rainbow sunset faded: dusk deepened around them. They followed winding, cobbled roads that led to the west,

with Carroll swaggering boldly down the street, while Ingulf
followed, slouching furtively near the walls of the buildings.

Dusk deepened: stars slowly burned through the dome of the
sky.

Then the sound they had been dreading, a wolf's high howl,
with a faintly maniacal human note blended into it. Carroll said
nothing but increased his pace, while Ingulf lurched behind as
best he could.

Twice Carroll had to stop and wait for the Islander. A wet
wind from the river blew in their faces.

There was a sudden, rapid patter of paws behind, and Ingulf,
turning, saw a massive black shape rushing straight toward
him.

He shrank back against the wall, as the other slaves were
doing all down the street, but Carroll whirled, and the flaming
blade flashed clear.

As the sunset died, two sleek shapes slid from the river.

"This water's foul, and the air is worse!" Airellen shivered.
"Sure a curse must lie on all this land of Sarlow! How can these
mortal men live so?"

"Listen!" Swanwhite hissed. "Hear that wail—that werewolf howl? And I hear mail jingling: soldiers running through
the town, hurrying to hunt Ingulf down."

They both had changed to human shape: weaving illusion
into a cape of river-mist around themselves, the two darted into
darkness.

Shouts rose as Carroll's sword flared. The werewolf's claws
clicked on the cobbles as it tried to brake its charge. The bright
blade whirled out, a wheel of glittering need-fire, and the
wolf's head flew from its body, changing as it bounced on the
cobbles.

But growls and shouts sounded further up the street.
Looking up, they saw mailed men charging, swords drawn,
and black shapes bounding.

"Run, Ingulf!" Carroll shouted. "Toward the river! That
way! I'll follow!"

Ingulf hesitated, useless arms twitching, then turned and lurched away.

Through narrowing streets he ran, the wet wind of the river in his face. The houses grew shabbier around him: the cobbles sank into mud.

Behind him, he heard the click of claws, and the hoarse breathing of a running beast. A glance over his shoulder showed him great red eyes glowing in the dark.

He was back in his dream, and in one of the tumbledown shacks ahead, Airellen waited. . . .

But which one, *which one?* His need for her was a sudden madness that far outweighed any fear of the hungry beast behind him. . . .

Was that it? Surely, that was the shack before him now! He ran toward it, hearing the feet of the beast racing at his heels.

His limp arms flailed. His numb hands would not close on the latch string. Then his fingers slipped into a crack, and he tore at the frail door. A leather thong broke: he pulled the rickety thing toward him and dashed through into the darkness beyond. . . .

Where was she? He felt dry earth under his naked, aching feet. His eyes saw only darkness. He smelled dust and mold. Was it the wrong shack, after all? Where was she? Where *was* she?

"*Airellen!*" He screamed, as the frail planks behind him shuddered as the werewolf's weight crashed against them. "*Airellen! Help me! Help me now!*"

She heard her name, and turned, to see a black-furred ravening beast clawing at frail planks of rotting wood, and from behind them the voice still called—*his* voice. . . .

The mist that cloaked her reached to blind the fire-red eyes, and from her mind illusion flowed, a spell to draw back the beast.

It ceased to claw the rotting boards, and whirled.

She knew only then that this was no true beast that her gentle spells could tame.

Its blood-mad mind seared hers like flame. She shrank from it, clasping mist tight around her. But now the wet wind from the river took her scent to the thing's nose, the scent of sweet Elf-flesh, and she sensed the sudden flare of hunger as it charged, dull mortal meats forgotten.

Then Swanwhite blurred away from her side, and the beast swerved to follow.

It was quick, but not so quick as the Elves. . . .

"Into the river!" Swanwhite called.

Then Airellen knew what she must do. Casting aside the mist that hid her, she sprang after the wolf in a blur of Elvish speed, and seized its tail.

She let go and sprang away, as the thing whirled to bite. Swanwhite wrapped herself in shadow.

Airellen whirled back toward the riverbank, the raging black beast close behind. . . .

It swerved as Swanwhite appeared again, and Airellen spun river mist and the smells of the wharf, to hide her scent, around her as she whirled aside.

The beast was fast: its teeth snapping within inches of Swanwhite's bare flesh. Again Airellen leaped out of the mist, on the creature's far side, and shouted, as mist swirled around Swanwhite. The baffled beast snarled and sprang, and she flitted back before it. Men in armor were shouting and running somewhere up the street, but she could pay them no heed: she was right at the bank, and dared not slow, but must dance over the slippery mud and down into the water.

Mist wreathed the river, and she could vanish at any time, but where was Swanwhite? Water splashed over her as the bounding beast gained.

She drew her hand back, and teeth clicked where it had been. Another great bound, and she had to twist her body back, as the fangs closed inches from her breast. She threw herself back into deeper water, and the beast paused, poised to swim after her. . . .

A white seal materialized out of the mist and hurled itself on the werewolf's back, driving it into the deeper water.

It tried to turn, but then a second seal reared up and gripped the wolf's throat, and all three vanished under the waters of the river.

* * *

"Trapped!" Ingulf wailed, *"Tricked and trapped! My love, oh my love, where are you? Why are you not here? Why are you not with me? Airellen, Airellen, come back to me! Come back to me!"*

"Ingulf!" Carroll's voice shouted, and then the scarred door was pulled back. "Stop your whining! Get up and *run!"*

"Why will you not leave me alone?" Ingulf raged. "She is lost here somewhere! I must find her—"

"Loon!" Carroll snarled. *"They'll* find *you*, if you don't hurry!" He seized Ingulf's helpless, twitching arm, and dragged him to his feet. "Why do I bother? You crazy fool! I should have left you hanging! If they weren't so cruel, I'd leave you alone, as you ask me to, and race myself back over the mountains!"

He dragged the helpless madman into the street. Bodies were strewn about. White mist was rising from the river.

"Let me go!" cried Ingulf. "She is always here, in this dream, in one of these huts! I fear for her, Carroll! I must find her! Please let me go to find her!"

"Loon, Loon!" Carroll shook him. "You'll not find her here! She's far in the ocean! You told me that yourself!"

"But what is it, then?" Ingulf whimpered. "Is it some illusion of the Elves that made me dream that she was here? Oh, let me go! I need her so!"

"It was only illusion," said Carroll. Ingulf quieted. "Whether of the Elves or of your own mad mind," Carroll muttered, "I cannot say."

"It was all a trick, then?" asked Ingulf. "Oh, evil Elves! What have I done, that such a fate is laid on me? That I should dream my love was here, and she out swimming the northern sea?"

"Will you not hush your raving?" whispered Carroll. "Even now, the werewolves are hunting. I must steal a boat, for crossing the river. Hush now, Ingulf. This fog will give us cover."

Ingulf quieted, and in the silence they could hear the shouting of the men who ran to and fro, searching for them.

In the mist, distant torch-flames were dim flashes of red. A werewolf howled, somewhere far off in the night. Ingulf ceased his weak struggles, but Carroll kept a hand on his arm as they moved toward the river.

But he released him at the water's edge, and throwing down his helmet and hacked shield, he unbuckled his sword-belt, and then bent to let the mail-shirt roll off, and then kicked off the boots and breeches before buckling the sword-belt over the pale brown tunic he wore underneath.

"Accursed things!" he said, casting the breeches into the water, and the helm and mail-shirt after them. "Accursed cowards! What kind of man is so afraid of a sword-edge he must weight himself down with iron? What kind of man would tie up his legs so? I hope I never have to wear such things again! But now at least I'll be able to swim if the boat turns over!"

They found a small boat tied near the end of the wharf, with the oars lying nearby. Carroll had to lift Ingulf in; the Islander's arms would only flail, as though they were made of wood.

The mist grew ever thicker as Carroll rowed across. Ingulf huddled in the bottom of the boat, limp arms hanging and occasionally flopping loosely and aimless.

"Airellen!" he muttered, his face wracked with self-pity. "Airellen, my love! What has brought this evil fate upon me? I am not a wicked man! How can these things be happening to me? Why is the world so cruel?"

Carroll's steady rowing stopped, as he stared in shock at something in the water. Ingulf, looking up, saw him staring and turned, but only saw a brief glimpse of something white that vanished in a swirl of ripples next to the boat.

"What was it, Carroll?"

"I thought I saw—" But then Carroll's eyes fixed on Ingulf's face, and he shook his head. "But that could not have been what I saw. It is too far from the sea."

"What did—?"

"Never you mind what I thought I saw, Loon. It was a white otter, perhaps!" He set to the oars again, and rowed on through ever-thickening mist.

On the shore behind them, dim orange light moved like fireflies in the mist, and the shouts of men and the baying of wolves came across the water.

Lights clustered at the wharf, and then a great cloud of them seemed to swarm onto the water, and there came a sound of oarlocks. Ingulf heard Carroll grit his teeth, then heard his breathing change as he rowed harder.

"Two large boats, at least," he said, "and no telling how many men—or wolves—in each. . . ."

There came a sudden burst of shouts, and a cloud of fireflies reeled and vanished, and screams mingled with the sounds of men and wolves struggling in water. . . .

The second swarm of lights hovered—and then it, too, toppled and was gone.

Carroll cursed as his oars snagged, and then realizing they had touched bottom, and that the keel of the boat was brushing mud, he jumped out and dragged the boat ashore, then helped Ingulf out.

"What was it?" Ingulf asked. "What happened to the evil enemies in the boats behind us? What tipped their boats over?"

"How should I know what monsters lurk in the water of Sarlow?" Carroll snapped. "Some Sorcerer's pet, I expect! Curse this mist! It hides us from our enemies, but it keeps me from knowing where we came ashore. There is grass underfoot, so we must be either at the pastureland or the edge of the fields. I know not whether to go left or right. There is a wooded strip, if we can find it, that will give us some cover, but if we go the wrong way, we'll still be in sight when the dawn comes." He stared about for a moment, and then sighed deeply.

"No help for it! Straight ahead! We've got about thirty miles to cover, and then we get out of the settled areas, and into the forest. Then we have a chance, at least!"

"Shouldn't you push the boat back into the water, and let it drift away?" asked Ingulf, looking back. "Otherwise, in the morning, they'll just come to the boat, and pick up our trail from here."

"Loon," said Carroll, " 'tis a better brain you have this night than my own! I am so tired that your brain is working when mine is not! You are quite right, and I a fool not to have thought of it! My thanks!"

Turning, he dragged the boat out into the water, pushing it out where the current would take it.

Ingulf, watching, saw the boat vanish in the mist as Carroll splashed back to his side.

"It's a long walk ahead of us," said Carroll. "We'd best start now."

"Hush!" said Ingulf, listening.

It was a faint music that he heard, summoning, compelling. . . .

He felt strength sweep through his weary body, and pain vanish, even from his arms.

The mist was shot with mysterious flecks of mystic golden light, and shimmering somewhere beyond was all the beauty and wonder of the world. . . .

"Airellen!" he cried. *"I am coming to you! Ah, wait for me now!"*

For now he heard *her* voice, sweet and high as some distant bird, while other birds' songs wove in chorus behind her. . . .

> *Ohone-a-ro!*
> *Where will you go?*
> *Why do mortals struggle so in vain?*
> *Why is their world so filled with hate and pain?*
> *Sorrow and strife?*
> *This mortal life?*

He heard Carroll shout his name, but he was past caring. He broke into a run, toward the golden track he glimpsed—so dim in the mist—toward *her* voice, and its promised joys. . . .

> *Let these horrors vanish from your mind!*
> *Leave war and hate and torture far behind!*
> *Run with me now!*
> *Run with me now!*

He ran through glowing mist; through golden light. Behind, hunters' voices faded in the night. Carroll ran by his side.

> *Let your sorrows fade; your terrors fly!*
> *Run with me: forget that you must die!*

Come, Mortal Boy!
Live now in joy!

Ingulf's feet were driving up and down: air hissing through
his lungs was sweet as wine. The mist rushed by and vanished:
overhead, bright stars and moons were gleaming. Trees rushed
past, and vanished behind, lost in a blur.

Leave victory and glory, deeds and fame!
I need no bloodstained tales to know your name!
Leave such things behind:
Gentle be, and kind.

Now the golden track was at his feet. He ran upon it, and
the giddy world whirled, his aching heart a wild rattle of
drums. . . .

"Swanwhite, stop! Swanwhite! Take off the spell!"
"Why? Here their enemies can still reach them! If they run
all the way to the mountains, they will be safe."
"If they run all the way to the mountains, they will be dead!
Dorialith told me! Take it off now!"

They ran in a dizzying whirl, the golden track beneath them
flowing under their feet, wild exaltation filling them, telling
them to run on! On!

Glory throbbed through them, higher and higher—brighter
and brighter. They were dimly aware of others that ran with
them in the night.

Suddenly, the golden glory vanished, and they reeled, hearts
pounding, muscles aching, lungs empty. . . .

Carroll and Ingulf fell together to the ground.

"Ingulf!" a high voice wailed, but he did not hear it. Airellen
raced out of the night to kneel beside him. "You've killed him!
Swanwhite—" She was still a moment, then straightened.
"No! He lives! But—so weak!"

"I was only trying to help," said Swanwhite, then, cruelly,
"and I thought you were waiting for him to die?"

"I—" Her head dropped to Ingulf's breast and she wept.
Swanwhite knelt beside Carroll.

"This one, too," she said. "But what happened to them? We lent them strength, and—"

"I do not understand it myself, Swanwhite," said Airellen, her long dark hair still hiding Ingulf's face and hers. "I only know what Dorialith told me. I have never known any other mortal. But Dorialith warned me. Our spells can only give a semblance of strength to mortals, and they will use all their own strength as well as what we give them. Then, when the spell is taken off . . ." She gestured, eloquently, at the two still forms. "If we had run them much further—even a third as far as you planned—then when the spell came off, they would have dropped down dead."

"Well, don't blame me! I didn't know! I never even saw but one mortal before in my life! Up close, at any rate. Well, they should be safe enough for the night."

"Who is this other one, Swanwhite?"

"No knowing in me, but I saw him once, in a werewolf's mind. He bears an Elf-sword—perhaps even one of the great Swords of Power. Except for that, I know no more than you." She studied him a moment. "But I think it is due to him that we did not have to steal your lover out of the dungeons—"

"He is *not* my lover!"

"Is he not? Well, have it your way, then. Whatever he is, this man freed him."

VII

Heart's Desire

EVERY MUSCLE ACHED in Ingulf's body, and he lay still, eyes tightly shut, waiting for them to come and begin the day's torture.

It had all been a dream, then . . .

A bird called softly nearby.

Another answered, closer. And then another, further off.

And in the distance was a constant twittering and chattering . . .

He opened his eyes to green grass-blades, and tried to roll over.

Sharp pains in his shoulders were at first the only response: his arms were still dead. After a while he managed to kick one leg over the other, to twist his hips around, and flop slowly, agonizingly, over onto his back . . .

He found himself staring up into leaves. Tall tree-trunks reared up all around him, black and brown and gray, reddened by the dawn suns' light, their branches swaying gently in the sweet dawn wind.

Carroll lay huddled a little way off, face down, bare legs drawn up as though running.

"Carroll?" Ingulf croaked, his throat dry and sore.

The big man roused, and slowly lifted himself on hands and knees, shaking his head groggily.

At last he sat up, and blinked at the forest around him.

"Where are we?" he rasped, and then broke into a fit of coughing.

"No knowing," said Ingulf. "I never know where I'm going to wake up next."

"We must have blundered into the wooded strip after all," Carroll muttered, shaking his head. "With that mist, it was—" He coughed again, and shook his head. "I hope we find water soon. What a thirst is on me! But we will have to be careful. This strip of woods is narrow, and they'll be looking for us by now."

He rose slowly, grunting, and when he stood at last he was bent, and walked stiffly, like an old man.

"It's sick I am, surely," he said at last. "Every muscle and joint in me is as sore as though pins had been driven in them, and my throat feels as though I had been breathing fire." He limped over to Ingulf, and stooped to lift him. "And my feet! It's raw they are! Well, I did a powerful lot of running and fighting last night." He rubbed his eyes. "I don't remember lying down to sleep at all—only wild dreams . . ."

"How do you know they were dreams?"

Carroll laughed.

"Poor Loon!" He chuckled. "It must be hard for *you* to know the difference. But indeed, the dreams I had were not so strange, when I think on it, since for the most part, I dreamed of running."

He lifted Ingulf carefully in his arms, and heaved him to his feet, and then stood, breathing heavily.

"It's sick I am, indeed," he said at last. He looked for the rising suns between the trees, then turned around. "West must be that way." He pointed. "Let us go! I hope there is water ahead."

Away from the men's sight, bare flesh went drifting between the trees.

Swanwhite stood on a swaying branch, gazing in raptured

wonder and delight across the broad mystery of the forest. The miles of trees rippled. Airellen dropped to the ground and gathered dry leaves.

"Whatever are you doing now?" Swanwhite asked.

"Weaving myself a dress," Airellen said, her magic turning the separate leaves into brown cloth. "Why do you not do likewise?"

"I'm not cold!" Swanwhite laughed, then sprang to the topmost branches.

Wooded hills stretched away all around them, the beauty and the mystery of the solemn oaks, cedars, pines, and spruce, mile after mile of waving emerald treetops. Birds were everywhere. Wind shouted through the tallest trees, and tossed leaves and boughs up and down.

Airellen danced into deep shade. Thick, leaf-colored light delighted her, here where the forest roof stained the sunlight like the green light undersea.

The forest was the more ancient part of her heritage: long before her people had turned to sea and beach, they had dwelt in deep woodlands. Now she felt the trees call to her blood, as she turned again to the weaving of a spell of bright soft cloth, the needle of her mind threading leaves together, binding the leaf of an autumn red to that grown golden-pale before it fell, weaving the two, combined with the seal-magic of her rich brown hair, into a long gown.

"Now what do you want of a long dress like that?" Swanwhite's voice demanded from the branches overhead. "Will you not be forever tripping over the skirt of it?"

"I will not!" Airellen laughed. "If you wore clothes more often, you'd know how to manage them!"

"I wear them too much of the time as it is!" the other retorted.

Airellen said nothing more, but listened to the forest around her as the birds sang and the brush rustled. No beast moved in the forest but her keen Elf ears heard: the breeze brought her myriad scents of animals strange to her.

Something slid soundlessly through a thicket near where

Airellen sat. The wind blew away from her all but a faint hint of a sharp scent.

Onto the sun-gilded grass of a tiny meadow a rabbit came, to nibble the soft petals of flowers.

Airellen shivered.

A fox leaped from leaves in a flash of red fur.

Quick jaws snapped. The rabbit squeaked. Blood smeared the long muzzle.

Then the fox was trotting away, the limp little body dangling from its jaws, and Airellen was crying. Swanwhite, dropping from the trees, stared at her.

"What is it? asked Swanwhite, after a moment.

"That—wolf—wolf-man—whatever it was that we drowned," said Airellen. "It—struggled so, and then it was only a—a Mortal Man—after—at the end, and his lungs full of water . . ." Death was not part of her people's heritage; but part of a cruel world she had always tried to avoid.

"At least Ingulf is—alive!"

There were birds everywhere. The trees were filled with rustles and chirping. Strange bird-calls that Ingulf had never heard before sounded among the endless trees.

As they went on, Carroll, gazing about him, began to frown. The ground was rising before them to a little hill, and at the top they turned, and looked about them.

In every direction, treetops hid the land. Carroll shaded his eyes, and peered under the rising suns.

"Strange," he muttered at last. "We should still be able to see the river and city from here."

Ingulf stared out across the mysterious forest's roof, and listened to the constant calling of the birds. Squirrels in the trees below them swarmed through the branches, red against the green.

West of them, where birds circled against the distant rising and falling splendor of the forest, a blue line of hills hung, far away above the green, wind-tossed roof.

"There are the mountains of Drumairod. Once we cross them, we're in Galinor, and safe." He looked north and south, and then back to the east.

"It makes no sense!" exploded Carroll suddenly. "How could we have got so deep in the forest so quickly?"

"It is some illusion of the Elves," answered Ingulf calmly. "Every time I go to sleep, now, the evil creatures change the whole world around before I wake!"

"There are no Elves *here*, you loon!" Carroll snorted, and turning, limped angrily away toward the west.

Hidden in the branches of a nearby tree, Airellen watched him go.

On a branch beside her a cardinal sang to his mate.

The vast numbers of the birds here delighted her: she loved birds, and wanted to make friends with every one. When she left that tree, and sprang to another, following the two men as they staggered wearily down the hill, the cardinals followed.

Here another bird flew bristling at the intruders, but a soft, near-inaudible call and stroking thought from the Elf-Woman soothed him, and when she moved again, he too followed.

As the day wore on, and Airellen moved from tree to tree, she met and tamed more and more birds, until she moved in the center of a twittering cloud.

Laughing, Swanwhite joined her.

"You will have every bird in the forest in the same tree," Swanwhite teased, "if you keep this up! And *you* were the one who did not want them to see you!"

Airellen blushed.

All around, flocks of birds called. Below, the two men slowly hobbled along. Carroll had cut a staff to lean on, but Ingulf, arms still numb, could only totter along on aching feet, and Carroll had to stop often to let him rest.

"The birds will help hide me."

"Indeed!" Swanwhite laughed. "And it will never occur to them to wonder why this growing flock of birds follows them everywhere they go? Well, now! But while you have been gathering birds, I have found water for our thirsting friends— or will you be telling me that they are not our friends, either? Whatever they are, I've found water, and a place where they can lie up and rest, and even find food. Now, how are we to get them to change direction to keep them from blundering past it?"

For answer, Airellen sent a dozen songbirds whirring down in a line across Ingulf's path.

He reeled and almost fell as beating wings thrashed the air beside his ears, and brightly colored shapes darted across his sight.

"Evil creatures!" he wailed. *"Why are you doing this? What are the evil animals doing to me now?"* His arms flopped clumsily at his sides as he tried to raise them to ward the hurtling birds off. He stumbled into Carroll's arms.

"That *is* strange," said Carroll, watching the birds flashing by. "I have never seen birds of so many different kinds flying together—except once," he added thoughtfully, "near an Elfmound."

If he heard Swanwhite's merry laugh, he thought it but a bird-call.

"Indeed, Airellen!" she laughed. "Off to the left indeed! Herd the heroes with birds! Turn them, curve their path south, and they'll stumble into the stream."

Eyes lit with mischief watched from the leaves as Ingulf steadied and stepped away from Carroll. . . .

"What are they doing to us now?" He whined, pettishly, as another flight of birds skimmed past his head. He staggered to the left. Carroll's staff lashed out as feathered shapes flew across his path.

"Why will they not leave me alone?" Ingulf began to run, useless arms flapping helplessly as he tried to lift them. *"Why are the evil murdering animals doing this to me?"*

Birds swirling around him, he blundered down the hill, and tripped over a tree-root. He fell, and the birds whirled away and flapped into the trees.

Silent as a ghost, Airellen swung into the branches above him as Carroll came running up.

"This makes no sense!" Ingulf whined shrilly. *"The evil animals! Why will they not leave me alone? I do not understand!"*

"I do not understand either," said Carroll, kneeling beside him, "but they have stopped now."

He lifted Ingulf to his feet, and they stumbled on together down to the hill, while the branches above them rustled with birds.

Carroll stopped. A broad beam of sunlight slanted across their path, red-gold in the green gloom, pouring down from a gap between the trees off to their right.

"We're going the wrong way," he said. "We should keep the sunlight in our faces."

He stepped into the sunbeam, and started to lead Ingulf toward the glare of the westering suns—and suddenly ducked and dodged as wings whirred past his head.

Ingulf, too, staggered aside, wings fanning his face.

"Why are they doing this?" he shrieked. "The evil things! Are they trying to drive me insane? Why are they trying to drive me insane?"

"We are being herded," snarled Carroll, glaring at the green around them. "Driven like cattle! But why— *hush! Listen!*"

He stood still, and Ingulf—and even the birds—quieted.

"Is it water that I hear?" Ingulf asked, after a moment.

"It might be," said Carroll, "or it could be the wind."

They followed the sound south, hurrying now despite aching muscles and feet, while above them ghostly presences followed, through branches that trembled with chattering flocks of birds.

The faint murmur swelled, and soon, even over the twitter of the birds, they recognized the sound of swift-moving water rushing over stones.

They pushed their way through thickening underbrush, and then they were reeling down a low bank, at the bottom of which a little brook purled noisily in its dark bed, and the two threw themselves down at the stream's edge, gulping sweet cold water.

In the branches above the stream, Airellen sat surrounded by her birds.

Below her, the thirsty men were drinking and drinking; farther down the stream, she heard the shrieks of an unwary muskrat as it was torn by the fangs of a mink.

Far off yet, but drawing closer, she could sense the hunters who sought the men below.

This was a cruel world, and Ingulf was part of it.

Even though she saved him from the soldiers who marched behind, he must die at last, and nothing she could do would save him.

She saw the other, Carroll, rising from the stream, and watched as he lifted his injured friend, gentle as a mother.

Then, standing again, Carroll looked up and down the long tunnel of brush-fringed gully through which the stream flowed.

"It curves away," he said at last. "If we'd held to our course, we'd never have heard this stream, much less seen it. If it had not been for . . ."

He did not finish the thought, but instead waded out into the swiftest, deepest water, and then crouched, hands and face close to the water.

It would be dark soon. She sent her birds home, back to the trees from which she had gathered them, and sat lonely and cheerless on the branch.

Swanwhite sprang into the tree beside her, from another tree further down the stream, and was about to speak when Carroll shouted and came dancing out of the water, holding in his hands a large fish that thrashed wildly in its attempt to get away.

"Here's our dinner, Loon!" the big man shouted, joyfully. "Now for a fire!"

He tossed the fish down, well up on the bank, and danced joyfully about as he gathered firewood under the trees. Ingulf sat up, his arms flopping awkwardly as he struggled to rise and help.

From the tree the two Sea-Elves watched the fish beat its head and tail against the bank in pain.

In the emptiness his life had become, Vildern found little satisfaction in the command of Klufbirk.

He never allowed himself to take out his rage and pain on his men, as another commander might have, nor did he allow his numbness to keep him from his duties, and discipline never lapsed. Indeed, discipline improved: the men somehow sensed the difference in him, and it frightened them. They became very quiet, alert as he had never seen them.

He vacillated between regret that he had killed the witch-wolf, and regret that he had failed to kill her sooner, before she had put her spell on him. She haunted his dreams and intruded into his work. He would find himself thinking of her instead of the fort's business when he sat down to check the records of the fort.

And it was her he was thinking of when Kelldule came bursting in.

Vildern turned to fix the invader with a stare; then, as he saw who it was, began to kneel, but Kelldule forestalled him with a wave of his hand.

"No time for that," the Sorcerer said. "Yotnir himself has summoned me to Kunzig. Your prisoner has been rescued from Svaran—by Elf-magic, they think. A man with a fire-sword was somehow brought into the dungeon while the prisoner was being questioned. He killed five men, fought Grom Beardless and Black Svaran together and defeated both—"

"No!" exclaimed Vildern, shocked suddenly out of the numbness which had gripped him since the wolf-girl's death. Grom's face filled his mind. *"Grom? Dead?"*

"What?" Kelldule blinked. "No, no Grom's not dead, but badly wounded, and Svaran's hand is broken—even that armor has its limits!" He chuckled, shaking his head.

"All the prisoners were turned loose, though most were caught very quickly. But the Islander disappeared. The guards at the gate were killed, and several werewolves, and the night after, two boats on the river were overturned by seals. . . ."

"Seals? That far upstream?"

"Yes, seals. And it is in the form of seals that the Sea-Elves go abroad. And there are subtler things that suggest Elves. Old Yotnir himself has asked me to join the hunt. I leave tonight, downriver. And there is no one but yourself that I would ask to go with me."

Even though common sense assured Vildern that this outland Sorcerer must be trying to trick him into something, such trust touched him. It was too bad men could never trust each other. . . .

Then he remembered the sudden suspicion with which Grom had turned on him. Suspicion was not always deserved, he knew. . . .

He thought of the violence of his reaction to Grom's death; his relief at learning it was not true. Fears stirred inside him. That was another barrier the priests had reared between men. . . .

No sin was more speedily or horribly punished than desiring another man: it was said that such men were really women shape-changed.

Yet, while mourning the woman he had murdered, it had occurred to Vildern that if she had not been a woman, an incomprehensibly alien creature, whose thought processes were inherently unknowable, he could have been happy.

There were old stories, he remembered, that had been forbidden by the priests, and he wondered if that was why. For by driving barriers between men, the army was weakened, and the power of the Council increased.

"I do not know what help I can be to you," said Vildern, "but I will go."

After two days' rest beside the stream, Ingulf was able to move his arms, although they still felt as though they were made of wood, and the hands at the end of them were still lumps of limp flesh, which he could neither feel nor move. But he could now push himself awkwardly up from the ground, and if he was careful, he could press the numb things at the ends of his arms together to hold things between them, like a squirrel, which meant he could feed himself after a fashion, and no longer had to have Carroll lift every morsel to his mouth.

Carroll now was almost completely recovered, though many muscles still ached. On the third day they broke camp and began to follow the stream west, toward the half-seen mountains.

Ingulf could feel some ghostly presence that followed them through the mysterious forest, and he knew that, although the big man would never admit it, Carroll felt it too.

As they walked, Carroll, trying to ignore the unusual flocks of birds that gathered about them, told tales about the life he had led after his escape from Sarlow, and of his wanderings in the Three Kingdoms, as well as in the Forest of Demons.

He told Ingulf of the Seynyorean Sword-Master he had studied under at the Court of the Two Kings of Galinor, and of the day the Immortal King had chosen to join them in their practice.

He told of the Battle of Girt Fulluv, where the army of the King of Elantir had been annihilated by a horde of savage raiders from out of the Forest of Demons, and how at the end of that long day, only the King's Champion of Elantir had stood alive beside Carroll, and two of them had fought shoulder to shoulder against more than a dozen of the raiders, and slain them all.

He told of ambush and foray in the forests along the Sarlow frontier, and Ingulf in his turn, told of sea-battles in which he had fought in the Eastern Isles, when the fleets came down from Noria, raiding the Airarians for slaves and loot, or sometimes the galleys of Sarlow came.

So the day passed. They covered many miles, while the bird flocks followed them through the forest—thrushes, robins, wrens—and some unknown presence haunted the trees just behind them.

Ingulf tired quickly, and they had to stop often to rest. At last Carroll knocked over a duck with a stone, in an area where the brook widened out, and as he went about gathering wood, Ingulf rose and helped him, lifting sticks by pressing them between his hands, and sometimes his wrists. He could only carry a stick or two at a time, and after he had clumsily carried seven or eight to add to the pile Carroll had amassed, Carroll stopped him, with a startled look at his face, and seized his hand: Ingulf saw that it was running blood.

Holding them up, he saw that both hands were covered with cuts and scratches that he had been unable to feel.

Cursing, he washed his cut hands in the stream while Carroll built the fire.

"I talked to a man who had been tortured much as you have," Carroll said at last, as they ate the duck. "He said it was—what? Five, perhaps six months before he was able to feel anything with his fingers. I think he said it was three or four weeks before he was able to grip with his hands, before he could hold a knife, say, or even a piece of bread."

"Six months," said Ingulf dully, staring at the limp curled fingers. "Months! Ah, it is a curse that is on me! Ah, why did you drag me back from the sea, oh seals?"

There was a sound in the leaves, as of a disturbed bird.

"Well, it's alive you are, at least," Carroll demurred, "and it is worse things they would have done to you. And it was only by great luck that I was able to reach you at all. If I had doubted that—dream, or whatever it was— "

"What are you babbling about now?" snapped Ingulf.

"Ah, I forgot, I'd not told you!" exclaimed Carroll. "I told you about the fight with the werewolves, and that Torvar had your sword—"

"Aye, I remember that much."

"And do you remember my telling you that we found your robe all bloody, near the body of the man who'd carried you? Well, I despaired then. I was sure you were dead, and so were Rakmir and all the rest. So I guided them back to the pass, to the Cave of Garinvel, and there we lay down to sleep. . . .

"I slept—I *think* I slept. For sure I dreamed. But I might have been awake when I dreamed. I saw—or I dreamed that I saw—a ghost—a vision, perhaps—of an old, white-bearded man—but the face above the beard was lineless, young—like a young girl's face!"

"Dorialith!" Ingulf exclaimed.

"And the dream screamed like a sea-gull, crying, *"What? Will the men Ingulf saved from the slave-pits abandon him now, and he being tortured by the men of Sarlow?"*

"And everyone leaped up in terror, shouting, and Torvar louder than any, shouting that he had tried to save you, but now you were dead, you were dead!"

"But Ingulf is alive, that bearded ghost said, *nor will his captors kill him soon. For they cannot dream that a man could come alone on such a mission, and they think there must be a secret army gathered to seek their destruction. And if now you strike against them, then they will be still more certain. In this lies his only safety.*

"Now I had drawn my sword when the—old man— appeared. He turned now to me. *So it is you that Swanwhite saw,* he said, and don't ask me what he meant by it. *Is that the Sword of Eruir, or the Sword of Kenual*? And I stuttered at him, amazed. *It is partly because of you, too, that Ingulf is alive! If you act swiftly you can save him yet!* he said, *And I will be there to help you as swiftly as I may*— and then, quite suddenly, there was no one there at all.

"And then the two children were pulling at me, and Rakmir was arguing with Torvar, and I was staring at the place where the dream had stood, trying to decide if I was awake or asleep, and if I was awake what had happened.

"The children were dragging at me, and telling me to run and save you. I heard Rakmir shout, 'At least give me the sword,' and Torvar answering it was some kind of a trick, that the Sorcerers were trying to separate us, so that the others would be defenseless when the werewolves came. . . ." Carroll shook his head.

"Finally, I went running back with only Rakmir, one other man, and the two children. Torvar led the rest of the slaves on through the pass. I tried to make the little girl go with them, but she wouldn't—she just followed. . . ."

He got up and threw more wood on the fire.

"I still don't—" Carroll looked around at the shadows around them, and sat down. He drew the sword from its sheath, and laid it across his lap. The blade reflected the firelight, but there was no hint of need-fire on the blade now.

"It was near dawn of the next day when we came close to Kirgiff. We saw torches on the road from Klufbirk—the fort in the pass. When we came closer I saw that slaves were being brought down from the fort, a long chain of them—I don't think I've ever seen so many. There were whole tribes on that chain. There were only a few men guarding them, but several packs of wolves. And werewolves.

"I charged: I cut the chains. I killed two werewolves, and the rest fled—all the wolves fled. The slaves made short work of the guards who tried to fight. Most of them ran. But among the ones that didn't, there were a couple that were near my size. So—I put on the clothes I was wearing when I found you. I was lucky, I was just in time to get on the boat!" He sighed hoarsely. "There isn't much more to tell, really. You know the rest. Get some sleep. We have more hard walking tomorrow."

In the darkness beyond their fire, Airellen stirred, keen Elvish senses reaching out into the night, testing the wind, listening to faraway howls and the soft sound of the rapidly running paws of werewolves that drew nearer and nearer. . . .

Swanwhite sprang into the tree beside her.

They are coming, she said, silently. *They have found the scent.*

Five of them, answered Airellen. *There are men, too, and common wolves, but they have been left far behind.*

The men will not be here tonight, and it will be easy for us to turn them aside when they come, Swanwhite thought. *It is the werewolves we must fear. This stream is not deep enough to drown them in. I think we should warn Carroll, and let him fight them. He has that sword.*

But Ingulf has no sword, Airellen countered, *and could not use one if he had. And even Carroll does not have his strength back. We must draw them away! How can we turn them before they come closer?*

We could weave phantoms to run before them, mused Swanwhite, doubtfully, *or we could try to lay a false scent-trail. But it is dangerous. Their senses are as sharp as ours and the magic that is about them is brutal and strong. Werewolves have caught Elves before this, and eaten them.*

Can they climb trees? asked Airellen.

They do not, replied Swanwhite, *but they can jump very high.*

Let us go, then, and lay a false trail for them to follow, said Airellen, *And come back safe through the trees. Come away now, before they come any closer.*

First smell your—smell Ingulf carefully, and then go sniff at his tracks, said Swanwhite, *and fix his scent clearly in your mind. I will do the like for Carroll. But it must be a well-wrought illusion that will fool the nose of a werewolf.*

They breathed deep of the air around the sleeping man, until each of them was sure just what blending of different odors gave each man his distinctive tang.

Then the two swung away through the whispering trees, following the gurgle of the brook until they reached the place where Carroll and Ingulf had come blundering down the bank two days before.

Here they dropped out of the swaying branches, and bent over tracks of the men, to learn how each man's scent wove itself into the mingled odors of the soil and leaves and herbs, to leave a perceptible trail.

We must lay an illusion to hide this track, also, said Airellen.

That will be harder, frowned Swanwhite. Together then the two wove odors to cover the men's spoor, weaving leaf mist and thin and rusty smell of the dry soil and the thicker, richer smell of the wet loam, and blending in the musky scents of beasts and the sweet, subtle aromas of grasses and herbs. . . .

It was a fragile web of illusion at first, but as they neared the spot where Airellen's birds had turned the men from their original path, the charm became surer, more practiced, and it was the scent of undisturbed earth that cut off the men's trail. But a determined nose would still find the true spoor beneath. . . .

Now Airellen began to breathe into the earth the reek of Ingulf's sweat, the savor of his flesh, while beside her Swanwhite scented the soil with the trace of Carroll's feet. . . .

Behind them in the night the distant baying grew.

Bushes and leaves crashed with the passage of fleeing beasts, frightened from hiding by the noise of the nearing wolves.

Airellen and Swanwhite ran west, veering slowly toward the north, carefully hiding their own fragrances as they wove the false trail behind them.

Louder and nearer came the shuddering song of the hunting wolves.

"Swanwhite!" cried Airellen. "Turn off to the north, now, towards the sea. Divide the track and split the pack!"

"Now, what good do you think that will do?" Swanwhite demanded.

"When they turn back to mortals in the morning, they will be that much more alone and lost in the forest."

"I'll lead them into a bear's den!" Swanwhite laughed, and dashed away north, weaving her spell as she ran.

Airellen kept on to the west, listening as she ran. Keen ears told her when the test of her illusion came: when the hunting beasts left the true track for her own. She heard faint, puzzled whines, and poised to run to Ingulf's side.

Eagerly rang the hunting-howl, as hurrying wolves smelled her spell.

She raced away before them, leaving behind, on grass and leaf, the scent of Ingulf's flesh. With Elvish hearing she traced the chase through the forest.

She smiled as she ran when she heard them pause at the place where the scent-trail parted. There was a moment's confusion of whining and sniffing and crashing through the brush; then she heard the howling begin again as half the pack swept up the path to the north in full cry after Carroll's false scent, and the others gave tongue as they followed her.

Ahead she heard in the distance the rhythmic rumble of bullfrogs, and under their throbbing the shrill voices of lesser frogs, and the occasional muted splash of water.

Toward these she made her way, still breathing the scent of Ingulf's feet into the ground as she ran, while behind her the howling and hoarse panting and the drum of loping paws drew steadily nearer.

She hurried on. Ahead, moonlight appeared through a great gap in the forest's roof, and then, at last, she came to the edge of the bog she sought.

Then she was blending Ingulf's musk with odors of mud and reed, laying the trail out into the swamp, sometimes resting his scent on top of the water. A sleepy duck quacked, disturbed; the eerie whinny of a loon shrilled across the water.

She stopped and stepped back, wrapping her own scent tight to her body. Then she sprang lightly into the lowest branches of a nearby pine.

Leaping like a squirrel from branch to branch and tree to tree, she followed the track back into the forest. Before her now the baying swelled.

As it grew loud and close, she paused in the upper branches of a fragrant cedar, and wrapping its perfume around her, waited beside the trail watching a great moonbeam that stabbed slanting down between the wrinkled boles of the towering trees.

She did not have to wait long. The baying echoed all around her, trembling through the treetops; between the howls she heard the harsh breath rasping from the lungs and the crashing of leaves under the rapidly pounding pads; then the shadows under the trees clotted into two black shapes that bounded into the moonbeam, lean and swift and hungry and filled with terrible energy. As they coursed across the wind she caught their scent, a foul, pungent taint unlike that of any natural beast.

They raced the length of the light and were gone, and Airellen threw herself into the next tree and hurtled swiftly through the treetops back along the trail.

At the place where she had parted from Swanwhite, she stopped and sent out a questing thought.

Still far to the north, she touched a twinkle of malicious humor, and knew the white-haired girl was also on her way back.

She dropped from the tree to wait for her.

Barely had she touched the ground when there came a tremendous crashing from a nearby thicket, and she whirled to face fiery eyes and dripping fangs.

She sprang back into the branches, but the bounding black shape sprang into the air after her, and its snapping jaw ripped away part of the skirt next to her thigh, and then she was pulling herself up into the branches, and the black shape was falling back to the ground, with the brown cloth changing to dry leaves in its mouth.

It leaped up from the ground again, and as she sprang away, the great black body crashed across the branch where she had stood a moment before.

Whirling vision-blurring magic about her, she sprang to another tree—but looking down she saw the lean black shape rush across the ground between the trees, and then it was in the air, leaping toward the very branch on which she stood.

She sprang to a higher branch, and the dull claws scrabbled at the bark where she had stood. . . .

She stared as it clung awkwardly to the branch, hind legs and tail beating at the air, while the wood lashed violently under its weight.

Then one hind paw found purchase on the bark, and then the other, and the wolf drew itself up and launched itself toward her.

She whirled away in a magic mist, into another tree, and teeth clicked where she had stood. Claws scrabbled on bark and as she caught her balance on her new perch, the heavy body went crashing down through the leaves and hit the ground with a sound of snapping bones.

Even as she drew breath it rolled up, broken bones healing, and came after her again.

She left an illusion of herself in the tree as she sprang away, and saw the long fangs tear at the ghostly throat. . . .

Then the beast fell to the ground again, whirling and sniffing, and she realized that in her terror she had only thought of visual illusions, and it was following her by scent and sound. . . .

Already it was lunging up the tree trunk after her, and even as she wrapped leaf-scent around herself and leaped, its breath warmed her flesh as the fangs snapped, and the sudden surge of fear made her twist in the air, and she missed the branch she had leaped for.

She fell sprawling in a pile of crackling leaves, and as she rolled up the wereworlf was already rising above her, great jaws gaping.

A swift ripple of silken dark hair wrapped seal-skin around her in a rapid shift of shape, and the wolf's keen fangs slashed thick fat-backed hide.

The fangs barely pierced, but she felt the fierce venom of the werewolf's curse pour raging and burning into the wound, even as her own sharp teeth ripped away an ear and tore a great gash in its scalp.

The wolf sprang back in surprise, shaking the blood from its eyes, staring at the seal.

Must she kill the thing? she wondered in terror. Death was not part of her people's heritage: always she had tried to avoid it. . . .

It leaped in, slashing at her throat. She twisted, so its tusks only slashed the thick skin on her shoulder. Her own snapping teeth met empty air as the wolf sprang back out of range.

On land her seal-form was little use. As the beast poised to spring again, she writhed aside, shifted, and leaped to her feet, dancing easily aside from its charge.

A snarl like a low chuckle oozed out of the werewolf's throat.

Her wounds healed as she shifted, but she felt her hair sticky with blood, and felt the werewolf-spell raging murderously in her veins.

It leaped again, but now that she had tasted the spell by which it lived, she met it with a blur of magic.

The wolf stumbled, balance lost as bones and flesh rippled and changed.

It reared awkwardly on its hind legs, and a whimper broke from its throat as its skeleton reverted to human form.

And as it stood swaying in the darkness, its fur fading, sinking back into its skin, Airellen, tasting the curse that coursed through her blood, shifted herself into wolf-form.

The man before her screamed, and staggered back, reeling.

Airellen shifted back to her own form with a fastidious shudder and, masking herself with a simple illusion, melted ghostlike into the leaves.

She sped quickly away through gray night. Her counterspell would not hold long: soon the man would be back in wolf-shape, as dangerous as before, and by then she wanted to be well away.

Where was Swanwhite? The merest touch of the fires of Tirorilorn would burn the curse from her; she felt it as a battle in her blood, between dark flecks of raging evil like tiny night-things, that fought bright, immortal cells like stars.

The taste of the werewolf-spell sickened her, as her own shifting-magic fought it off. Yet she was glad to have learned the wolf-shape: her seal-form was useless in these woods, and once the spell's madness and poison were burned from her. . . .

"Cousin?" cried Swanwhite, sailing through the branches to her side. "What has happened? I feared that one of the werewolves had caught you!"

"One did," Airellen said, "and I am bitten."

"Bitten? Let me see!" Swanwhite demanded, and Airellen, obedient, showed her the gash across her shoulder. "I fear there is poison in it."

"Indeed," said Airellen, "it is a curse that would make a Mortal Man turn into a blood-mad wolf, filled with hunger and with rage. Burn it out of me, Swanwhite."

"What do you mean, burn it out?" snapped Swanwhite. "You mean—with *this*?" She touched the jewel at her throat. Airellen nodded.

"*No!*" Swanwhite exclaimed, her voice shrill but firm. "Why, I'd be as like as not to burn you to a cinder! I am not my grandfather! What do you think this is? Would you have me sew a seam with a spear? Would you ask me to part your hair with an axe?"

"Tell me, then, what other choice I have, Swanwhite! Thrust your mind into my wound: taste the evil that seethes there, and then tell me what I should do. Can you call up the Hasturs to heal me? Or will you counsel that I wait until some other healer can be found?"

"Indeed, that is what you should do!" exclaimed Swanwhite. "Can you not fight it off with your own magic, while we . . . " Her voice softened, and stilled. She touched a finger to the edge of the wound, and her brows knotted.

After a moment, she looked up, and there were tears in her eyes.

"I am sorry!" she sobbed. "I did not understand! Let me think—"

They were still. In the distance, they heard faint, frenzied howling. They heard a crashing in the brush, and another howl nearby, that diminished and faded in the distance. Swanwhite looked up, startled, and for a moment her frown was replaced by a malicious smile.

"What did you do?" she asked. "Lead them into a bog?" Airellen looked away, then nodded, shyly. Swanwhite laughed.

"I didn't think you had it in you!" Her laughter rang eerily through the branches.

"Nor did I," murmured Airellen, softly.

"Those I led will be on the sea-strand by now," said

Swanwhite. "I think they may well follow the trail right into the cave. They *should* reach the cave before the tide comes in . . ." Another merry laugh trilled, and then she sobered. "Do you think you can drive all of the poison back into the wound? Grandfather would be able to follow it right through your veins, but I cannot."

"I'll—I will try," muttered Airellen, with a quick, jerky nod. She pressed her eyelids tight, and frowned to tighten them more. "Only hurry, please," she whispered timidly. "I cannot bear it longer."

Swanwhite stared up into the shadowy leaves above them, drew a deep breath, then gently gathered up the long dark river of Airellen's hair and lifted it up to fall over the unwounded shoulder and flow down over her breasts to her lap. A touch, and the brown cloth fell to separate leaves again, and dropping from bare flesh went drifting from the tree, spinning in the night breeze as though autumn had come.

Placing a finger on each side of the wound, Swanwhite spread the gash apart. Airellen gasped as the blood flowed.

"That's it!" Swanwhite said. "Herd them all together, gather them in the wound!" The branch swayed slightly as she moved, and lifted the jewel in her hand. "I fear this will hurt," she added. "But it was you who would be insisting."

"I feel—unclean," murmured Airellen.

A needle of light flared from the stone: leaves flashed emerald all around.

With a strangled scream, Airellen thrashed wildly, and would have fallen from her swaying perch had Swanwhite's arm not caught her, and pulled her tight against her breast.

"Is it done?" she cried. "Are you healed?"

"It is done!" Airellen sobbed. "They are gone. I am healed! I am clean! I thank you!" She wept, and Swanwhite wept with her, holding her tight.

"Clean! But I can still take wolf-shape when I want!"

The two sat together weeping in each other's arms on the swaying branch, until dawn turned the moons to gold, and they heard the frantic howls of the trapped werewolves change to the distant shouting of men.

* * *

As the Twin Suns climbed the sky, Carroll and Ingulf slogged west along the brook. Between the leaves they caught occasional glimpses of the jagged mountains ahead. Bird-flocks followed them, chattering and piping mysteriously.

Carroll stopped suddenly, and held out his hand for Ingulf to stop also.

"Listen!" he said. "Is that not wolf-song that I hear?"

Ingulf listened, as well as he might through the whistling and piping of the birds. A jay scolded, and the warbling softened for a moment, and above the muted twittering he heard a distant wail that for a moment he took to be an owl.

Then the hooting shifted pitch, whining away in a dirge, and he nodded, even as his ears picked out another sound mingled with it, a rasping grunt. . . .

"Men's voices as well," he growled.

"I expected the Hounds of Sarlow on our track long before this," said Carroll. "It is good we had these few days to rest."

The distant howling was drowned again as more and more birds came trilling through the wood, to gather in the trees around them, fluting and crooning as though to fly north or south in autumn or in spring. . . .

"Come!" Carroll waded out into the stream. Ingulf followed cautiously, his aching arms outstretched for balance.

As they waded up the stream, there came a loud crashing of brush behind them. They whirled, hearts choking them, but it was not wolves that burst from the bushes, but deer.

As they stared, the deer swung to the right and ran along the riverbank, over the tracks of the men. Carroll's jaw dropped, and he looked as if he were about to speak, but then he shook his head and turned away, and waded on.

More and more birds gathered in the flock about them as the day went on. Ingulf's bare feet turned as numb as his hands in the ice-chill water.

Now and again they could hear above the chatter of the birds the baying and shouting of the hunt behind. But as the day wore on the noise seemed to come more and more from the north, as though the pursuit had missed their track, and passed them by.

But it was chiefly on the north bank that the birds flocked.

Toward sunset the birds scattered, whirring away to roosts in distant parts of the forest.

Even with the coming of darkness Carroll dared not stop, and the two blundered on against the current, while owls haunted the right bank. Far off in the night they could hear the cry of the pack, and knew that werewolves now swelled its ranks.

At last Ingulf's foot slipped on wet rock, and his flailing arms could not keep him from falling. Cold water splashed loudly around him, and then he was holding his breath and trying to find his numb hands, to lift himself out of the cold water, and then Carroll's arms were around him and he was coughing water against Carroll's chest.

"Breathe, Loon! Poor Loon! You must rest! I'm sorry, Loon. . . ." Carroll kept babbling like that as he half-dragged, half-carried Ingulf up to the left bank of the stream. "No food all day, and no fire now. . . ." Ingulf felt himself laid on clammy grass, and shivered with cold.

Then a gradual warmth drifted over him. He still heard Carroll babble, and the brook as well, but he was not sure which was which. . . .

He dreamed that he lay on a plain of ice, with a cold wind blowing over him, freezing his bones and driving spikes of ice into his joints.

And he dreamed that two seals came out of a hole in the ice, a white seal and a black, and one lay down on each side of him, and then they turned into a warming fire. . . .

The dream changed. . . .

Beyond the screening leafy roof, something flew, hunting for him. . . .

Nearer it drew. But it was no bird, nor any other winged creature.

A fat man rode on a staff, as though it were a horse. It looped and turned in the air like a dog hunting, quartering the sky above the trees. . . .

It drew nearer, and now he saw that the face of the crouching figure was familiar, one of the faces that had looked at him during the long nightmare of torture. Familiar, too, was the

voice that seemed to fill all the night with chanted nonsense
words. . . .

Schufaheer, Schufedar. . . .

The bald head was bent down to look from the stick-steed's
side, and Ingulf saw the fringing gray tuft of hair, the merry red
cheeks, and then the twinkling blue eyes met his, and he knew
he had been seen. . . .

Only then was he aware of the woman at his side.

She rose, and it seemed that the light of her presence cast
shadows far across the forest, as though a moon had risen
above Ingulf's shoulder. . . .

But the man on the stick threw his hands in front of his face,
and the stick was suddenly swept away as though by the tide.

Ingulf glimpsed the fat man falling, while the staff was torn
away, swirling round and round as though caught in a great
wind. . . .

Then it seemed that a roof rose to cover him, and he lay as
though in a tunnel under the earth, small and round and safe.

Then it seemed that he waked, and *she* was spreading a
blanket over him, and he snuggled down happily, glad to be
safe back home.

And after that his dreams were only wandering, meaningless
images. . . .

Sunlight woke him, to the frantic chittering of a squirrel. He
lay warm and happy, smelling grass and pine-trees. He opened
his eyes slowly. Over the two of them was spread a warm
blanket of bright rainbow colors.

Blinking, he stared at it. It was thick like wool, and every
color shimmered in it. Where had Carroll gotten it?

He sat up, and reached to take it in his fingers to feel the
weave, forgetting his hands were numb, but at his touch the
cloth dissolved, and fell away into hundreds of separate
feathers.

He sat up, startled fully awake. A tiny breast feather, falling
from his shoulder, drifted to Carroll's nose, and in a moment,
Carroll was sneezing himself awake.

The squirrel's chittering grew louder. A jay dived into the
clearing, shrieking a warning, then whirled and flashed back

across the stream, to where other jays were circling and screaming.

"What the—?" Carroll surged explosively to his feet, scattering down. He stared around. "Feathers?"

"It was—like a blanket when—I woke," said Ingulf, stupidly, then realized that Carroll would not have understood.

Something red dropped suddenly from a tree, and the squirrel raced up to them, chittering madly.

Three jays flashed across the stream, and Carroll ducked as they drove straight for his eyes.

Ingulf laughed as Carroll ducked, and then the squirrel ran in and bit him on the leg.

"Why are you doing this?" Ingulf shrieked. *"Evil little animal! What are you doing to me?"* He leaped to his feet, in a cloud of feathers.

There was a shout from beyond the brook, and a whirring of wings.

"Ingulf!" Carroll shouted. "Run! They are closing in on us!"

"Evil animals!" Ingulf shrieked. *"Why are you destroying me? Leave me alone!"* Carroll seized his shoulder.

"Run!" he shouted, as a flock of birds dived from the trees.

As they staggered aside, sudden mist rose from the stream, but not before they saw a glint of mail among the tossing bushes.

The mist thickened as they ran. But all around they heard a whirring of wings. There was a loud splashing behind them.

Glancing back over his shoulder, Ingulf glimpsed a dim wolf-shadow in the fog, and then it vanished with a startled yelp as birds swept down upon it.

Then, from out of the wood, a herd of deer came milling in panic, and they bounded into the misty wall, and splashing was followed by a wild chorus of curses, yelps, and screams.

They ran on, hearing shouts and curses behind them, while on their right the stream was a solid wall of clammy mist. Deer rushed past them, and foxes, a pair of badgers, and once a bear. The air above them was always filled with birds.

If they slowed, wings fluttered about their heads, and twice beaks pecked Ingulf's hair. Before long, Ingulf could think of nothing but the pounding of his heart, and his fight to pull air into his lungs.

Behind them the racket in the thickets diminished. Birds herded them down a trail away from the water, and badgers and foxes followed.

"Why are the evil animals doing this?" Ingulf sobbed, under his breath. *"Has the world gone mad?"*

"They are helping us!" Carroll gasped, his feet pounding. "Must be—Elves . . ." They ran on, Ingulf reeling and staggering, until the birds let him collapse at last.

Far behind they could still hear occasional shouts, but the sounds were muted by distance. A jay scolded overhead, and then Carroll turned back to Ingulf's side.

"This is madness," Ingulf wheezed, as Carroll lifted him, "or else a nightmare! This cannot be happening!"

"No need to talk like that," gasped Carroll. "'Tis all a simple matter. There are still Elves in these woods, that is all. I thought they had all been driven out, but I was wrong."

"What?" Ingulf started, and looked up, grinning. "Now I know I'm dreaming or mad, or under spells! I thought I heard Carroll Mac Lir say he could be wrong about something!"

"Well—" Carroll seemed at a loss for words. "Why—I had wondered why—why these woods had been left standing, and now—now I know. But before I did not."

Ingulf laughed.

Vildern had only seen old Yotnir, the head of the Council of Sorcerers, once before, and that from a distance. He studied the ancient carefully.

Yotnir's skinny hand gripped his staff with an intensity that showed his age, and his pale blue eyes peered at them carefully. His voice, when he spoke, was shrill and cracked.

"I fear I made you waste your time, Kelldule!" he cackled gleefully. "We may not need you after all. Ramaukin has found them, *and* the elves that guard them. His men should be closing in on them now."

Yotnir sat throned in the midst of a mass of soldiers. Behind him more than a dozen Sorcerers stood against the wall. For all the frailty of his flesh, Vildern sensed a power in the old man, a rage and hunger that made him dangerous.

"Let us all hope Ramaukin is right," Kelldule answered, stroking his pointed beard. "Where were they hiding?"

"They had somehow gotten all the way beyond the Alak, and were following the Dourinvaquil toward the mountains. Does that make you unhappy, Outlander?"

"No," said Kelldule, "but there is a spell at work right here in this room." Startled, Vildern looked at him, saw the narrowed eyes open like sudden blue glass.

Kelldule pointed at one of the men behind the throne.

"Who is that man—?"

Before he could close his mouth the black-robed Sorcerers behind the throne were suddenly thrown about as though by a whirlwind in their midst.

Vildern gripped his sword-hilt and sprang, but before his sword had cleared the scabbard, a great wind met him and hurled him flying to the floor.

He rolled up in time to see the guards at the door blown aside, and the heavy door ripped from its hinges.

"*Fools!*" Kelldule raged. "An Elf was in this chamber, listening to every word! Dorialith himself, more likely than not!"

After Ingulf had rested, the gathering birds herded them on again, and all through the day they were hurried along.

At last the sounds of pursuit faded, far away to their right, and the birds began to scatter to distant roosts for the night. Carroll and Ingulf found a thicket in a hollow fold of a hill, and stopped there to camp.

In the twilight after the Twin Suns fell, Ingulf stood watch while Carroll picked berries and gathered deadwood, in case they should want a fire. Treetops stretched away in the distance, and stirred in the wind like the sea.

Ingulf started. Under the fading shimmer of sunset, an eerie blue flicker appeared.

"Carroll?" he called, straightening. "There is a light ahead in the wood."

Carroll scrambled up the hill to his side. Ingulf pointed with his limp curled fist at the strange glow.

"Surely that is no fire," said Carroll, after a moment. The light was far ahead, but on their line of march, if they continued to follow the stream. "Sorcery, or—"

He stopped, listening, as both heard harpstrings, and then a high voice singing, sweet and serene. . . .

"Elves," said Carroll.

"Dorialith!" whispered Airellen, cringing on the tree-limb where she sat.

"I wondered what was taking him so long," Swanwhite said. "Between the three of us, the mortals will be safe enough. Shall we go meet him?"

"No!" Airellen cried. "I do not want him to see me! I do not want him to know I am here! I cannot face him now!"

"What—?" Swanwhite stared a moment, then sighed. "If that is what you wish." Airellen hunched more deeply into herself, her eyes on her long fingers, knotting and twining in her lap.

Ingulf and Carroll woke with the sunlight, and soon were on their way, trudging along the river.

They set off with their spirits high, cheered by the light they had seen, and by the realization that some power guarded them. Yet, as they went on, their nerves began to fray, and they walked as though constantly listening for something.

"The birds!" Ingulf cried suddenly. "Where have the bird-flocks gone?"

Carroll stopped, and stood listening. A thrush sang nearby, a jay scolded off in the woods, a blackbird fluttered across the path ahead—yet they seemed to walk in uncanny silence now, without the constant whisper of wings and rustle of shaken leaves, and the endless undercurrent of whistling and piping which they had heard for days.

"True," said Carroll. "It is gone they are. Now what does that mean?"

"It means they have tired of us, or forgotten us!" snapped

Ingulf. "We do not matter! They have found some other game!" His voice was bitter.

"Ah, Loon, Loon!" murmured Carroll. "The birds are gone, but so are the wolves! Perhaps there are no more dangers between us and the mountains, and they feel no need to guard us further. And indeed, I do not miss them. With their racket, I could hear nothing in the woods, and could neither hunt nor hide."

"They care nothing if we suffer!" Ingulf shrieked. "*She* cares nothing if I suffer!"

"Calm yourself, now, Ingulf—"

"*What do they care if we suffer?*" Ingulf shrieked. "*She* cares nothing if I suffer!"

"Calm yourself, now, Ingulf—"

"*What do they care if we suffer?*" Ingulf's scream woke echoes through the wooded hills beyond the stream. "We do not live long enough for them to notice us!"

"Ingulf—!"

"They do not care if we live or die!" Ingulf wailed. "*She* does not care! The evil Elves, with their harping and their illusions—!"

"*Will you not hush?*" roared Carroll. "This is worse than the birds! Soldiers are hunting us, hunting to kill us—half of Sarlow could be creeping through those woods now—"

A wolf-howl rose in the wood behind.

Carroll froze, listening.

Wind blew. Around them, thick trees creaked, and the limbs tossed as the wind bent them.

Nearby, the wolf-pack sobbed. Then men's voices echoed.

"Hear you the wolf-pack?" Carroll hissed. "Hear you the echoes? Men's voices, too?" He drew his sword. "Our foes and their wolves are seeking us, closing in on us, and you, stupid Loon, start screaming! Screaming!"

A great wind came soughing through the treetops. Trees bent like grass.

Harpstrings rang.

And out of the wind, a high voice rose, as though the wind itself sang.

"Feel no Fear!"

Carroll's face turned white. Ingulf felt his heart lurch.

They both stared up into the trees.

Wind pressed treetops down: trunks bent and groaned.

And out of the wind's blast, words formed, throbbing, in a rapid chant. . . .

"Friends of the spell-charmed
Power of the Sea-Elf
Need fear no steel-armed
Warrior nor werewolf!"

"What was that?" Carroll gasped.

But the wind and the voice went away. Off to the north and the east they could see trees bend like grass. And although they no longer grasped words, they heard the voice singing.

Screams of terror answered, and shrill yelping from the wolves.

Faintly, under the roaring of the wind, they heard the crashing and stamping of a panicked army fleeing. And trees bent and swayed as the wind followed.

"Abandoned, are we?" snorted Carroll, looking into the trees above.

The wood was still about them, as they took up their journey down the stream. Through gaps in the leaves they saw clouds fill the sky. All that night they expected to hear the sound of harping, but the forest maintained a peaceful silence.

Sometime after noon the next day it began to rain, softly at first, then strengthening. A light wind blew the cold rain in their faces wherever they turned.

At last it slacked off again, and they plodded on through rain that was more like a wind-driven mist.

"Look, Carroll," said Ingulf, suddenly, pointing with a limp hand. "What do you think that could be?"

On the opposite bank, great blocks of squared stone lay everywhere, and the stream spread into a wide pool; then it flowed over a falls formed of the blocks.

On Carroll's face Ingulf saw a pitying frown.

"It must be the ruins of some house that stood here long ago, before the Sarló came out of the north, when this was a peaceful land."

They waded across the stream. The blocks were scattered in patterns about a low square wall; on some could still be seen the black mark of fire, though most had been washed clean by the years of wind and rain. Inside the ragged remnant of a wall, a set of stone steps led down, into cellars that were now open pits, the floor long gone above them. Dim shapes lay at the bottom.

Ingulf stepped up on the wall, and hopped down onto the stone platform above the top step.

"Ingulf! Loon! Come back!" Carroll shouted, as Ingulf started down the stair. "There's nothing here you need to see!"

Ingulf went on down the stairs. After a moment he heard Carroll following.

Water, black and foul, covered the floor: there was silt at the bottom. A broken stone chair lay face down in shallow water, short legs stuck forlornly in the air.

Other, less identifiable shapes lay tumbled where they had fallen, centuries ago.

Ingulf stepped off the bottom step, into slimy, ankle-deep water, and began to wade toward the fallen throne, heedless of the scum that stained his bare feet.

"Loon?" Carroll called after him. "Loon? Be careful now! You do not know what you might step on or—"

"Leave me alone!" Ingulf muttered under his breath. "You stupid, nagging, bothersome, nosy, snoopy . . ."

He tried to seize the broken, pathetic throne, but his fingers would still not obey his will, and he could not close his hands on it. Crouching, he pushed his arms under the thin broken slab that was its back, and tried to lift it that way, but it was too awkward and heavy.

He heard feet splash in water, and then Carroll's hands closed on the stone.

Together they heaved it up and rocked it back, and as they struggled they felt their hearts and breath pounding together, and it was only when they had heaved it upright and stepped back, breathing hoarsely, to survey their work, that they heard the music that linked the rhythm of their hearts, a harp that played a tune they had first heard while wind bent trees like grass above their heads . . .

A voice rose: words sprang to the tune . . .

> *"I fear no reaving*
> *Warrior nor foemen*
> *Out on the heaving*
> *Waters of the Ocean!"*

Turning, they rushed up the steps, leaving filthy footprints.

> *"Fearing no evil*
> *Sorcerer nor werewolf*
> *I searched the vile*
> *Fortresses for Ingulf!"*

They stopped, stunned, at the top of the stair; there, atop the flat stone of the wall lay folded woven wool, bright with the colors of their own clans.

And, on top of the tartan of the Clan Hua-Eliron, lay a great bladed flail, and a scabbarded sword.

"Frostfire!" Ingulf whispered, reverently, and fell weeping to his knees.

The music slowed; the tune shifted.

> *"Hear in air the charm around you!*
> *Deep Sea-magic is around you!*
> *Green Sea-magic is upon you!*
> *Fear no wrong when I am near you . . ."*

A tall shape walked along the wall, resting a small harp against his breast, his fingers dancing on the strings. A silver beard covered his chest.

"You!" said Carroll. "I *dreamed* you!"

The Sea-Elf laughed.

"Dorialith?" Ingulf said. "Then that was you in the trees?"

"It was I," Dorialith said, and let his fingers fall from the strings. "The winds on land are much the same as on the sea; air is like water, and has its currents and its tides."

"Dorialith is with him now," murmured Airellen, "and he will be safe enough. Let us go back now."

"Not yet!" said Swanwhite, sharply. "I want to hear what Dorialith tells him about. . . ."

"Please!" Airellen sobbed. "Please, I'm afraid that he will see! That he will—make me talk to Ingulf again! I cannot face him—cannot face either of them. . . ."

"Go on along with you, then," snapped Swanwhite, crossly. "Go on ahead and I'll catch up with you!"

"I will wait for you on the hill of the apple trees," Airellen murmured, and fled away through the treetops.

Vildern squinted against the glaring suns that hung like fiery enemy eyes above the leafy forest wall ahead. All around him he could hear the tramp of feet and the clatter of armor. As he urged his horse after Kelldule's, even with all the noise of the army, he was aware of Yotnir's cold voice.

"Only those who are purged of the womanish weaknesses which corrupt mortal flesh will be deserving of immortality," Yotnir said, "and the rest will be food and sport, for us to enjoy—their pain and their blood. Thus we shall approach the perfection of the Lords Beyond the World, as the Council—"

A man's hoarse scream cut through the thin voice.

Other voices, too, stopped.

"It's coming!" The voice screamed. Leaves and brush crashed, and an armored figure burst through the screening leaves at the wood's edge. *"It's running above the trees!"* he screamed as he ran.

The soldier's pasty face was twisted back over his shoulder to watch the branches above him. Kelldule's horse reared.

Other screams sounded from deeper in the wood.

Exclamations rose from the front ranks, and men further back shouted. There'd be panic in a minute, Vildern thought. The man turned as he heard the voices in front of him, and then ran toward Kelldule and Yotnir and threw himself on his knees before their horses.

"Save us, Masters!" he shrieked, spreading his arms imploringly. *"It will get us! The trees bend under its weight as it runs!"*

Another man burst shrieking from the bushes, and a murmur

rose from the army. Vildern cursed. They'd all be running in a moment. . . .

He whirled his horse around, and his deep voice roared out.

"Stand firm!" He heard other officers' voices echo his order as he spurred his horse toward the second man.

"Run!" this one screamed. *"It's closing in! The wind from its wings will—"*

Vildern's fist struck the man from his feet. But already a third and a fourth man were crashing out of the forest, and more were behind.

"What's coming?" he roared at the man on the ground. "Stop screeching like a girl on the rack and talk like a man!"

The white-faced man stared up at him, swallowed, and then stammered, so that Vildern had to listen closely.

"It's—it is huge! Like a—hawk—or an eagle, but—but so big—so big its wings—" The man choked. "The wind from its wings bends the trees like grass! It's a giant eagle, a—a—"

But Vildern had stopped listening, and he whirled his horse away. What was it the first man had said? *The trees bend under its weight as it runs.* . . .

He straightened in his stirrups, looking into the trees. There was only the barest stirring of branches in a light breeze, and he had seen nothing either flying or running as he had approached the wood from the river. Or earlier, when he had looked across the river from the fortress. . . .

Still more men came running from the trees. As one bolted past, Vildern heard his shout.

"They are coming!" this man cried. Vildern spurred his horse after him, and caught him by the scruff of the neck, and shook him.

"What do you mean, *they* are coming?" he snarled. "Who are *they*?" What are you babbling about?

"The *Dead*!" the man wailed. "The Wild Hunt rides on the ghost wind, and all I ever tortured or killed are there, waving their broken limbs and screaming! They fly on the wind like leaves, and I cannot escape them!"

Vildern dropped the man, and turned to find Kelldule at his side, and Yotnir watching.

"I think it is all illusion—"

"Yes," said Kelldule. "I heard. Not one of them sees the same thing. Some illusion of the Elves, no doubt of it!"

"It is time this wild land was tamed!" Yotnir shrilled. "I've suspected before that Elves might lurk here, or were coming over the mountains from Galinor."

"These, I suspect, come from the Sea-Elves' City," Kelldule asserted. "This was no simple illusion! Some powerful figure cast this spell—Dorialith perhaps, or Ciallglind, or Ethellin the Wise."

"We have tried to attack the Sea-Elves' City," said Yotnir, "but always their spells have brought our armies to disaster, and they have overcome our magic and banished our sendings."

"Only the Stone of Anthir will give us power to overcome them in their own city," Kelldule answered. "But once that is ours, we can walk in and slaughter them."

"So you have said before," sneered Yotnir. "But that does not help us now."

"I do not think that even the greatest of the Elves could enchant so great an army," said Kelldule, waving an arm at the host that flooded all the land to the river's edge, and the boats that were still ferrying more across the river.

"If we can find them at all, in this forest," snarled Yotnir.

"Then let us destroy the forest," said Kelldule.

"And how would you do that?" asked Yotnir.

"By calling up the *Guirndoel*, the one you call the Leveler of Mountains."

"That can only be done at one of the Great Gates," scoffed Yotnir. "And still it takes much blood. Even with the blood of this whole army, I do not see—"

"I can summon the Leveler of Mountains here," said Kelldule. "And use no blood at all." He laughed at the expression on Yotnir's face, and stroked his black beard. "It is true! Have you not heard how I summoned the Leveler of Mountains to shape my new citadel, out of Sgur Alain—the mountain you call Saraly?" He laughed as Yotnir stared at him.

"All of your spells work with blood and pain to lure the Great Ones to open the Gates themselves, in places where the barrier between the worlds is weak. But I—and I alone—know how to open a new Gate! For I have learned how the barrier is woven, and I, alone of Mortal Men, know how to part the threads. But you shall see."

On the hill of the apple trees, Airellen waited, her heart awhirl with conflicting desires.

From the apple trees, she sprang to the topmost branches of the tallest spruce, and stood on a swaying branch, gazing over the miles of forest, to where Ingulf and Dorialith had met.

White, fluffy clouds drifted peacefully in bright blue skies all around her; at her feet stretched green miles of treetops. And when she called, birds came fluttering up from the trees, to gather around her as she sang.

> "Ages pass me by,
> So why must he die?
> Why should I seek sorrow time never can mend?
> Is it now too late
> To fly from this fate?
> Why should love be wasted on life that must end?
> My Love! My Love!"

At her feet the beauty and mystery of the forest stretched away like a green sea, a broad sweeping vista of wooded hills rising and falling, waving treetops mile after mile. But she saw it through a mist of tears.

> "Oh why is it so?
> And where can I go?
> Is there no shelter to which I can flee?
> Night, day, morning, dawn,
> All pass and are gone
> Yet longing and sorrow stay ever with me.
> Ingulf! My Love!"

Her birds flocked about her, twittering as though to comfort her, perching on her shoulders and her arms, preening her long brown hair, fluttering around her in bright-feathered clouds. Still tears ran down her face as she sang.

"Men and flowers pass away,
Their lives last but a day.
My Love, my sorrow haunts me:
Empty my life must be!
Whether I draw near or stay away
From you, my darling,
An endless parting waits for us on some sad day.
Ingulf, your longing haunts me
Would that I could set your free!
My cruel spell still rules your mind—
You think you love me.
What happiness do you think that we could find?

Her birds whirled and fluttered with sudden agitation as her song changed, and became swift and passionate as the breath of love.

"Could you live forever—
Could we live together—
If your love were no illusion—
We could then all sorrow shun:
Then we could become as one!
But my magic binds you,
Makes you see a false view:
My power takes its toll—
Ingulf! Ingulf! My sorrow's soul!"

Her voice sank: her shoulders hunched as she drew in upon herself, her hands clasped tightly in her lap, long fingers writhing about each other in anguish. Her birds settled to the branches about her, and when she sang again, it was softly and sadly.

"My spell still draws you to me.
Cruel magic, set us free!
Why torture us with desire's dream
of a life that could never be?
Cruel love! Set us free!"

A sweet cold wind tossed the branches all about her up and down: she could still taste in it traces of Dorialith's spells. The whole tree swayed, and she had to reach out and seize another branch. She looked out across the sea of moving leaves that stretched away to the west, her eyes seeking out unerringly the fold in the forest where the stream cut through, the rougher, tattered patch of leaves about the ruins where Ingulf talked with Dorialith, and suddenly her voice soared, wild as birdsong, in loneliness and longing. . . .

"I know what you offer me, Ingulf,
The Mother of Gileran Half-Elf
Still mourns by the grave of her lover,
While Centuries move stars above her.

When Gileran's Children are dying,
And Gileran, too, wanders sighing,
She knows, and she wails in her sorrow
To mourn those who will die Tomorrow.

Gileran, Gileran, Where are your children now?

Ingulf, you are mortal and human,
But I am an undying woman,
Now doomed to be evermore weeping,
For one who in death's grasp lies sleeping!

Miles behind her in the cleared land at the river's edge, Vildern watched, mystified, as Kelldule ordered great blocks of men to change the position of boulders, and to stand beside them.

He knew that the Sorcerers who watched were equally mystified.

They were still more mystified when Kelldule assembled them, and sent them to stand in ranks beside the soldiers, and then, at his order, to raise shields of Dark Power against something they would not see.

Kelldule himself strode past the blocks of men, and past the half-circle of stone. Vildern, following him closely, felt a sudden vertigo. Fear prickled through him.

The earth at his feet and the forest beyond seemed to ripple like a mirage, and grass seemed to writhe and twist as though in agony. The light changed, and all colors sickened.

Sudden flocks of birds swirled up from the trees, shrieking frantically, and there was a loud crashing of brush under them as they scattered and flew away.

Kelldule laughed.

Behind them Vildern heard exclamations from the ranks, and turning saw outside the lines of men tiny fountains of sparkling white and gold light, hanging in the air. He tugged at Kelldule's sleeve and pointed, but the Sorcerer only nodded.

"It is only the sparks struck where two deflected lines cross," he said, then, turning, strode forward, raising his arms above his head, and spoke, his deep voice rolling like thunder. . . .

> *"Hawshjkfethek! Come forth now!*
> *Come forth now! The way is clear!*
> *The way is open! Come now!*
> *Hawshjkfethek! Come now! Come now!"*

As he spoke, the dim light grew dimmer. Vildern felt his feet against the ground, but no longer felt as though the ground were down. . . .

A wind began to spin. It stripped the leaves from the writhing oaks, and tore needles from the pine, and whirled them round and around in a swirling cloud. Vildern heard wood rending as branches were ripped away. . . .

Then, from nowhere, blackness came.

Vildern could not be sure that it did not rise out of the earth, to grow towering into the sky. He could not be sure that it did not pour down out of the sky, to sink into the earth. Nor could he be sure that it had not come from some faraway point on the horizon. His eyes seemed to see all these things at once, and yet he knew it was none of them he saw, but something else: something his eyes could not interpret to his brain.

One moment there was only the whirlwind, and the next moment there was something more: something all writhing limbs and barbs and mouths and eyes, all whirling and lashing and knotting as it spun and swirled. . . .

Beside him he heard Kelldule's voice boom above the growing whine. . . .

"Westward go! Eat the hills!!
Crush the Forest! Trunk and root!
Earth and Stone: blood and bone!
All are yours, beast and plant!
Eat them all! Eat them all!"

It rose up into the sky, high above the trees, taller than the tallest tower. . . .

It moved away, with a crash of splintering trees as it moved into the doomed wood. And where it had been, only smoothly polished stone remained.

Airellen still sat on the hill of the apple-trees, gazing west from her treetop perch.

Suddenly the air was filled with crying flocks of bright-colored birds, flying all together out of the east.

A Wood-Elf, familiar with the Forest of Demons, would have known what that meant. But Airellen only stared at the splendor and beauty of the sight in raptured wonder and delight. Below she glimpsed the bobbing tan backs of bounding deer, amber against the green.

Not until her own birds rose in a whirring cloud, and she reached for their minds and found only terror, did she think of danger.

She sprang up, spinning in the air to face a sky unaccountably darkened, as though by storm.

But then she saw it was no storm that reached from earth to sky. At first she thought the advancing tower of darkness to be the smoke of a forest-fire, then she thought it was a whirlwind. . . .

Birds flew past her, crying, crying. Sudden wild wind plucked at her hair, and she had to grasp another, smaller branch to keep her perch.

Then she felt the gaze of a thousand hating eyes, like filth-soaked whips against her flesh, and saw through the smoky dark the whirling, tossing, barbed limbs, and saw the trees at its base sucked up, roots and all from the earth, and saw trees and earth and the very stone showering upward into whirling, gaping mouths.

A moment she bore its hate-filled gaze, defiantly. From the distance came the sound of splintering trees.

Reluctantly, she turned to flee. Her extended Elvish senses heard all about her the silent dirge of the doomed trees.

Springing with Elvish speed from tree to tree, she soon caught up with the fleeing birds, and moved in the midst of a bright-feathered crowd, racing through the mournful forest. Below, she saw the low bushes over which the yellow-brown deer leaped shaken with the flight of thousands of smaller beasts.

All the forest fled with her. But ever louder and nearer sounded the roaring of splintered trees; and now behind her the hill of the apple-trees itself was suddenly shaken. The apple-trees and the tall evergreens that rose above them were ripped away: earth and grass showered upward, and the hill dissolved into a mist of flying earth that vanished into writhing, sucking mouths.

She threw herself across the dizzying gaps between tree and tree with reckless abandon, her only thought now to reach Ingulf and die beside him if she could not save him.

Tall pines and cedar scraped the sky with emerald wreaths. All the forest mourned about her as she leaped from limb to limb, racing through the highest branches, while the gloom deepened behind her, and louder and louder came the crackling of ripping wood.

An ill-smelling wind caught up with her: it ripped leaves from the trees and sucked helplessly fluttering birds backward in their flight. Leaves and feathers swirled around her.

Her voice rose in a wordless song of warning and of mourning, and now the trees through which she sprang shuddered in loosening soil.

"*Airellen!*" a voice cried. On the ground below she saw a slender, white-haired shape.

"*Swanwhite!*" she cried. "Flee! Get away if you can!"

Dark barbed tentacles reached for her, and she felt the tree snatched whirling out from under her even as she leaped. . . .

But Swanwhite did not flee. The jewel at her throat blazed out, and rainbow light clothed her as she lifted her arms. From between her lifted palms stabbed a beam of white fire, burning into the heart of the darkness.

Kelldule screamed: boulders burst; broken rock flew.

Vildern stared as cursing Sorcerers broke ranks and scattered, some flailing flaming patches of their robes' dark cloth.

He caught Kelldule as the Sorcerer reeled like a drunken man and fell into his arms.

Dorialith whirled as great flocks of birds came crying through the trees, and the ground was stirred with the rustle of many paws.

Need-fire flared on his blade as he drew.

"Swords out!" he cried. "Something comes— some sending of the Sorcerers—some great Demon out of the Dark World— or—"

Carroll's sun-bright sword was already drawn, but Ingulf could only paw helplessly at *Frostfire's* hilt.

Dorialith's hand, too fast to see, flashed to Ingulf's side, and pulled *Frostfire* free: the tall Sea-Elf stood facing the east, a flaming blade raised in either hand.

Dimly through the roof of leaves they saw the sky darken; then the leaves flared emerald with light, and the earth shook to a distant rumble as of thunder.

Evil-scented wind slapped Airellen to the ground almost at Swanwhite's feet.

Earth and sky shuddered; she heard great trees crash all around her.

Then all was still, and she felt sunlight warm on her skin.

Carroll let out his breath in a hoarse gasp.

"It—it's gone! What—?"

They could all see the need-fire fading from their swords; the leaves plain green against the sky.

"It is gone, indeed," Dorialith agreed. "Some other power has come to our aid. I can only guess that the Hasturs must have sensed the opening of the Gate through which—whatever it was—was summoned, and came to drive it back before it could burst into Galinor."

"What power is *this*," gasped ancient Yotnir, hobbling up, "that can drive great Hawshjkfethek, the Eater of Mountains, out of the world with a single stroke?"

"Finn! It must be Finn!" moaned Kelldule, his voice weak and weirdly shrill. "Arnim Finn must have escaped from the Maze, and now he has come to hunt me down! Where can I hide?"

"I never heard this name until you spoke it," Yotnir mumbled, "but I have seen your power, and I am wise enough to fear what you fear.

"Come!" the ancient shrilled, turning to the Sorcerers gathering in a milling mob about them. "We are finished here. It is time to return to Bluzig, and assemble the Council!" He turned back to Kelldule and lowered his voice. "With all the Council assembled, and the shield of the citadel raised . . ."

"Not even the defenses of Bluzig can stand against the fire of the Stone of Tirorilorn, if Arnim Finn comes again. Only with the Stone of Anthir, perhaps, might he be defeated. And I do have—"

"That will be a matter for the Council to discuss!" snapped Yotnir. "Come!"

He turned and strode toward the crowding Sorcerers, and they made way for him. Kelldule pushed himself away from Vildern, with a scant nod of thanks, and followed the ancient, still staggering slightly.

Vildern watched him go, uncertain whether to follow. It had all happened too fast. . . .

"*Wait!*" a voice shouted, and a powerful, richly dressed figure, with one arm in a sling, came riding up on a horse. Sunlight glowed on gold hair, and Vildern studied the cruel features for a moment before he realized that it was Svaran, without his armor.

"We cannot simply turn and—leave!" Svaran exclaimed. "Something must have fought your sending. It must be that the fire-swords are still there, many of them! Now we have a clear road to march on, and with no forest for them to hide in, we can catch them!" He pulled his arm out of the sling and waved it: the hand was splinted. "I want to catch that udder-sucker that broke my hand!"

"The army may be safer than we," Kelldule muttered to Yotnir. "Arnim Finn will hesitate to use his power against Mortal Men, if there is no magic used against him. And while he hesitates, he might be cut down."

"Do as you will, Prince Svaran!" cackled Yotnir. "It is nothing to me! In the end, our masters will eat us all. Your puny swords are nothing to the Powers of the Dark!"

Svaran sat his horse, frowning after them, as the Sorcerers marched away in a long column, back toward the river and the boats. Soldiers watched uncertainly.

Vildern waited until the Sorcerers were out of earshot, and then strode up to stand beside Svaran's horse.

"I'm with you!" he said. "It's time the army remembered its proper role, and did something on its own! Let the Sorcerers run!"

Svaran started and stared down at him.

"It has been a long time since the king and the army ruled Sarlow," he said, softly, "and it is near treason to remember that once they did."

"Yes," said Vildern, meeting his gaze. After a long moment, Svaran grinned and laughed.

"*March!*" he shouted, waving his arm toward the new-planed stone to the west. "March! We'll teach these womanish pityboys what pain is! We'll cut them into gobbets!"

"March!" Vildern echoed, and the mighty army surged across the smooth stone plain.

"Airellen?" Swanwhite's voice trembled. "Was that not one of the Great Dyoles? Terror stirs, indeed! I felt the very threads of the barrier between the worlds unraveled! Some Sorcerer had *made* a new Gate! I closed it, but—I do not know whether they can open it again—"

Winded and bruised, Airellen rolled over on the soft moss and sat up slowly. One arm was broken: she hurled healing magic through it until she felt the ends weave together.

Fallen trees lay all around, but beyond Swanwhite she could see tall trees rearing crests of emerald mist against the blue.

But when she glanced over her shoulder, she saw only two trees still standing, and both leaned against loosened roots. And there, too, lay a thin tangle of fallen trees, green branches quivering like a curtain, before a vast flat of polished stone that stretched away for miles. Far away light shimmered, like sunlight on water, or on thousands of tiny moving bits of metal.

All the way to the river, she thought, shivering. The solemn, ancient cedars and pines, emerald needle and leaf, oak and beech, the apple trees in the deserted orchards that had grown around the pathetic, crumbling ruins—all were gone, and even the earth from which they had grown was stripped away, and the hills and valleys ground to a flat plain of polished stone. . . .

"Ingulf?" she asked. "Is Ingulf safe? And—and the others?"

"Safe?" Swanwhite laughed. "Not yet! But alive, and able to move, and not even aware they were in danger as far as I know! But they still have some distance to travel before they reach the mountains. The passes there are guarded, Dorialith was saying, and—"

She stopped suddenly, shading her eyes, and peering intently over Airellen's shoulder.

"—and there is a great army of men marching now across the stone."

Airellen turned and, shading her own eyes, looked back across the rock. The distant sparkle she had thought the river was flooding across the plain, and now she could see that the tiny dancing sparks of sunlight leaped from the moving mail-rings of the armor of many thousands of men.

"They are still far away. . . ." she whispered.

"But they march steadily across the flat," said Swanwhite. "And Ingulf can move only slowly, and even Carroll is hurt. They may well be trapped between these and the guards of the passes, and I do not know if even Dorialith can enchant so many men all at once."

"Perhaps not," Airellen breathed. "But *we* can!"

Swanwhite looked at her in sharp surprise, and was met with a daze of wonder and beauty.

"Cousin!" Swanwhite exclaimed. "You have grown, Cousin! You know your own power now!"

"Yes, let us go and meet this army."

Together the two sprang through the tangle of broken trees, slid down the slope of loose earth, and strode out onto the stone plain, out to meet the advancing flood of men, and the wonder and the magic of their singing went before them, a wild loneliness that tore the hearts of men who knew neither trust nor friendship, and had never imagined love.

> *"Foolish men*
> *Shallow men!"*

To Vildern it was Eluvorg, alive again, who came striding across the vast waste of stone, and passed through the ranks of the host, singing. . . .

> *"Cruel men*
> *Hollow men!"*

Vildern turned and followed that singing ghost, not knowing whether he followed to regain the joy he had lost, or to kill her again and be free at last. . . .

> *Empty a loveless life,*
> *Knowing only*
> *Hatred and strife!*
> *Loveless men are lonely!*
> *Would you own the*
> *Wandering fire?*
> *World's Desire?*
> *Ecstasy?*
> *Follow me!"*

He reached for her, and drew back singed hands, for she was clothed in a cloak of flame.

All around men fought and killed to lay hands upon her, but those who tried either drew back, burned, or else their hands found empty air. . . .

> *"Folly's fee beware!*
> *Love me who dare!*

Let him beware!
Power cannot find me!
No chain can bind the
Wandering fire!"

Sometimes there seemed to be two women, and sometimes a dozen, or a thousand or more. And Vildern saw that although at a distance they seemed to be different women, whenever he drew near it was always Eluvorg's face he saw, his lost witch-wolf bitch.

"Heart's Desire!
Wild and free!
Follow me!"

The rest of the day he followed her, and on into the night, by the light glow from her flesh. And his heart ached, as though pierced with arrows.

"Come follow me!
Love and life am I,
Joy and laughter,
Hope and despair!
Follow who dare!"

Svaran's horse reeled and fell, ridden to death. Men reeled and cursed and staggered and fought.

"Come, follow and find me!
None can bind the
Wandering fire!"

At the bank of the river she changed into wolf-shape, and plunged into the water.

"Heart's Desire!"

Then he saw that there were two, a black wolf and a white, that swam away downstream.

And men reeled into the water after them, and in the press many were dragged under and drowned.

And others raced along the banks, still following.

But Vildern stood on the bank, and wept for his lost Eluvorg, without fear that his unmanly tears would be seen.

"Airellen!" Ingulf sobbed. "You are lost to me! I have failed! My hands are crippled, and what was the use of it all!"

"You did not fail, Ingulf!" answered Dorialith. "There are many who were slaves in Sarlow, who now are free!"

"But I am still a slave!" Ingulf cried. "An abandoned slave, with no hope, lost and alone!"

And he would not be comforted, for he did not know that she whom he loved more than life had come up out of the sea to save him.

But not even Dorialith knew that.